DAKOTA MAN

Center Point
Large Print

Also by Frank Bonham and available from
Center Point Large Print:

Trago

DAKOTA MAN

Western Stories

Frank Bonham
EDITED BY Bill Pronzini

CENTER POINT LARGE PRINT
THORNDIKE, MAINE

This Center Point Large Print edition
is published in the year 2014 in conjunction with
Golden West Literary Agency.

The text of this Large Print edition is unabridged.
In other aspects, this book may vary
from the original edition.
Printed in the United States of America
on permanent paper.
Set in 16-point Times New Roman type.

ISBN: 978-1-62899-194-9 (hardcover)
ISBN: 978-1-62899-195-6 (paperback)

Library of Congress Cataloging-in-Publication Data

Bonham, Frank.
  [Short stories. Selections]
  Dakota man / Frank Bonham. — Center Point Large Print edition.
  pages ; cm
  Summary: "Five western stories about men who stood their ground"—
Provided by publisher.
  ISBN 978-1-62899-194-9 (hardcover : alk. paper)
  ISBN 978-1-62899-195-6 (pbk. : alk. paper)
  1. Large type books. I. Bonham, Frank. Texan buys a gun-bride.
    II. Title.
  PS3503.O4315A6 2014
  813'.54—dc23
                                                    2014019478

Table of Contents

Foreword

This new collection of Frank Bonham's fine stories once again demonstrates why Bonham was among the most acclaimed Western writers of his generation. Well-researched and diverse frontier backgrounds, attention to period detail, strong character-motivated storylines, dramatically choreographed action sequences—all these qualities and more make the five novelettes in these pages compulsive reading.

"The Texan Buys a Gun-Bride" (*Action Stories*, Summer 1949) is a powerful historical tale set in the Republic of Texas in 1841. Rich in the lore and language of the period, it features a fiddle-playing, bullwhip-wielding hero caught up in land squabbles and land fraud among ranchers, cavalrymen, and a group of feisty Scottish emigrants. Oregon's rough-and-tumble Rogue River mining country is the scene of "Whiskey Creek Stampeders" (*Dime Western*, 1/49), the chronicle of one man's struggles to compete against an overland freight line by building a fleet of ore-carrying boats to run on the tempestuous Rogue.

The locale of "Bonanza Railroad" (*Blue Book*, 12/45) is Nevada's rich silver mining country, the time 1874, and the central story ingredient a partnership between a rancher turned miner, a highballing railroad man, and the daughter of a refining company owner to build a sixteen-mile shortline railroad between Virginia City mines and smelters on the Carson River. "Cowman-on-the-Spot" (*Dime Western*, 5/47) tells the action-packed story of a violent war between cattlemen and lumbermen in Wyoming's Wind River region. A Tex-Mex border yarn set in the years shortly after the Civil War, "Dakota Man" (*Dime Western*, 2/47) concerns an ex-Union soldier's purchase of 2,000 head of longhorn cattle, the pitfalls of cowhands at work in the harsh Mexican brasada, and a band of gun-running former Rebel sympathizers.

Enjoy.

Bill Pronzini
Petaluma, California

The Texan Buys a Gun-Bride

I

Jim Croft rode into Pistol Creek settlement with a whip tied before his saddle and a fiddle lashed behind. He had thought of tying the whip behind the saddle, but in the end he had decided to keep first things first. He knew no way of fiddling a train of land-starved immigrants out of sight, but he knew ways of encouraging them with a buckskin popper.

Croft was a long shake of a Texan in a leather shirt and britches, his hat low-crowned, with the brim pinned up in front and a mockingbird feather stuck in it. He was twenty-five, Tennessee born, optimistic about himself, pessimistic about Mexicans since the war, contented with ranching but hungry for white ways and white women. He owned forty-six acres of Cross Timbers range. He ran longhorn cattle, fed a few hogs, and raised enough corn for himself, his Mexican, and the hogs.

He would take an oath that no land in the world gave back so much for so little. The Cross Timbers had everything but civilization, and sometime it would have that. Nails, needles, bolt cloth, and tanned leather—these were the icons of civilization, to be treated with reverence. Yesterday he had had to discard the socks he had bought from the wife of the Pecan Point ferryman. So he was wearing no socks today, and, as he rode, the stirrups fretted his ankles a bit. The old wooden tree under him twisted like a fractured arm.

His emotions when he thought of the immigrants were mixed. He had been a landless man himself. He knew the hunger for land that dominated a man's thinking when he had worked too long for others. It might be these people were confused and had camped at Pistol Creek by accident. The Republic of Texas was patch-worked with grants, headrights, and scrip parcels. He had heard these people were refugees from Scotland. Well, they were confused about Texans, if they thought they could take refuge here. And every rancher in Smithwick County was riding in to tell them so.

He reached the red bluffs above the settlement. Pistol Creek followed a moist, shaded valley in a foam of greenery. Among giant pecans and elms, a few small farms, fenced with bois d'arc hedges, displayed poorly aligned crop rows. Shank's Tavern, tiny hub of a tiny wheel, was hidden in the trees, but a tang of smoke rose from the site.

About a quarter mile north of town, Croft made out the immigrant camp, a white square of wagon tilts enclosing a sort of village square congested with children, dogs, clotheslines, and fires. It was like a punch in a slack belly to see all these things at once, women salaaming solemnly before washtubs, kids at play, wagons drawn up civilized-fashion. It was the biggest gathering he had seen since the war. A thin rag of sound ascended to him—the wail of a new baby. He had a thought that showed how long he had been away from it: *A late drop, that one.* . . .

As he passed, a young woman emerged from the trees carrying a blackjack limb for firewood. She was tall and slender, wearing a woolen gown pinned to the knees to rescue it from the mud. Her hair was reddish, pulled back into a sleek knot low on her neck, and she had a figure so completely unlike a squaw that he had almost forgotten was to be found. Her calves and ankles were more for dancing than for carrying burdens. She was full-breasted, slender, dauncy as a mockingbird, and the way her waist had the delicacy of a redbud stem and her hips flared to womanly fullness were astonishing. Croft stared at her like a trapper.

The girl rested the branch on the ground to wave at him. "Howdy!" she cried.

Croft grinned but solemnly raised his hat. It sounded like "Hoody!" A Scotsman's stab at being Texan, he reckoned.

She picked up the branch and walked on. He watched the way her skirt swayed from her hips. She seemed incapable of moving without grace.

Croft rode on along the rutted trace known as the Central National Road of the Texas Republic. Near the tavern, on the east side of the road, was a gloomy fieldstone structure—the courthouse of

Smithwick County. Beyond, on the meadow sweeping up to the bluffs, a couple of settlers had their gardens and dog-run cabins.

Horses were staked on the muddy ground about Shank's Tavern, wild ponies captured and tamed, and, in this early spring, still shaggy with winter hair. He saw Frio Gorman's Pothook brand, Bigfoot Morgan's Chain, and five or six others. Yonder stomped Colonel Saul Lightfoot's red mule, a sorry mount for a Texas Quixote, but heroes were a dime a dozen these sober days of 1841.

The tavern was a large, pitch-roofed stone building with a gallery across the front. The roof was of hand-hewn shakes and the sash windows were paned with saggy, oiled rawhide. Shank's liver-spotted hounds slinked forward, obsequious as footmen. Croft dismounted, leaving the fiddle on the saddle but carrying his whip.

Shank's was a dim cavern of ham, chicory, and sour-leather smells, the puncheon floor littered with shoddy merchandise. Near the plank-and-keg bar, in the rear, eight men were deployed on boxes. A low thread of conversation broke. Colonel Lightfoot, rising from a keg like a man lifting a yearling steer, called: "Hee-yowdy, Jim!"

His hand was like a vise on Jim's and he struck him on the shoulder. Lightfoot was a buckskin legend that had amassed itself a belly. His long hair was coarse and black, but streaked like a badger. His brow was an anvil and his shoulders unbelievable. He wore a medal on his buckskin shirt, which the colonel was prone to rub significantly and yarn of a dismal swamp at San Jacinto, where he had pulled Sam Houston from under a dead horse. He had degenerated into an officious old gaffer nibbling at the crust of his glory.

"Feared you'd forgot the day, Jim!"

Croft turned to Shank. "How's the whiskey supply, storekeeper?"

Shank set out a pottery cup of purplish liquor. He was a gross-bellied man in tight breeches, his cheeks shot with broken veins. "Blackberry brandy's the caper today. Yancey's boys have cleaned me out of whiskey."

Croft pushed it back. "Give it to somebody with summer complaint and save a few drinks of whiskey for your steady customers next time."

"Anybody steadier than a cavalryman?"

He made his howdys to the others. They were, in the main, shy, unlettered frontiersmen who would not have known what to do with civilization if they had it, men who bottled their emotions under the cork of terseness until it had fermented sufficiently to be fit to bring out.

Someone kicked the door open and a man in fringed buckskin pants and a patched military shirt entered. Dollar-size Amozoc spurs chimed at his heels. He came on and picked up the blackberry brandy Jim Croft had rejected.

"Bin down?" he asked Jim.

"Came by."

"Got some women down there." Captain Joel Yancey's eyes, black glints beside a lean nose, sparked with deviltry. "*Young* women."

"They've got some men, too. Old, ugly, and greedy, by the look of them."

Croft did not find Yancey a necessity. He was a tough, rangy, and irreligious man, gaunt and heavy-lidded. Nothing about him pleased Croft except the Sam Walker Colt at his right hip, a magnificent weapon carrying six heavy slugs and taking copper caps. Yancey commanded a troop of Texas cavalry encamped just south of the settlement, licking its wounds after a Cherokee campaign.

Yancey had no stake in this game. He said: "You'll go right to howdyin' and civilizin' when you meet the McCash girl . . . hey, Colonel?"

"Reckon I'll uncivilize again, directly I meet her family." Jim glanced at Lightfoot. "Talked to them?"

Lightfoot cleared his throat and tucked in his shirt tail. "Had a little powwow with the old man last night, Jim. Kind of take to him. He's got an eye like a sharp-shinned hawk. Speaks flat out. Name of Thomas Alexander McCash. He's brought this gang of Scotch refoogies to Texas to find land. They've come a long ways, I 'low."

"Then they won't mind going a little farther."

16

Lightfoot hacked at a frog in his throat. "They're with an *empresario* named Brannigan. He sold them the land and he's getting tithes to help them get dug in."

"Sold them what land?"

Ira Mosher hammered his heel with his pipe. Mosher was a one-mule farmer and county recorder. "That's the joker, Jim. *Our* land! This jaybird says he was gave a grant by Houston for procurement work during the war. Our claims kind of seem to overlap."

A flame lighted in Croft. He had been hoping for some kind of bald-faced doings like this so that he would not have to kick his conscience before driving the immigrants out. He struck his palm with the loaded haft of his whip. "Let's get down there."

Lightfoot complained. "Brannigan seems to be square enough. I'm licked if his title don't date back earlier than ours."

The leather haft *thudded* against a molasses barrel. "There's my title, Colonel! Did you get that medal for bowing and scraping, or for fighting?"

Lightfoot's brows bunched. The others watched him; it began to be plain to Croft that all this had been hashed over before he arrived. ". . . Maybe we can work out a compromise."

Croft picked up a half-drunk cup of blackberry brandy. He placed it before Colonel Lightfoot. "Colonel," he said, "you set right here and take care of yourself. Button your shirt and drink this gut-shrinker. If you're afraid of these immigrants, I'll take care of 'em for all of you. Texans? Good Lord!"

Lightfoot threw the liquor on the floor. Croft turned his back on him and walked out through the dusky sprawl of merchandise. He heard Lightfoot and the others getting up to follow him.

II

Captain Yancey rode down with them. He was a gaunt blackbird of a man on a brush-scarred gray gelding, a back-country Texan who had acquired the habits of the animals from which he had learned survival. Forty years old, Yancey had fought in the Texas Revolution and stayed on to fight Indians for the Republic. Texas had given him the splendid Walker pistol he carried in a homemade holster under a thong; practice, Indian fights, and an eye like a scratch awl gave him the ability to hammer a sprig at fifty feet. Putting no stock in flourish, he let his men drink and hug what came to hand, let the refuse of his camp of four dozen rascally cavalrymen stew near the tents until the flies hummed like a bass fiddle.

"You're going to make forty-eight enemies when you send those Scotch lassies along," Yancey said. "My boys have been like stud hosses in April ever since they come. Six unattached females, by George! Five, not counting mine."

"Which 'un's yours?"

"Guess when we git there."

The colonists' camp was on high ground near the road, the white tilts of the wagons rain-washed and shining in the sunlight. The nearer they drew, the more a wonder and furtive excitement kindled in Croft. The whole camp swarmed like a beehive. A blacksmith was shrinking a tire at a forge. The *thump-thump-thump* of a churn made Jim think of golden spring butter.

They dismounted. This was a moment of decision. Croft was halfway ashamed of the whip on his saddle, but stubbornly he reached it down and slung it over his shoulder. The others followed suit, all but Lightfoot and Yancey. The cavalryman led the sober file of eight into the improvised plaza. "McCash!" he called.

A girl called to him from the back of a wagon, the same girl who had been carrying firewood when Croft entered town. She set aside a hand loom at which she had been working and, with care to her skirts, descended. She gave Yancey her hand in greeting, but it seemed to Croft she was a little impatient about pulling it away. He grinned at Jim, implying: *This is the one!* And when the captain introduced Jim, a tempest of eagerness shook him and he had to take himself firmly in hand.

Her name was Janet McCash, daughter of the clan leader. She said—"I'm pleased to know you."—with an accent you couldn't have duplicated if you tried. It was like the fragrance of heather, delicate but intangible. Her hair was like washed copper, braided and arranged low on her neck.

It seemed to Croft that she looked at him in a very personal way. "Colonel Lightfoot has told me about you. A real Texican, he said, and a hero to boot."

Croft did not know how to answer a thing like that, and merely scratched his neck. "We want to talk to your father and Brannigan," he stated.

"Father and Brannigan have gone down to get Prince Charlie. Come and look about while you wait."

There was not a wagon, it appeared, where someone was not about a trade. A tanner was fleshing the hide of a recently butchered beef. Another was grinding corn in a mill. Croft thought of the hours he put in every week pounding corn in a mortar. A wheezing old Scot was hammering nails into the heel of a boot. Croft stopped. In a box were many boots and women's shoes. He picked up a boot of close-grained black leather. Just about his size, with fine stitching and the salty odor of good cowhide.

"Need boots?" Janet McCash asked him.

". . . Fixing to. Feller," he said, "you want to make a swap?"

"I ain't keen," the man said.

"Don't be sharp with our guests, Bob." The girl laughed. "Of course he'll trade. What'll you give?"

"A steer. Make you a dozen pairs, and some eating besides."

"Bring it over when you're ready," the girl said. "See what you can find to fit."

Jim pulled off his boot. He heard her make an amused sound, seeing his bare foot. He carried it off the best he could, pulling on boots until he achieved a fit, and then standing up and testing them. "They'll do."

They walked on across the square, catching the spiced fragrance of a burgoo the women were preparing. It made Jim a little giddy to stand in the full draft of it. Somewhere bread was baking, riz bread with wonderful brown crust. He pulled his forehead into a scowl, not to be seduced by civilized doings. He spoke over his shoulder to the rest. "All right if I talk for you boys? I and the colonel may not fiddle the same tune."

Then he saw that Frio, Bigfoot Morgan, and the others were joshing a clutch of girls fifty feet in the rear. Lightfoot looked at Jim, solemnly stroking his mustache, and Yancey chuckled. Croft whistled peremptorily through his teeth. The Texans jumped and came along. Jim put the question again.

"So's you don't get too wrathy, Jim," Frio said, "we don't want a scrap till we try every other way."

21

Frio was red-headed as a kinglet, a small man whose toughness was that of gristle. The more he was chewed on, the bigger he got.

"Here's a Texan who talks sense," the girl said.

Two men came through a gap in the wagons, leading a bull. Croft gathered that Prince Charlie was a shorthorn. His study was more for the bull than the man. Short-legged as well as short of horn, it had a mellow coat and breadth of loin that caught Jim's eye. Why, the brute packed more meat than any two shaggy brockle-faced longhorns in his herd! A bull like that could be the making of a county; it could send its bloodline down the ages.

The man, McCash, knew it. A thick-legged Scot whose brows were broad and level, whose mouth had lines from being firmed often, he led the incredible bull by a rope and nose ring. He handled it as though it were the granddaddy of all bulls, smiling to see Croft stare.

"Bates strain, M'ster Croft," he declared. "None of the randy Booth line in this man! The day we get settled, Prince Charlie goes to service."

Jim shrugged. "I reckon the climate will kill him, if our cows don't. But if you're close enough, we'll ask about service."

"I think we will be."

Croft moved his gaze after a moment to Dock Brannigan. Here was a man whose mouth was too fleshy to bear any but false witness. "You're Brannigan?" Jim snapped. "Let's see that grant of yours. At Goliad, eh . . . ? You ain't black enough for a Mex, but I didn't see you in our camp."

Brannigan's eyes contained his resentment. "They took me out of it the first hour. All I could do for the next year was to write letters, but I wrote some that Houston figured helped win the war. An army marches on its belly, I've heard. You might say I was a belly general." His laugh was hearty as a handshake. There was good humor all around. But Croft stood there evaluating the *empresario*. He was a big man who looked as though appetite, both for food and women, were a dominant factor in him, a hearty man all around, a spinner of yarns and hoorawer. He wore a black coat and pants, and a gray beaver hat protected by an oiled silk cover. He smoked a slender pole-green cigar. From his right boot protruded a pistol.

McCash, seeking to take the edge off the encounter, clapped his hands together. "How long since you've tasted Argyll whiskey?" He led them to his wagon and handed a stone jug to Croft, who drank and passed it to Brannigan, standing nearest. The whiskey tingled like a spring brook, and left a man feeling as though he were just an inch taller than any man in the world.

Brannigan handed the jug to Lightfoot. "*After* heroes, Colonel . . . not before! I've forgotten whether you said the horse was a roan or a gray. . . ."

"A roan," the colonel responded quickly. "And

Big Sam's boot was full of blood from a wound he'd got. He said to me, as I pulled him out . . . 'Lightfoot, you're not light in guts, I'll swear!' "

"Did, eh?" Jim grunted. He had heard the story for five years, but the pun was new. "Got that grant handy?" he asked Brannigan.

The contractor drew a roll of thin Morocco from a pocket in the tail of his coat. Jim's education was only tolerable, but he could make out the language of the grant. It was signed at Washington-On-The Brazos, December 15, 1838.

"Three years . . . you weren't in any hurry to get up here."

"I had no reason to be. Then I met these good people in Nacogdoches, wandering like the children of Israel. I plan to see them well settled before I leave."

Jim looked at the women cooking dinner, and the kids romping with the tame coyote pup, at the wagons with the mud of thousands of miles on their wheels. "Well, this is plain hell, that's all . . . plain hell! You might have checked your bounds before you brought these damned greenhorns up here."

"I checked the lines in Washington-On-The-Brazos. There are no prior grants here."

"Nobody said anything about grants! It's headright and scrip land."

"Proved up on?"

Ira Mosher's narrow fox face was beginning to heat up. "In process!"

Tom McCash raised his hands. "I've never yet found a knot that couldn't be untangled. And we'll untangle this, if we take it slowly."

"McCash," Croft declared, "we went through hell served up Mexican style for the scrip we bought this land with. Damn it!" he said, "why does everybody who comes to Texas turn over leaves looking for gold pieces? This isn't heaven."

"It seems like heaven to us, after trying to raise crops on stone, and giving half what we raised to landlords. We've been pushed along from Pennsylvania to Texas. This time we'll stay until we know we're encroaching. We've a saying that it's ill work taking the britches off a Highlander. Don't try it."

On the Texans, the novelty of seeing women and civilized fixings had suddenly worn thin. They had been treating it as a joke, but what McCash said was plain enough. Someone snorted and someone swore.

Brannigan did not heat up any more than a water jug in the sun. He said coolly to Ira Mosher: "I happen to be a lawyer by trade. I'll be over directly to examine you men's titles."

"Then come with a court order," Mosher snapped. "There won't be any title tampering while I'm recorder!"

"It's not your place to decide who shall see the records. They're public property."

Mosher merely grinned with the complacence of

the man with the keys. Brannigan's brow began to darken, but Janet McCash came into the awkward moment. "All we ask right now is a compromise. If we're to have food next winter, we must put our crops in. We'd like to move out to the land while Judge Stinger deliberates, do the clearing we must, and plant our crops. If our titles are not upheld, you'll be ahead some cleared fields."

Colonel Lightfoot began to nod enthusiastically. "Said they were honest folks, didn't I?"

Croft shook his head. "I'm principled against letting a man break his back for nothing. Let Stinger set on it till it hatches. But nobody is going to camp on my ranch longer than to say howdy." He decided: "Let's go, boys. I guess that makes it clear." He slung the whip over his shoulder and walked off.

III

About halfway to town, Croft turned to glance back, a little ashamed, yet still angry. Brannigan was the powder in this charge. He was sorry for the Scots, anxious for the things they could bring to Pistol Creek. But they would not stay while they were harnessed to Brannigan.

The camp once more looked as though nothing had occurred; the ripples of a small, dropped pebble had been absorbed. He resented this. He resented hearing a distant *tinkling* of laughter as Janet McCash laughed with Yancey.

In the enclosure, the great shorthorn bull peacefully grazed. Suddenly Croft said: "Any of you want a shorthorn cross for your herds? Think I know where we can borrow a Bates bull."

Frio took off his hat and scratched his sweaty scalp. "Jim, you're plumb devilish. That'd be cow stealin', wouldn't it?"

"Not if we bring him back. When they come askin', we'll tell them they can have him back the day they shake Pistol Creek."

He swung off a few dozen rods in the deep thicket along the creek. He left the trees then and guided his big steel-gray gelding back toward the camp. He began to feel mean about it, but Lord, camping in another man's dooryard and refusing to move off! That was the real grit, for nerve. What they had to learn was that the Republic was a hard-knuckled shake of men who had fought for their land and knew how to keep it.

A grudging thought of the girl pried into his head. Hope she knows about soldiers. Her own look-out, though. He mused on the other girls he had seen in the camp, with their young waists and bosoms, but his mind came back to her. Hair that gleamed like a handful of copper priming caps. Lips you watched form a smile or a vowel with a tingling in you. The sport she'd have been to swing in a reel! But there was depth to her, too, a womanly treasure of tenderness and gentle wisdom. Jim knew, the way a buck knew when to scrape the velvet off the horns, that she could be for him. . . .

From the edge of the wagons, he could see her again, still with Yancey. He scowled, raised the bullwhip off the horn, and gave the gray a slap with the haft of it. The horse dug and jumped. Croft was aware of the Scots staring at him. He loosed a yell and bent over the horn. He sent the whip out in a stinging *pop,* and the bull swerved toward the wagons at a scared run, his head flung high.

Men were yelling. One of them was Yancey. "Croft, you damned idiot . . . !"

Prince Charlie made for a table of Scots at their meal, which happened to block the nearest avenue of escape from the enclosure. Thomas Alexander McCash arose, picked up a poorly little gray woman beside him and ran. Less gallant, other men cut and ran alone. But the table was empty when the shorthorn's curly head dynamited it. Iron cutlery, tin plates, and white crockery flew high.

Yancey, having put Janet behind him, calmly stood his ground. As Croft passed, his hand snapped up with the Walker pistol. He let the long barrel line out on the shoulder of the horse. Jim acted with the brilliant sureness of instinct. He threw the popper of the whip over from left to right, flinging it out at the last with a hard *snap.*

The plaited rawhide came down with a *crack,* winding about Yancey's forearm. Jim raked the whip back and Yancey lost the pistol and his balance and fell in front of the pony. Croft freed the whip and put the gray over Yancey's sprawled lanky form in a long jump.

The bull ran clumsily across the splotchy ground, turf flying. In the trees, Croft slowed and followed him by the trail of torn underbrush. Finally he caught up and hazed him across the creek. He had in mind a thicket where the immigrants would not find him in a month of quartering.

He should have been prideful of his success. He was not, entirely. What he remembered chiefly was the look Janet McCash had given him, which had made him feel small enough to hide in a boot.

Ira Mosher rode over to Sheep Bridge that afternoon to summon Judge Amos Stinger from his farm. Stinger arrived at the stone courthouse before sundown in a big yellow carry-all. He dismounted, carefully wiped the mud from the wheels and dashboard, staked the horse, and struck his hands together as he walked toward the courthouse. He was a peppery little man like a whang of sunburned cartilage. He could quote at great length from the Bible, the Laws of Texas, and *Pilgrim's Progress.* There was not a man who could consume more whiskey with less show of it.

In the small courtroom there waited Brannigan, McCash, Jim Croft, and the remainder of the ranching crowd.

Stinger's shotgun personality made the pine table as pontifical as a Boston jurist's bench. "The case of Dock C. Brannigan *versus* one Ira Mosher," he said in his raw, nasal voice. "Mosher, how's it you won't unlock the records for this man?"

Mosher said contemptuously: "How long do you think the records would be around if this snake-oil lawyer ever got his hands on them?"

Stinger's scrutiny went over the *empresario* like a fleshing knife. "I know. But it's the law, Ira. You got to let anybody examine the records that asks to."

Mosher's keen eyes followed the progress of a lizard along the window sill. "Principled ag'in' it, Judge."

Stinger smote the desk with his gun. "Principles, hell! The law takes no account of principles . . . or, if it does, it's coincidence. You'll open 'er up!" He looked at his watch, which indicated 3:45. "You've got till tomorrow morning. I'm dating a bench warrant nine a.m. Captain Yancey will be empowered to open it at that time, if you haven't already."

Croft was grinning when he went outside. Brannigan saw it and in his broad brown countenance his large, dark eyes retreated into watchfulness. Stinger was a man of honor, thought

30

Jim, a law man but not without imagination. They had all night to think about how to protect those land titles of theirs.

By the time Croft had ridden back to his camp in the trees, he was feeling a need of solitude, like a hurt animal crawling away to be by himself. He was not hurt, but he was confused. He did not understand how you could be so hot for something and so set against it. When he recollected the bewildered stare the girl had given him when he drove Prince Charlie out of the square, it made his toes squirm inside his new boots.

I wonder if they call her Jan? I wonder if she's bespoken? She couldn't be, the way she and Yancey sashayed around together. Lord, if she got herself engaged to him! It made him coldly sick in the belly to think of it. *Yancey, the lying, gambling off-scraping of the wilderness! He bragged that he'd loved Caddo squaws before he was fifteen, and hadn't passed one up since. She couldn't know that, and who could tell her?* Seeing Yancey's hands on her was like witnessing desecration.

And another lady who was making some wrong friends was Texas, he thought sourly. She couldn't hang on the arms of such men as Brannigan and Yancey without starting talk. She was making fond eyes at the States, hinting at annexation, but it would be a cold day before anybody annexed a strumpet whose sweethearts were title forgers and renegade soldiers. She had some beaux to say good

31

bye to, some mascara and carmine to wipe off her face before she could put that star of hers on another flag. Nobody would buy land where you could hold it only with a rifle.

Needing comfort, he picked up his fiddle. He leaned against a tree and catgut and horsehair begot a little melody. Jim was purely an Arkansas fiddler, but the music scratched an itch nothing else could. He was warming up with "Will You Come to the Bower?" when someone did.

The girl said: "A man who can fiddle like that, James Croft, can't be so hard." It was Janet McCash.

He laid the fiddle aside.

"Play it out!" she begged him.

Jim's face was hot, but in the dying light of the day, with the smoke of his fire tangy in the woods and the girl sitting on the tarpaulin by him, he finished the tune.

"Is it for dancing?" she said.

"Or for fighting. It was our regimental march in the war. We didn't have time to find a better one."

He kept thinking he ought to be standing, that it was unseemly to sit, but she was warm and friendly and he began to loosen.

"So you have wars over here, too," she said.

"I thought we had a patent on them. What do you fight over?"

"We fought over being moved from our crofts so the landlord could feed sheep instead of us feeding ourselves. And we fought over alien kings. We hoped we were through with fighting. But they're close to singing clan songs tonight, James."

"What's a clan song?"

"A fight song, like yours. We paid four passages on that bull to bring him from Scotland. He was carried in a wagon most of the way from New York. He's had grain when the rest of us were eating roasted acorns."

"Where'd you eat acorns?" He had eaten them, too, and knew about how hungry you had to be to resort to acorn meal.

"In Tennessee. We laid over there one season to plant a crop, but we got moved along. We were eating the acorns before we got the crop off."

"You're plumb land hungry, you Scots. It's dull music, ain't it?"

She closed her eyes; the lids were faintly blue. "Starved," she said. "Do you know what it is to be moved along for two and a half years without ever having a roof over you?"

"Know what it is to be without land. My father was a one-mule cropper before the war, back in the States. I've put down roots here that not all the forging land swindlers in Texas could rip up."

"Why do you think he's a swindler?" She did not sound angry, so much as curious.

"Why would he wait three years to claim a grant?"

"I suppose he was busy."

33

"Busy learning to write Sam Houston's name. Jan, I'll make you a swap. Throw Brannigan out and I'll sell you a quarter of my land cheap. And I'll talk the rest into it, too."

Her eyes went thoughtfully over his face. They borrowed their color from her dress, which was gray and purple. He noticed how tiny the pores of her skin were, how the planes of her face were as delicate as his mother's old cameo.

She shook her head. "We haven't the money to buy land twice, Jim." Then: "How did you know they call me Jan?" she asked him, smiling.

Jim's heart was running like a horse. "Something about you," he said. "You act spoiled. That's it."

She laughed. "I'm a good clanswoman that knows her duties and her failings. One of which," she said, "is not knitting. I knit better than my mother, even. Look at these socks."

She was pulling them out of a fold of her shawl. She laid them across his arm. They were of the same mauve-gray everything else seemed to be in the Scot camp, long and soft, blanket-thick. He knew why she had brought them. His impulse was to accept them and say: *Prince Charlie is in an ironwood thicket across the creek.* But a stubborn reaction made him growl: "What's the matter with your men? Are they afraid to come and ask for your bull?"

"They don't know I've come. You won't find them afraid to come, Jim. They'll come in their own time, but I hoped to save trouble all around."

She got up. Jim rose with her. He felt like hell about the bull. But what kind of a Texican would he look to be if he traded it back for a pair of socks? He tried to give her the socks; she put her hands behind her.

"Perhaps we're of different stuff. But a Scotswoman could not sleep for knowing there was a bachelor running around barefoot because he had no one to knit him socks. Keep them. They might be a lesson to you."

"I'll walk you back," he said.

Jan shook her head. "They'd tie you up in place of Prince Charlie."

He let her go, but after a few moments he followed quietly, standing at the edge of the woods until the slender form with its shawled head and swaying skirt reached the fires. The darkness was more lonesome and more cheerless than he had ever known it.

Ira Mosher was sitting by his fire when he went back. "Thought I'd wait till your company left." He grinned. "You ain't selling us out, are you?" He was looking at the socks in Jim's hand.

Jim shrugged. "Tried to give 'em back. What's on your mind? Yancey gunning for me?"

"Well, that of course . . . but the caper is we're holding a buryin' tonight, Jim. An old friend of ours, known as the land records of Smithwick County. Coming along?"

35

IV

Day broke, clear and blue, over Pistol Creek. The new leaves of the pecans glistened with the still wet varnish of dew. Smoke of breakfast fires drifted through the bosque, and on the ridgepole of Shank's Tavern a mockingbird, singer of a thousand songs, but none of his own, gave a melodious series of imitations.

Croft arrived early and sat on the gallery of the tavern, smoking. Shank's woman took a rocker and began pounding maize, with a howdy for Jim. She pounded a handful of corn for ten minutes, poured the meal in a pottery kettle, and measured another handful of Indian corn into the mortar. At a quarter before nine, a dozen men and women from the immigrants' camp walked up the road to form a group before the stone courthouse. Brannigan, McCash, and McCash's girl were among them.

Colonel Lightfoot, who had slept at the tavern, strolled behind the building a while with his hands clasped behind him. His thick black hair was gathered into a brief pigtail by a rawhide string. He coughed frequently, spat on the ground, and paced again like a man disturbed in his mind.

Captain Joel Yancey, with four of his troopers including Corporal Greaves and Sergeant Billings, arrived just before nine—lean, leather-skinned men on half-starved ponies. The only show of regimental insignia, other than greasy shirts and unshaven chins, were their blue-and-yellow saddle blankets. Colonel Lightfoot joined them. Jim heard him say tartly: "Why don't yo' make them pot lickers of yours wash their shirts once a month, Yancey? You should've learned soldierin' under me. My boys were slicker'n wet rawhide every day we weren't fightin'."

Yancey made his short-stemmed corncob gurgle. "We run more to fightin' than fancy doings."

"We ran to both," the colonel snapped.

"Seen Mosher yit?"

"No."

Lightfoot lowered his voice. "Be careful. There's a yarn goin' about that Mosher . . ." He turned, saw Jim, and delivered the rest *sotto voce*. Croft smiled.

It was now nine o'clock. The door at the side of the courthouse, which opened into the room where records were stored, was still locked. Brannigan stepped from the group of Scots. He cupped his hands and shouted:

"Nine o'clock, Mosher! Open up!" When there was no answer, Brannigan started for the door with Thomas McCash. Yancey called a warning. They waited for him. While they conversed, Judge Amos Stinger came down the front steps of the courthouse to join them. He carried a paper. There

37

was more talk. Croft sat on the gallery of the tavern with the other ranchers and waited.

Yancey took the paper and squared off at the building, hands on hips. "Last warning, Mosher!"

There was a movement at the dark slot of a window, but no answer. Turning back, Yancey said: "Take the women back to the trees."

He remained with Greaves and Billings. When the immigrants had reached safety, he suddenly flung himself to the ground behind a boulder. The troopers sprinted for shelter. Yancey drew the wonderful Walker pistol. Jim leaned forward with his elbows on his knees. He wanted to see this shot; he wanted to see the officer make an ass of himself. It was about ten rods from where he lay to the door, and the lock was a small target. Jim thought he could hit it himself, with luck, but a lot of Yancey's marksmanship was talk.

Yancey pulled a bead. The Walker gleamed in the sunlight, long and trim, the brown metal parts burnished. The revolver leaped in his hand, a cloud of smoke bursting from it. There was the stinging *crack* of the shot. Yancey's thumb caught the hammer and he eared it back. Jim stared. He had shattered the lock with his first shot, torn a hole in the wood, and mangled the metal! There were calls of encouragement from the Scots.

Jim sat back, frowning. So the man *could* shoot.

Yancey remained there a moment longer. Then his long legs drew up and he sprinted forward.

Again he fired. This time the bolt was broken and the door stirred inward. Jan's voice carried with a note of alarm: "Cannily, Captain Yancey!"

Yancey waved. The drummer boy going unarmed into battle. Abruptly he lunged forward, reached the door, and hit it with his shoulder. He sprawled inside. Greaves and Billings stood tensely with guns at the ready. A commotion was heard, then brief silence.

A face appeared in the doorway, large and bearded, the eyes bloodshot. Prince Charlie stepped through, his sides scraping—it had been a struggle to get him inside after they stole the records, Jim recalled—and after a glance about to see that the world was still there, he limped toward the Scots' camp.

Yancey appeared in the doorway. He was disgustedly brushing smuts from the sleeve of his shirt.

Jim Croft exploded into laughter. Lightfoot tried to bottle his, but broke into deep bass guffaws as the others shouted. Even the Scots saw the humor of it, and their laughter rang.

Thomas Alexander McCash caught the bull's lead rope, and brought him gently to a stop. He followed up the rope and patted the shorthorn affectionately; it seemed to Croft that any minute he might kiss him. He started to lead the animal off, but noticed his limp. He seemed trying to understand that something—anything—could be wrong with that horned god of his. Suddenly he dropped to his knees and started examining the favored leg. His hands came away blood-smeared. Jim's heart thudded.

McCash wiped them slowly on his trousers. He rose, gave Jan the lead rope, and came stolidly toward the tavern.

"He-boar's on the prod," Frio said.

"Damn Yancey," Croft grunted. "He must've shot him."

He watched McCash come onto the porch. The fun was off the prank. He was ashamed, but not ready to admit it. It had been a way to return Prince Charlie without seeming to back down. The more he thought about it, the more righteous he felt.

McCash's deep-socketed eyes burned. "He's shot!" he said. "If the screwworms get into it, we'll lose him. Croft, was this your joke?"

"Mine as much as anybody's."

McCash crossed the rough puncheons. He was an enormous man, a patriarch of blacksmiths. "Get up!" he roared suddenly.

Of all the men Jim did not want to fight, the Scot was first. "McCash," he said, "if the bull's hurt, I'll doctor him. I've got creosote and blue vitriol."

McCash seized him by the arm and gave it a heave that hurled Jim over his hip, across the porch, and onto the ground. He lay on his back with a roaring in his head, the wind pounded out of him; the trees were a slowly revolving pattern.

He instructed his limbs to action, but for the moment they lay flaccid as ropes. He managed to roll over on his face; the singing in his ears lessened, but now a misery began in his back, as though pegs had been pounded between the vertebræ. His lungs rasped at the air.

McCash stood at the edge of the porch, fists knotted. "A man among cattle, but puny among men!"

Jim Croft pushed himself up on all fours. McCash jumped down beside him; the Texans merely watched. It was Croft's fight, but their faces indicated that he'd better make it a good one or walk softly around Pistol Creek.

Jim had the wit not to get up until he was ready. Then he went forward in a rush, plowing into the Scot's belly and bearing him back. McCash's blacksmith's arms locked about his chest. Jim felt himself being lifted off the ground, his feet thrown high over his head. He relinquished his hold, startled. The Scot raised him higher. Jim began to struggle; by luck, he got McCash's head between his knees. McCash tried to throw him down, but Croft's leg locked the way they locked on the barrel of a pitching bronco, and the pair of them fell heavily. McCash whipped over like a wildcat on a stove and dived at him. Jim's open palm met him on the side of the head. He bounced up, McCash after him. McCash circled, long arms feinting and reaching, his face hard and red.

Somewhere Jim had heard that the Scots were tolerable wrestlers. He'd been called a handy lad in a rassle himself, but there were tricks in the Scotsman's book he'd never heard of. There was only one gambit he knew, and it was rough fun, but something told him it would have to be a quick fight.

McCash slashed in low. Jim stumbled backward, but, in falling, he got both hands under the other's chin and sank his middle fingers deeply into the soft flesh of his underjowls. Grunting, McCash released him. Jim smashed his palm down on the top of McCash's head and forced him down, and with the Scot floundering he got a handful of the thick short coat, and another handful of the seat of his breeches, and heaved him off the ground. He was the largest man he had ever fought, and, for all his grunting and straining, Croft could not raise him over his head. It was harder going than hogging down a two-year-old steer.

Jim began to pivot. He swung the Scot out in a flat arc, so that McCash was at the end of Jim's arms and moving in a slow circle. "Got you, old hoss!" Jim panted. McCash was flashing swiftly over the ground and across the edge of the steps. Jim kept moving in a mincing circle, backing away from the gallery. Suddenly he hoisted the Scot with a rising heave that flung him into the road and sent Jim reeling back. McCash sailed and dropped and rolled three times before he rocked to a stop.

He did not move.

Yancey drifted over and stood, staring down at him. He squatted, then glanced across the big loose form at Jim, with a raise of one eyebrow that shot Jim's heart into his throat. He started into the road, but Jan McCash came running with her skirts held knee high and knelt by her father. In a moment McCash stirred and lurched up, blindly striking out. He calmed. They got him on his feet. For a moment Jan stared at Jim Croft.

"Lordy!" Jim said. "I didn't mean . . ."

The McCashs walked slowly toward the immigrant camp. Jim turned to Shank. "If you got any more of that blackberry brandy," he said, "I'll be taking a shot."

V

Around midday, Jim Croft saddled his gray, tied behind the cantle a sack of flour purchased from Shank, and gave his fiddle a pat. Well, he'd come with good intentions. It was a sour affair, start to finish. Diplomacy had failed, and now he could only retreat to fundamentals, barricade himself behind the knowledge that he owned what he owned.

Judge Stinger and Colonel Lightfoot came from the tavern as he mounted. Stinger's hands were clasped under the tails of his claw-hammer coat.

"You're going too far and in the wrong direction," he declared. "There was no call to steal the records."

"There was if we didn't want them stole out from under us. Once they're gone, our powder's mildewed."

Stinger shook his head. "Get 'em back. Brannigan's asking an injunction to oust you, if the records aren't returned by the time the trial comes up."

"What trial?"

"To show cause why you shouldn't vacate. I'm with you, you know that. I've got land myself, though it's outside the grant. But what's done will be within the law. The Republic will make an adjustment if we find his case is legitimate. Why don't you let them come onto the land and put in their crops?"

"The easiest way to get a rattlesnake out of a privy," Jim said, "is not to let it in."

"We'll find out about that," Stinger snapped. "In the meantime, I've appointed Lightfoot county recorder. Mosher is out."

Lightfoot pulled in his belly an inch. He knotted his heavy brows. "You get them records back, Jim," he said.

"Better trail Prince Charlie around, Colonel. I've got a suspicion he ate them. Better wear hip boots, too. Didn't know what kind of work you were getting into, did you?"

44

In the tavern, somebody laughed. Lightfoot's face reddened, but hardened at the same time, and he lowered his head a bit and said: "I'll git 'em, Jim, if I have to git you. Some fellows like to fight just to fight. No reason the rest of us should get our noses skinned just because you want to skin yours."

"I reckon not. Only that was practically the reason you and me joined the army. I came all the way from Tennessee to fight. I guess a man's ideas change as he goes along. But I hope I never sell my friends down the river for a two-bit county job."

He rode on, leaving the settlement as he swung northeast toward his ranch. He passed the Scots' camp. He wanted to look back and find Jan, but disciplined his eyes. He stared straight ahead along the trail winding up out of the bottoms and across the broken range. The sweet scent of grass was in the air. A covey of fool quail ran into the trail and hardly moved aside as he went by. All he could think of was Jan.

He came up through a gap into a grove of walnut, and suddenly he saw a horseman blocking the road. It was Joel Yancey. Yancey had his rifle across his saddle. At the side of the road were a dozen of his men, all holding rifles, all mounted, and the focus of their attention was Jim Croft.

Jim eased the bit back into the pony's mouth. He was only fifty feet from them, and he didn't like the look of the outfit.

"Come on!" Yancey called. "We want a little talk."

Jim let the horse move ahead. He thought bitterly: *A man in love ought to be knocked on the head.* Wool gathering had brought him to this, where with a little attention he'd have noticed their sign a mile back.

Yancey kept moistening his deep underlip. "Better git down, Jim," he said.

Croft dismounted. He let his revolver and powder and ball punches fall to the ground. Yancey handed his gun to Corporal Greaves, a big pock-faced fellow with simple features, who handed him a coil of hard rawhide rope. Jim's heart convulsed. He saw the play now, but it was too late to back out of it. Yancey's long face was hungry; his hands handled the rope nervously as he walked toward Jim. Jim suddenly slipped to his knees and snatched at the carbine lying in the road, but in the same instant the cavalrymen swarmed over him in a rush.

Sometime during the fracas, Captain Yancey's rawhide rope got around Jim's neck. A short length of grass rope was lashed about his wrists. They hurled him on his back beside the road and Yancey put the barrel of his rifle on Jim's chest and leaned on it, regarding him with lean satisfaction.

"A real ripsnorter, Jim," he said. "Going to take Pistol Creek country apart and put it back together to suit you, huh?"

46

"I like it the way it is," Croft told him. "Dock Brannigan's the one that's trying to take it apart."

Yancey chewed on a cud of kinnikinnick, spat close to Croft, and asked suddenly: "Where'd you cache the records?"

"Can't tell that."

"Stand him up," the captain ordered. Corporal Greaves and a private hauled the rancher up. Yancey gave the rawhide a tug. "Think she'll bear him?" he asked Greaves.

Greaves fingered his pitted chin. "Well, sir, if she don't, we'll keep on splicin' her till she do."

Yancey nodded reflectively. He turned and studied the great walnut, half shading the trail, its bark black and sodden, its branches festooned with small leaves like children's hands. He turned back, his lank, heavy-lidded features thoughtful. "Well, we might as well get to it, though I'm constitution-alized ag'in' such affairs. But what can you do with a man that's busting out with meanness like this? You boys walk over and have a smoke while I administer sacrament."

Sergeant Billings hung back, a thick-necked, sober young fellow who looked more like a farmer than a soldier, his yellow hair cut crudely and his features overly reflective. "Captain," he said. Yancey glanced at him. "This man's got friends, Cap'n. Do you reckon . . . ?"

"I reckon I'm still doing the reckonin' for this outfit!"

47

The sergeant hesitated, scratching his head, and ended by moving away.

Yancey offered Croft a chew of Indian tobacco, but Jim shook his head. Yancey swung the rawhide like a skip rope, fretting Jim's neck. "Still don't want to talk about the records, huh?"

Jim regarded him without replying.

"I'll tell you what, Jim. I'm thinking of settling down. Been soldiering a long time. Thought I'd buy a little piece of land, get a woman and some cattle, and be a rancher. Want to sell that land of yours?"

"Get the woman first," Jim advised. "You'll sicken of doing your own mending."

"Aim to. Got her picked out. She may sound like snappin' twigs when she talks, but she's sound as a yearling heifer."

"She can knit, too," Jim persisted. "I've got on a pair of socks she gave me. She was down to my camp last night."

A pucker deepened between Yancey's eyes. He studied Jim, and suddenly the edge was off the joke for him. Jim still did not think he intended to go through with it; he still hoped one of the other ranchers over this way would happen along, but, looking into the captain's face, he was not so sure as he had been. Yancey's voice sharpened.

"Do you want to sell your iron to me? . . . Or do you want to give it to me?"

"I want to keep it. You've got no show to pull this. Who said I took the records?"

Yancey's mind hung with bulldog tenacity to the main issue. "Jim, I'll pay you five hundred dollars for your outfit. No grit just now, but if the place is any good, it'll work it off." His face was unbecomingly eager.

"I can't gar'ntee title, you know." Jim smiled.

"You let me worry about that."

Jim said soberly: "I'd rather be buried on that land than give it away, Captain. Let's quit jawing and admit you haven't got anything on me. Stinger's the authority around here. He'll haul you before a firing squad if you go through with this."

A moment longer Yancey regarded him, then he raised an arm in signal. The troopers came back. "Put him on his horse." Croft kept his eyes on Billings, wondering if he could be used as a lever. He sat above them, Yancey retaining the rope, Billings holding the reins of the horse. Yancey moved his head toward the tree. The sergeant walked the pony under a high branch.

Suddenly Jim was scared—scared and nauseated and sweating, with groveling words just behind his teeth. An instant from the past swam before him. A Mexican spy caught near Buffalo Bayou, yellow with malaria and fear, facing the firing squad with a black cigarette in his lips and contempt in his eyes. *Little fella,* thought Jim, *you had guts!* He wanted to say something light-hearted and scornful, but was afraid, if he opened his mouth, his teeth would chatter. The soldiers were watching him thinly, hungry for a show of cowardice.

But it appeared he must be doing better than he'd reckoned, for they seemed almost respectful. "The Pistol Creek War," Jim drawled. "I'll put a *toston* on the card that says Lightfoot musters enough Second Infantry boys right in this county to tromp this troop out like a hog-nosed skunk!"

". . . Cap'n," Billings said.

"Shut up!" Yancey snapped. With sudden decision, he stepped back. He hauled on the rope so that Jim was yanked out of the saddle. Hands still lashed behind him, he landed heavily on his side. An explosion of pain carried him up into the thin atmosphere of giddiness. The rawhide noose was torn away. Yancey stood over him, breathless and smoky-eyed, coiling the rope with swift jerks of his wrists. Then his right arm began to rise and fall.

There was little to add to Croft in the way of pain. The hard coils smashed his back. His body writhed, but his mind was separate from it. Yancey flogged him steadily, snorting through thin nostrils. He continued to lash at the slowly stirring man on the ground until blood began to stain the leather shirt. Then he straightened, breathing with quick, shallow breaths. "Put him on his horse," he said. "That'll set him to right any time he thinks he can rig Captain Joel Yancey for a clown!"

VI

Croft's cabin was at the edge of a deep stand of post oak in the Cross Timbers, facing south into a snug valley, well-watered and heavy with grama and buffalo grass. Pecans grew along a stream and furnished both scenery and a change to the eternal diet of maize, jerky, and fat pork. In summer and fall there was an additional blessing in the squashes and sweet potatoes from the field Croft's Mexican tended. It seemed to him that the land gave a square shake—a good yield for a minimum of effort—and, by Joe, it was his! No greasy cavalry renegade was going to take it from him by bluff, nor any snake-oil lawyer. This was the thought that kept his mind off his misery during the days that followed Yancey's flogging him.

It was a beating to cripple a man for days. But the frontier was not a place where a man could afford to puny around, so Croft was out mending harness in the sun on the second day. Something in his back pulled whenever he moved. Abelardo, the Mexican helper, doused his wounds with a mash of boiled pokeroot that seared the raw flesh agonizingly, but started it healing immediately. In every way he endeavored to forget that all he could think of, all he wanted to do, was to kill Joel Yancey.

It was a full week before his fury annealed into more governable metal. At the end of this time, he was glad he had waited. Yancey would have loved to toll him into a foolhardy attack, for he had not half drunk his fill on the Pistol Creek road. With a healthy fear of Colonel Lightfoot and 100 other Texans who would have made lynching impractical, he had backed down. But Yancey was the gun of the law, where Judge Stinger was only the bullet. He could not be attacked without Jim's taking on the whole troop and a shelf of law books.

Yet he might be vulnerable to a duel. They said Sam Houston had fought seven duels so far. He had given the practice prestige. Partly for something to do during his convalescence, but largely with forethought Jim Croft stretched a tape of bleached hide belly-high about a tree and began practicing. Hitting dead center was no trick for a marksman, but getting the range was a matter of patient practice. Jim began to cut the tape with regularity.

Every morning, when he drew on the marvelous gray socks, he thought of Jan. He dreamed of slim fingers and the kind of cleverness that could achieve such miracles of knitting. It stood to reason that she could cook and keep house, as well. His mind fingered that hour by the fire threadbare. He extracted the quintessence of meaning from everything she had said. *A man who can fiddle like that can't be so hard, James*

Croft! She was the dream he had dreamed so long, made mortal for him.

Out here, a man was purely in a pocket. Women broke down into two basic groups: good ones and strumpets. The good ones, town girls who regarded coyness as a talent to be cultivated, were not to be carried off by a cowboy with burrs in his hair who came courting and gave her twenty-four hours to make up her mind. She was not to be rushed, but neither would cows and calves wait for him to come back and tend them. So he would likely never penetrate the screen of corsets and bleaching towels.

The strumpets, while they supplied the coddling and excitement so badly needed, were hardly what a man wanted to carry back as a wife. Some men subscribed to the services of a procurer who brought wives to the wilderness for a stipulated fee. To Croft, this smacked of the barnyard. So he had been waiting, and all at once two trails crossed, and one of them was Jan's, and one was his. But right at the crossing stood Yancey—and Brannigan—and trouble. Jim's position was no better than it had been. It was merely different.

On a cold day of low clouds and weak rain, fine as salt, Colonel Saul Lightfoot rode out to Jim's Panther Scratch ranch. He brought with him the *empresario* of the Scotch outfit, Dock Brannigan. Two big men on large horses, they found Croft and Abelardo branding calves in the stone corral at

Conejo Spring. A small fire burned smokily on the damp earth. Jim was kneeing a calf as they rode up, but neither he nor the Mexican acknowledged them until the colonel said heartily: "Well, Jim! Never one to let a stray run long, eh?"

"Cows nor women," said Jim.

Brannigan vented his laugh of deep pedal notes. His shiny box coat was streaked with wet; beads of moisture stood on the oiled cover of his beaver hat. The bootleg pistol shoved into his right boot glinted as he lit down. He leaned on the wall to watch the work.

"Look a little peaked, Jim," he said.

"Fell off a bronc'," Jim grunted. "But I'll ride him again, and leave the gaffs in him next time." He looked up coolly.

The exchange puzzled Lightfoot. Shaggy as a Mexican badger, ponderous of body and mind, he blinked at it. He gave it up, shrugged, and said with an attempt at the old camaraderie: "Jim, I wrote Houston last week. Got to get this cleared up, you and me. You could help, you know."

With mild protest, Brannigan came in: "Some fellers lead better than they push, Colonel. Eh, Jim?"

"You've got better sense than I thought."

"Jim," Brannigan said, "I'd like to lead you to a little stack of gold coin totaling three hundred dollars."

"For what?"

"For your ranch."

"You already own it. You've got a paper that says so."

Brannigan looked thoughtful. "I'm going to break a rule of mine," he said. "I'm going to brag a little on myself. I want you to know that I'm not like just any fellow who wrote himself a grant and came butting in hoping to make it stick."

"No. You sold a bunch of immigrants into the deal so they'd have to side you or lose their money."

"I sold them what I thought I owned, what I still think I own. Now, that title of yours may look to you like the gospel according to Houston. All wrote down legal and signed." He shook his head and sighed. "It ain't that simple. Look at Texas as a big patchwork quilt . . . biggest in the world! The patches are grants . . . headrights . . . scrip . . . colonies. Every new politician sews in a patch of his own, and he gives or sells a shake of grants without looking too close into prior rights. I've negotiated five grants and only got stung once. That was where another *empresario*'s grant predated mine. Open and shut, I bowed out. It goes back to prior rights, you see. Now . . ."—he cleared his throat—"what's the date of your headright claim here?"

The bland wash of oratory had hardly touched Jim. "Don't recollect right off," he said. "Let's just say . . . earlier than yours."

"We could settle that in a minute, if you'd dig up those records."

Lightfoot stared hungrily at Croft. The king without a kingdom, the recorder without records. . . .

Croft went back: "I still think it's wasteful to buy something you already own."

"I've got an obligation to those immigrants. I don't want to get them into a county war. I've got a reputation all over Texas for getting things done without fuss. I wish you could see my colony down at Owl Creek. Those people are taking off crops you'd have to see to believe. They've got their own church and community storehouse. A school's a-building. Over at Buffalo Gap they've put in cotton and sugar cane, and it looks like they'd make a killing. I don't leave a colony until it's on its own feet, and even then . . ."

He talked on. He seemed to see himself as the Moses of Texas, leading her to greatness. Brannigan was a mighty orator, and even Abelardo, understanding none of it, stood open-mouthed. His cigar went cold, darkening along the top with moisture. And finally his boots again touched earth, and he looked at Jim Croft and said gravely: "If I've got a calling, it's to build empires. The Titan of the West! That's the future I see for Texas! And, even though I may be a small wheel of the machine, I want to be part of it."

"Wheels have a way of rolling," Croft said. "My guess is that you'll roll just before things get too rough. Are you buying out the rest of the boys for three hundred, or just the ones that make enough noise?"

Brannigan dropped the cigar and stood down. "We may as well go back," he told Lightfoot.

Lightfoot hesitated.

"Colonel," Jim snapped, "you used to have a little savvy. Does it look like a man would buy his own land just because there was a squatter on it? Or does it look like he might use a forged grant and a herd of immigrants as a cannon to blow a dozen settlers out of his way?"

Lightfoot was confused. "Why . . . I don't know, Jim. But I know I don't want to go to war again. If we stand trial and lose, Yancey's empowered to run us out. But Dock says he can talk the Scotchmen into letting us 'bide, till it's been appealed. Just so's we let them come on and put in their crops. They got a most unholy yen to farm, just got to sink a plow or die, seems like. If they lose the case next week . . ."

"Next week, eh?"

"Sat'day. Jim, if you and Mosher don't produce the records, ain't no use even coming to town! Stinger's a bear cat for doing things reg'lar."

"Do you know what would happen if I brought those records to court?"

Brannigan looked curious. Lightfoot unconsciously rubbed his medal with his sleeve, in the old gesture.

"Somebody would want to examine them. He'd bring a quill with him and change a date or two. Or there'd be a ruckus outside the courthouse, and, when we came back, the job would be done. Or maybe the damn' courthouse would burn down. Been happening all over Texas. Those records are like the preacher's hope of heaven. As long as we've got 'em, hell can freeze solid, but it don't change a thing."

Brannigan walked to his horse. He mounted, and Lightfoot, momentarily pulled in two directions, lingered. Then, with melancholy decision, the colonel gathered the reins of his pony.

Croft watched him lay the leather across the horse's neck. "We've been building to this," he said. "You've been a good neighbor, even though you've let other fellers chase your cows home and pull your critters out of the bogs. You're lazy as hell's first fiddler, and you pack more wind than the cow that got in the grain shed. For all that, we've pegged you for one of the best. But the day you let them pin a tin title on you and set you to lay traps for us, I laid Colonel Lightfoot away in his shroud. You ain't the colonel any more. You're plain old Saul Lightfoot, and no friend of mine."

VII

Two days before the case came up, Jim Croft carried a sack of cornmeal and some jerky to a hedge apple thicket about two miles from his cabin, a thorny jungle few men would enter by choice. He left the food under a cairn of rocks. There was no telling what would break loose after the trial. But he'd learned long ago the value of a final firing line.

Then, on Thursday, Frio Gorman, Ira Mosher, and Bigfoot Morgan rode by. They wore clean buckskins, boots rubbed with tallow, and a holiday look. "Coming along, Jim?" Frio had whacked his red hair off stylishly.

Croft looked them over. "You going to a trial or a shindig?"

"Maybe both. When I was in the other day, them Scotchmen were getting ready to throw the dangedest *baile* you ever seen! That'll be tomorrow night, before they break up camp. They aim to leave out right after the trial."

"The mail carrier must have got lost," Jim said. "He never got here with my invite."

"Do as you like, Jim. But I heard Yancey's gang saying they'd show them lassies how we dance in Texas. So we thought we'd mosey down and show the soldiers how we dance in Smithwick County."

This made a little more sense. It might be inviting trouble to raid the party, but Jim might be able to get Yancey in a corner, too. Yancey, with his bragging of the squaws he'd bedded, whirling a girl like Jan in a reel!

Gorman rattled his rowels against the dun's hide. "Well, take 'er easy, Jim."

Jim said: "Hold on. I'll go along."

In a matter of three weeks, leaves had come out on the last of the naked trees. The ground, drying, bristled with new grass. Heel flies attacked stock in biting swarms. Pistol Creek brawled. The immigrant camp was as neat and ordered as ever. No refuse had accumulated, no loose gear lay about. It was as clean as the inside of a church. And Croft thought: *It was a black day you tied up with Dock Brannigan. But for him, we'd make room for you.*

Yancey's men strutted about the camp like cocks, watching preparations for the feast, and pretending to help. It was a dingy picture for Croft to take to his blankets with him. Next morning he drank the chicory juice Texas called coffee, and then stood at the edge of the trees to watch the Scots' camp coming to life. Jan was just beyond the wagons, stretching a large square of cloth on the grass. Jim walked over. "What are you doing that for?"

"Bleaching it. Don't you ever bleach your sheets?"

Jim chuckled. "Not since I tore them up for lamp wicks."

"You mean . . . !" She gave a small shudder.

"How's Prince Charlie?" he asked her.

"Blooded stock heals quickly. He's as fine as ever. No thanks to you."

He stood awkwardly, watching the slim, strong fingers work, noticing the slender waist and wondering if he could span it with his two hands. Well, not quite, but he'd come a lot closer than trying to span it with his arms.

"Are you coming to the feast tonight?"

"Haven't been asked."

"You can come if you don't start another fight. The soldiers will put you out if you do."

It was an odd thing. Jim got the impression the whole thing was with design. That perhaps the celebration was an unguent to soothe some irritated tempers. "We're pretty peaceable as a rule," he said. "Will your father let me in?"

"He's all but forgotten the mill you had. He was the best wrestler in our town. He admires a man who can beat him. Tell your friend, Frio," she said abruptly, "that Margaret is saving the first reel for him."

"Who's Margaret?"

She laughed. It was a light, golden sound. "He'll know! He's been in every week to see her. In fact, every Pistol Creek rancher but you has been in."

"If I come, do I get a dance?"

The reddish braids gleamed as she moved to stretch the sheet. "Captain Yancey asked me to save all my dances for him."

She looked up quickly, the gray eyes lively, but Jim said casually: "Well, I was really coming for that Argyll whiskey, anyway."

As he started off, anger boiled up in him for the way he had been tricked. He heard her rise.

"Jim!" She came to him and stood there, slim and sober. "Of course you can have a dance. But I'll have to explain it to Captain Yancey. If I give you the last dance, will you do me a favor?"

"Might."

"Bring the titles back to the courthouse." She saw the stubborn ruts form between his eyes. She reached for his hands. "Jim, for your own sake! We don't want a falling out. If we're wrong, we want to know about it. Because it will be no loss of ours if we are . . . Brannigan will have to return our money. We'll only have to move on."

At that moment Jim saw the big, casual form of the contractor pass between two wagons, on his matutinal round of inspection. An idea of what seemed great cunning occurred to him. Just how unscrupulous, and how incautious, was the *empresario*?

"I'll make a dicker with you," he said. "For a kiss I'll bring them back."

She searched his face, and then colored a little and smiled back at him. "You can't scare me out,

Jim Croft. But how do I know you won't trick me?"

"I'll give you a bond. If I don't bring them to the courthouse by noon, you can have the kiss back."

"And you say the Scots drive a hard bargain!" Jan closed her eyes and stood on tiptoe with her hands clasped behind her.

Jim framed her face with his palms, tilting it a little on the side. "I'll just try on a few for size first the way I did with the boots. This may have to last me longer than the boots."

He kissed her on the forehead, and she caught her breath. He kissed her cheek and she sighed. Then he kissed her mouth, slowly and sweetly, and she made a little sound in her throat. When he took his lips away, she whispered: "Oh, Jim. It's got to come out right. Let's make it."

"Honey," Jim said, "that's the only reason those records are coming back."

The Texans were gathered at Shank's Tavern when Jim rode up. They sat in the thin spring sunlight on the gallery, smoking, chewing, whittling, waiting. Somber and spiritless, Jim eased himself in the saddle and looked down at them.

"Anybody want to help bring the records back?"

Lightfoot sprang up. "Jim, boy . . . !"

Frio headed inside. "I'll git a shovel!"

They reacted like kids to a stick of candy. Sex was a wonderful thing, thought Croft. Put a parcel of grandmothers down there instead of those long-legged Scot lassies, and they'd be tough as gar soup. But here they were falling over themselves to risk their land titles for the chance to swing a few girls!

West of the settlement, on a bluff overlooking Pistol Creek, was the cemetery, a lonely colony of crosses and hand-chiseled stone markers. At a spot marked by a splintered board, they dug. Colonel Lightfoot knelt to raise a square box. Frio opened it with the shovel. The fat cowhide ledger was undamaged, damp and moist to the touch, but not mildewed.

Croft told him coldly: "If anybody tampers with that book, it'll be two feet of hide off your backside."

"By God, I'll sleep on it."

All day, barbecue fires smoked in the ground and the succulent odor of exotic come-back sauce tortured Texas salivary glands. Yancey arrived about three with a dozen of his men. The rest of the crew straggled in later, uninvited, unwelcomed, hanging around to watch the doings and ogle the girls. The Texans rode down shortly after. They left their ponies staked beyond the wagons. McCash met them at the head of the wagons, frosty, gray, stern as a deacon, and wearing his purple and gray tartan across his shoulder.

"If you come in peace, welcome. We'll have no

brawling nor swilling. We're Borderers, Croft, temperate with everything except our tempers."

Yancey and the troopers strolled about with chunks of beef to gnaw on. Judge Amos Stinger was there, never getting far beyond the whiskey jugs. Out beyond the wagons, some of the younger men were playing a game that involved tossing a log from a scratch line. An unearthly whining of bagpipes came from where three men played a clan song.

All this foofaraw was lost on Croft. He was tense and anxious until he saw Jan emerge from her wagon and come across the square toward him. She smiled as he came to meet her, giving him her hands while he filled himself with the presence of her. She wore a gray merino gown he had not seen before, nor anything like it, a snug, civilized gown to hug her waist and fall with tiny, crisp flounces to her ankles. She wore high Balmoral heels that just showed. Croft took a long breath.

"I've changed my mind about that bargain," he said. "I was too hard. I'll give the kiss back."

"Not this night, Mister Croft." They started back to the fires.

Jim glanced down at her. "Well, then do I get my dance?"

She shook her head. "Don't ask me for it, Jim. Captain Yancey is holding me to my promise."

Jim's glance found Yancey. "You think I'm an

upstart, don't you? What would you think if I took all your dances from him . . . without a fight?"

"I'd think it was wonderful." Her eyes said: *Take that any way you want.*

Jim walked over to Yancey. Yancey had the smell of sweat and liquor on him. He had a smile that involved only his mouth.

"Looking good, Jim," he said. "Taking better care of yourself, I hear."

"Been keeping out of street fights with more than six men at a time. Captain," Jim said curiously, "they tell me you're pretty handy with that Walker Colt of yours."

Yancey kept his dark, sad eyes on him. "Jim, don't start anything you don't want me to finish. You don't think you scared me out that day, do you?"

Jim shrugged. "Why should you be scared, with twelve men to back you up? But that's done with." He nodded at Yancey's revolver. "I hear there's a lot of back flash with those things. No good for target work because you get to flinching."

"That what you heard?" Yancey raised the gun and spun the cylinder. He glanced about. In the wiry grass just beyond the open end of the wagons, a whistler squirrel sat piping its monotonous call. Yancey cocked the gun and brought it down. The shot exploded. Through a haze of black powder smoke, the squirrel could be seen kicking its life out on the ground. Yancey holstered the gun.

Jim regarded it respectfully. "Quite a piece. How are you at a dueling tape, for a prize?"

"What prize?"

"Backwoods stakes. Winner take all . . . the loser's gun and gal."

"That's no stake. I've got the best of both already."

"You could use two guns, couldn't you?"

Yancey hesitated. There were a lot of men to hear his reply. "You still ain't matching the gal."

"That's a fact. Reckon nobody could. But I'll bet I get her anyhow, when she hears you crawfished. She wanted to see a Texas shootin' match. This was really her idea. Well, all right . . ." Jim didn't finish.

Yancey spoke as Jim turned away. "Throw in your pouches and I'll go you."

A black-trunked elm was girdled with a strip of rawhide. The tree stood about 100 yards from the wagons, in a strip of meadow. Judge Stinger was enlisted to referee the match, Frio and one of the troopers walking to a point near the tree as judges. All the kids in camp had run down to the course, and most of the men and a good showing of women had come down. Jim emptied and reloaded the Paterson. It was a five-shot, .34-caliber weapon with a twelve-inch barrel. It had its failings, one of which was not target work. But Yancey's Sam Walker was the kind the angels carried—a six-shooter with a trigger guard and built-in ramming lever.

They paced off the distance and laid a branch for a scratch line. Yancey won the toss for first shot. Judge Stinger, red-faced and pompous, reviewed the rules.

"Half the width of a ball will be counted a hit. Ten seconds to make your shot after coming up to the scratch. First man to cut the tape wins the match."

Yancey stepped up. His stance was careless—feet wide, half faced from the target, his left thumb hooked over his belt. A long and gangling figure with buckskins bagging at the knees and elbows, there was nothing heroic about him, but something deep and steady.

Stinger held his big silver watch in his hand. "Time!"

Yancey raised his gun high, slowly bringing it down on the target. Almost as it reached eye level, he fired, the gun leaping in his hand. Yancey blew smoke from the barrel.

The judges ran from their places near the tree to examine the mark. Frio placed a peg in the hole, dead center but six inches above the tape. Yancey regarded it a moment and turned away.

Jim felt his heart begin to thud. He had more than a gun and a dance on this. He had his chance for partial retaliation for the flogging Yancey had given him. Yancey would be like a fighting cock with his spurs cut if he lost that Colt. He would lose prestige with his men and with Jan. Jim glanced at her in the crowd as he came up to the mark. She put her fingertips to her lips. Her father glanced down sharply, but her eyes and her smile were still for Jim as he cocked the gun.

"Time!" Stinger said after an instant.

Suddenly everything seemed to slow down. This was the tree behind the cabin, the tape was the old, much-hacked piece of harness spragged to the elm so it wouldn't fall when cut. He had all day, but he wouldn't need all day because it was as simple as holding your breath and pointing your finger.

He let the shot go. Through the blur of powder smoke he watched the judges run to the tree. He thought he could see the mark, but the distance was too far to be sure. Then the peg was driven into the bark barely an inch from the tape!

The crowd shouted. Jim asked Stinger: "How long?"

"Six seconds."

Yancey's cocksureness was punctured. He rubbed his hand on a buckskinned thigh, licked his left forefinger, and held it up for windage. *Rattled!* Jim thought. A forty mile gale would hardly affect the range, and only range counted here. Yancey gave the priming lever a pull to seat the ball. He shuffled his feet and kicked a pebble away. Then he brought his right toe up to the branch.

"Time!" Stinger said.

Jim saw the trooper take a deep breath. Yancey held it, and once his arm wavered. His face was screwed up, but a black splinter of eye glinted, keen as the point of a scratch awl. Jim found himself flinching, waiting for the long-delayed shot.

Suddenly Stinger yelled: "Time!"

The Colt bucked, the shot overlying the sound of his voice. A man ran up and shoved a peg into the tape.

"*There's* one for you, Jedge! She cuts! Bring a ball to measure!"

Yancey grinned, levering a ball from his belt pouch, but Jim saw the unsureness of him. Little Amos Stinger was shaking his head. "I called time on you, Yancey. You forfeit the shot."

Yancey squalled; his troopers set up a howl on cue. "The shot was away!"

"Air you calling me a liar?" Stinger inquired.

Yancey let the interval gather tension. Then he slipped the ball on the ground. "Not the last shot I figger to make."

A fountain in Jim's chest was bubbling. So close! He'd have hated to be licked by a coin toss. He set his feet, let his breathing quiet, and watched the judges duck back.

"Time!"

Easy, Jim's mind whispered. Bring it down, slow and sweet, watch for rawhide. He was startled when the gun bucked, as a good target shooter ought to be. For a moment he was blinded by the quick burst of gases. Then he heard them yelling.

The tape hung in two equal lengths at the sides of the tree.

Captain Yancey waited smilingly for Jim to claim the gun. As he held it out, Croft flinched. Yancey was offering it muzzle first, on full cock. Jim smiled back in his teeth, and reached.

"Easy does it," Yancey told him. "I've filed the sear so she fires on a wink."

Jim held the barrel, but Yancey seemed to have trouble drawing his finger from the trigger guard. Jim's cue was to show the saffron by asking the trooper to uncock the gun and reverse it.

Yancey abruptly gasped: "Don't pull, dammit! I'm hung up!"

It was one thing to stand behind a gun when it discharged, an entirely different experience to have the hot, killing blast of it strike you like a cannon ball. Croft was shaken to the marrow. Flame ran up his sleeve, scorching and blistering; an engulfing roar staggered him. He stumbled back, clutching his forearm. Yancey dropped the gun. In tight-lipped concern, he strode to Croft, pulled back his sleeve, and examined his arm.

Jim heard him say: "Damn me for a clumsy one, Jim! You ain't hurt, but you're shore scorched."

He was standing that way, filled with sanctimonious sympathy, when something flashed in the air and he staggered and put both hands to his head. He fell to his knees, lunged forward on all fours, and remained that way.

Judge Stinger pouched his massive horse pistol. He had clipped Yancey across the ear. He watched Yancey's face tilt up and the sense slowly seep back into his eyes.

"Plumb mistook you for a murderer I hung once," Stinger said. "I was going to write up charges again' you for gambling with government property, if you lost. But we'll just call it a square shake all around."

VIII

Yancey did not return to the shindig. It seemed to take his blessing off it for the troopers. After that it was Texas night.

The Scots got in a reel or two of their own and a fling. But mostly it was mountain reels and shuffles. Jim had no idea of how long it went on. They had insulated this moment from reality, and they were drinking it dry. Barbecue fires cooled; whiskey jugs gave up their nectar. The Texans swung their ladies in the Texas style, got tipsy on whiskey, and sobered again before anyone thought of breaking up the party. It was the night before Austerlitz, with the Russians sharing their women.

At last Thomas Alexander McCash invoked the

curfew. "Last reel, friends! Time we were cooling the blood."

The bagpipes began their infernal whining and a fiddle scraped. But Croft sat with Jan and had not the heart to dance. She knew what he was feeling; he felt her hand squeeze his arm. "Jim . . ."

Firelight was golden magic; a plain woman was beautiful, a beautiful woman something to make a man's heart weep. He pulled her face against his neck and held her, his eyes closed. So gentle and so proud, so near to being his, so far from ever being.

Then they heard a man close by saying brokenly: "It won't be for long, Maggie. We'll break our heads till we find a way to work it out."

Frio Gorman was having his troubles, too, and all the other young bucks.

Suddenly, at the end of a dim corridor, a door opened and Jim Croft saw an answer. He began to chuckle. "Honey, we've been making this too hard. There's five bachelor ranchers in Smithwick County, and only two married. Stinger can marry the whole kit and caboodle of us! You move in, and the old ones come along."

He could not comprehend for a moment that she was not falling in with it. "No, Jim. They wouldn't be pensioners if this were the last county in Texas. Would you?"

Jim scratched his head, considered the valiant lie, and gave it up.

He left ahead of the others, riding solemnly down the fragrant night road and consoling his heart as a father might a hurt child. He was back where he'd been the day he rode into Pistol Creek. Nothing was better except that now he wore knit socks and bench-made boots.

He reached the turn-off to his riverside camp, glanced once at the straggling crescent of buildings, and hesitated. A light in the courthouse? He reflected—Stinger bunked there on court days. But this light was in the archive in the rear of the stone building. It was merely a furtive candle flame as unobtrusive as a cough behind a hand. But only Lightfoot had the key to the records, and there was no evidence of Lightfoot's red mule in the yard.

He dismounted, jammed twigs in the shanks of his spurs, and walked to the partly closed door and looked in. Dock Brannigan had a large cowhide volume open and was examining a page under the light of a fat beef-tallow candle. His thick, dark brows were gathered, but, as Jim thrust the door open, he came hurriedly to his feet.

Brannigan recognized Croft and sat back on the three-legged stool with a windy sigh. "Come in. So many fools around, Jim, that I didn't know what to expect."

Croft stood with his hands on his hips, a lank, unsmiling figure against the black rectangle of the open door. He said nothing, and Brannigan, reaching up to wipe perspiration from his fore-head, volunteered: "I had the key from Lightfoot. Had to prepare my case, Jim, now that you've brought back the records."

"You ought to have it prepared by now."

"But it's the first time I've had a chance to look at you men's titles, you know."

"If they look genuine," Jim said, "I suppose you burn them?"

Brannigan, the big, the hearty, the snake-oil spieler, seemed trying to get a foothold. "Stinger is a bear cat for facts. I can't go blundering in there without knowing where I stand."

Croft walked around him to see what he was looking at. The volume was open to a page headed: *The people of the Republic of Texas: Be it known that James Robert Croft, having . . .*

Jim reached forward, ran his hand across the page, and looked at his hand. No ink.

Brannigan's hand moved, but not quickly enough to hide a small silver ink horn. Jim seized his wrist and pulled it away.

Brannigan frowned. "What am I going to make notes with?"

Croft hit him with the angle of his fist. Brannigan went back over the table, spilling ledger and candle. In the darkness, he moaned softly. Jim stepped around the table and waited, but an intemperate fury was on him and he shouted: "Get up, damn you!"

Brannigan lay there, part and parcel with the darkness. *If I'd been two minutes later!* Croft thought bitterly. *If there'd been one spot of ink on that page!*

The tempo of Brannigan's breathing changed. It was controlled, careful. In this instant Croft saw a spark of metal on the floor; he put his weight on his left leg and sent his right boot forward in a kick that landed solidly and brought a pained grunt. Jim dropped on the warm lump that was the contractor, found his head, and slammed it once with his fist. Brannigan was not faking this time. He was out. Jim found the title volume and left.

IX

By nine o'clock, the wagon city had melted into a line of white tilts, an orderly column fretted by disorderly dogs and urchins. The wagons had been moved onto the road, the wistful wilderness trace called the Central National Road of Texas. The area where they had camped for six weeks was a bare reddish square in a green meadow.

Brannigan was up and down the column officiously, dapper in gray, well-combed beaver, square-skirted coat, and linsey-woolsey pants, visiting briefly his own canvas-topped carry-all with its two strong mules, and dropping back to confer with McCash or one of the others. He had not been visibly affected by the encounter with Croft the night before, other than by a knot of pink flesh over his right eye.

At a quarter of the hour, he assembled all the family heads beside the road. On the ground he had sketched a large map to approximate his tract survey. Yancey, looking gelded without the fine Walker pistol at his side, was on hand with a few troopers to watch the drawing of plats. Brannigan had numbered each section and now shook a handful of paper slips in his hat and with considerable ceremony delegated the first drawing to Thomas McCash.

McCash looked at the slip he had drawn. "Plat Number Five."

Brannigan indicated with a stick the position of the Scot's farm. "The Coon Rock farm, presently occupied by one Frio Gorman," he said. "A little inaccessible, but rich in bottom land. If you ask me, the best farm in the county. Kirk, you're next."

McCash wandered off to smoke his pipe in the shade of a tree.

Croft's Texans sat on the courthouse steps, watching this papier-mâché empire building. They had nothing to say, and, when Colonel Saul Lightfoot appeared on his red mule and joined them, they did not acknowledge his presence. Jim had told them of the encounter with Brannigan. He had brought the cowhide ledger. And now he tossed Lightfoot's keys on the ground and said: "I found these last night. Brannigan said you gave them to him."

Lightfoot looked stricken. "I must've been stiff as a ring bolt on that Highland tap water. I . . . I kinda remember. . . ."

He sat down, staring straight ahead. There was a blackness and a confusion in him not entirely attributable to his dereliction. The tufted brows were locked together, the anvil forehead corrugated. Once he started to speak, stopped, and sighed like a winded horse.

"Tell us how you saved Sam Houston," Gorman suggested.

At ten sharp, Judge Amos Stinger opened the door to the warm spring morning. The Texans walked in and took benches. They heard Brannigan bring his crowd to claim the rest of the seats. Stinger sat behind his table with an inkwell, sharpened crow-feather quills, and a few law books. Smelling of whiskey and chewing tobacco, he opened court. He then asked Brannigan for argument. The *empresario* arose and strolled to the bar. He unrolled the Morocco case and laid his land title before the judge.

"Right there's my case, Your Honor. There's nothing I can add to it, nothing my opponents can detract from it. Given in gratitude by the people of Texas, signed by the President of the Republic." He made a half bow. "Your Honor, I submit that . . ."

"Set down," Stinger snapped. "What have you fellers got to say?"

Jim brought the title volume to the bar. "There's our case, Your Honor . . . a catch lot of headrights and scrip. They happen to be legal. Big Sam's name is on some of ours, too. I guess your job is to decide whether Houston writes his name better than Brannigan does."

Stinger waved him back to the bench. He huddled over the evidence a long time, a little man with the build of a mockingbird and the bearing of an eagle. He looked up angrily.

"What do you want me to say? 'It's the big fella's' . . . run all the little ones out'? Or . . . 'It's the little fellas', renege on the Republic's promise to a man who helped win the war'? You Pistol Creek men are all friends of mine. Because my farm happens to be outside Brannigan's grant, it doesn't concern me any less than if I stood in Jim Croft's boots." He rested his head on one hand and massaged his eyes. "Been up all night," he grunted. "Couldn't find one hell-swiggered precedent for a decision. We're making policy here, making history the way we did at Goliad. Whatever I say, people are going to damn me all over Texas."

Another interval of shifting and scowling and waiting followed. Then Stringer laid both hands flat on the table.

"Well, there's only one thing I can do, only one thing I could do from the start, and you men didn't make it any easier to find an alternative. It's my opinion . . ."

"Your Honor," someone said. Colonel Lightfoot got on his feet, a big, shabby man in leather shirt and old cavalry pants with the seat bagging like a bushel basket.

"Well?"

"I've been trying to recollect. When did Sam go out of office on his first term . . . back in 'Thirty-Eight?"

"Same day Lamar took office. Second Monday in December. Same as now."

"What's the date of Brannigan's grant?"

Stinger's eyes flicked. "December Fifteenth, Eighteen Thirty-Eight." Then his back straightened, but he kept his glance on the colonel's face.

"That'd be later than the second Monday, wouldn't it?" Lightfoot sounded doubtful, almost apologetic.

The judge rubbed his hand reflectively over the parchment. "Seems like it. Seems like Lamar would have been signing papers by then. How's your memory, Brannigan?"

"Good enough to remember what Houston said to me when he presented it!" he flared. "He . . . well, never mind. You know the kind of clerks we had in those days. Any plow boy that had learned to spell his name was a clerk. If the date's wrong, don't blame me."

Something was about to break loose in the

courtroom, although hardly a man had stirred. But Stinger, red as brick, kept his voice under control. "No, I don't blame you," he said. "I'm right on the point of it, but I won't blame anybody until I get an opinion from the capitol. You and your party will camp right here at Pistol Creek until I do. That's an injunction. Yancey will enforce it."

Brannigan's temper broke like a storm. "He will like be damned enforce it! He'll give us escort onto the land!"

Thomas McCash said gruffly: "We abide by the law. We camp here until you return our money. You're a forger and a liar."

Brannigan stepped into the aisle and stared down at him. "You'll get your money the day after hell freezes. I contracted to settle you. I hold myself to that, and I hold you to it. I'll go out if I'm the only one. Yancey will see to it that I get where I'm going. The grant's genuine."

He tromped out of the courthouse. Yancey got up like a stalking timber wolf and followed him. Stinger shouted: "You greasy-faced devil's recruit! If you mix in this, you'd better be keepin' the peace rather than disturbing it!"

"I take my orders from the military, Jedge."

"Is a colonel high enough to give an order, Yancey?" Lightfoot asked.

Yancey smiled. "Not a colonel of the wind-broke cavalry."

They were gone from the courtroom.

For a while it was silent in the cold, stone-walled room. Pressure released stops and took a breath. Jim turned to look at the Scots. McCash stood alone, like a man lost in a desert with an empty canteen in his hand. He looked down and around him, at the people he had brought so far, to lose their money and gain no land, to be poorer than the poorest crofter in Scotland. And Jim felt the terrible guilt and bitterness of him—the clan leader who had led his people to ruin.

McCash's deep-socketed eyes came to him. "Mister Croft, we're sorry. We'll be going along."

"Where to?"

"To free land. Wherever that may be."

"The Cherokees will scalp you bald a week out. Go after Brannigan," he said impulsively. "Get your money back."

"Aye," McCash said with the air of a man repeating something he had not the heart for doing. He had struggled over strange trails for thirty months; he had reached Canaan only to find it a drier desert than anything he had come through.

He walked from the courthouse. The others trailed him. Jim heard Brannigan's carry-all grind along the road, hustling toward Yancey's camp. He strode with sudden resolution to Stinger's desk.

"Write up a warrant for that ripsnorter, Judge. I'll take it to Yancey. He'll serve it, or we'll do it for him."

"A warrant for what?"

"Fraud. Land fraud, man! I caught him tampering with the titles last night. Is that enough, or has he got to confess?"

Stinger squinted. "You'll swear to that?"

Croft raised his hand.

Stinger dipped a crow quill and scratched on a sheet of paper. A hive of conversation suddenly broke out. The cow crowd was at last launched on the kind of headlong, boastful talk men fought best on. Jim listened to it with a grin that seemed to sink down through him.

Through the benches came Colonel Lightfoot, moving slowly and with his eyes on Jim. He reached him, patted his shoulder hesitatingly, and let his hand fall away. "Die in your sleep, Jim," he said. "Die while you're still dreaming."

Jim gave his hand a hard pressure. "You weren't the only one he oiled for the slide, Colonel."

Lightfoot pulled off his medal. "Keep this for me until my face is clean enough to wear it again. A soldier! Me! Calluses on my back from him patting me, soaked in his damned whiskey and buttery talk. . . ." He started out.

"Where to?" Jim called.

"Down to reason with Mister Brannigan. I reckon he could be persuaded to leave that money before he goes on."

He went down the steps. A moment later they saw him jog by on his mule. The buckskin legend was going out to write another chapter.

X

As he went out, Jim was startled to see that the wagons were already in motion. McCash was taking his people on to some vague refuge. The clan leader's wagon, trim as a sailing boat, led the train south along the road from town. On a short chain beside the wagon ambled Prince Charlie, the incredible shorthorn. Dust swirled among the wagons like ground cinnamon. A bony, dour man on the second wagon began to adjust a bandanna over his nose and mouth.

With gaunt acceptance, the women were pulling the drawstrings of the canvas tilts. Only the dogs enjoyed the emigration, yapping at the wheels and darting precariously among the hoofs of the oxen.

As they passed Jim, McCash raised his hand. Janet stood behind him and her mother. She waved, without much spirit.

"We'll write, Jim! Wash those socks every night and they'll last. And never dry the boots over a fire, or they'll crack."

Jim laid his hand on the line and stopped the oxen. "The socks won't last forever, and I'm dead set against bare feet now. What happens when the boots wear out?"

"Ride over and see us," she told him.

"A better way would be if you stayed. McCash, I

can talk to you now without shouting through Brannigan, like an ear trumpet. Will you stay?"

The Scot's knuckled hands massaged his knees. "Even a farmer needs land, friend."

"Pick out a section that suits you, and I'll sell it for fifty cents an acre. We can put every family on a piece of land except the ones who want to raise cattle."

McCash frowned at his wife, who was beginning to cry. "Mother!" She straightened out. "It's beyond my ken, Mister Croft. It's doing a man ill and getting good in return. Brannigan was a liar and a cheat. And how could we be . . . ?"

"You're civilization," Jim declared, "and it's tarnal hard to tell civilization good bye. You're boots and butter and riz bread. You're wool pants and ground meal. We need you, McCash."

McCash's countenance still kept joy in the vestibule. "Then we come to the matter of money."

"Lightfoot's gone to see about that. We might ride along and see how he's making out."

"This is grief. We'll have it out with him ourselves."

"Ours, too. Brannigan still says he's going onto the land. It may be he'll come with Yancey. That's why I'm for getting down to the camp. Lightfoot's outnumbered."

McCash unlimbered a rifle and climbed down to borrow a horse.

Janet took his place. Jim saw how her eyes

complained and how she didn't look at them. "Worrit?" he said, joshing her accent.

She took yarn and needles from a box under the seat and gave him a look of cool censure. "Would a worrit woman be knitting socks too big for her own feet? Only, be back quickly, or we'll bring the whole train after you."

Jim thought: *I'll bet she would, too!*

Deep in the road were the bars of Brannigan's tires and the cup marks of Lightfoot's mule shoes. About a quarter mile out they caught a glimpse of the camp. Dirty tents, an offal heap, a pole corral, and a blur of smoke. They jogged on with saddle guns unbooted. The first thing Jim saw in the camp was Lightfoot's mule. Then he saw Brannigan's carry-all, and knew he had chosen to stay and fight. Now the game was to strike hard and quickly.

Jim waved his gun and plunged into the smoke, smells, and flies of the camp. Of Yancey's forty-eight, he saw a dozen. Most of them were with a man who sat on a chopping block near the fire. This man was big and black-haired, leaning forward as if with a belly cramp. It was Colonel Lightfoot. His shirt was off; a smear of blood matted the hair between his shoulder blades. Jim sprang down in fury, but Lightfoot glanced about and gasped: "No, Jim! They're with us!"

The story, as Lightfoot gave it, was that Yancey was a sneaking fox who refused to obey the order of a superior officer. He had declined to arrest Brannigan, who was in camp when the colonel arrived. Brannigan had his hands full of gold pieces and was trying to buy, not soldiers of fortune, but an escort out of the county. When the colonel turned his back, Yancey sprang on him with a knife.

This was while half the camp was out on some detail or other. About a dozen men went with Yancey and Brannigan, the contractor leaving his wagon and taking a horse. They left the colonel for dying, but Sergeant Billings, brought back with a wood-cutting detail, was doing him some good.

"He must be doing some good," Lightfoot gasped. "He's been scorching my hide with bluestone for ten minutes."

Jim examined the cut, a gash but not a deep one, by virtue of having struck bone. "If you don't get the screwworms," he said, "you'll live to let other men brand your calves as usual. But you're out of action."

"The hell!" Lightfoot said. He got up, winced, rose above his pain and said to Billings, the shock-haired soldier who had helped get Jim's neck out of a noose once: "Assemble every able-bodied man and put my mule under me."

Billings, who had not had to listen to the colonel's yarns for five years, was half out of his head with the honor of working under a Texas hero. He began shouting orders.

Lightfoot's eyes flicked about the ground in reconnaissance. "Ten men. Everybody else hunting floosies or meat. We still outnumber them."

Lightfoot had to be assisted into the saddle. Once there, he laid the reins over and kneed the mule into the road. They milled a moment on head-tossing, curveting ponies. Then Lightfoot spurred along the road after the renegade officer and the builder of paper empires.

Trees lined the road, leafy elms and chunky bois d'arc, a random forest offering ambuscade to a thousand men. McCash, more of a wagon man than a horseman, lunged along beside Jim, clutching a ponderous tape-primer.

Before long the hoof prints faded and the road traveled on through the woods almost unmarked. The horsemen had split into two parties, one heading right, the other left. Lightfoot pondered it, but pain competed for his attention and he seemed unable to make a decision.

"They won't split up for long," Jim offered. "Strength is what they want. They'll come back to the road."

They followed the main trail for a while. Then, from the brush, the tracks of one party came back to the road; not far beyond, the other horsemen merged with them. A weak fog of dust drifted down the aisles of the trees. They had gained ten minutes on Captain Yancey's stratagem.

Croft bore on at a lope until the dust thinned.

Here he halted. Yancey's previous trick had given him a window into his mind. His strategy would be the obvious—nothing was more obvious than to throw a half dozen men at each side of the road and clamp the jaws on his bear when it stepped in. Jim's eyes rummaged along the road. Ahead, a small branch crossed the road in a tangle of greenery.

"I'm guessing they're in the blackberry thickets, yonder," he told Lightfoot. "If we bring it on them from both sides, we might get two honkers with the one charge."

Lightfoot's face was bloodless as old buckskin. "The only honker I want," he said, "is Yancey. Take the boys around to the right. I'll take the troopers."

Yancey's force broke up the maneuver by suddenly pouring a shrill and headlong fire from the bushes. All about the Texans, trees *thudded* and brush *crackled* with balled lead. A horse went down, wriggling and squealing. Yonder, at twenty rods, overly eager cavalrymen stood up in the thickets and sent a stinging offhand fire down the road.

"As you were!" Lightfoot yelled. "Bring it on them!"

He sent the mule into the brush. Jim led out to the right. They cut off angularly, like a pair of ant mandibles closing. Yancey's men boogered. They came into the road and tried to run out of the trap; they fell and got up, emptied their guns, and spilled powder horns trying to reload. Yancey bawled advice and stood there, waving an off-breed pistol in each hand. Jim saw Lightfoot bearing down on him with his horse pistol lining out.

Off to the right, a horseman was moving delicately through the woods away from the road, neither slowly nor briskly, rather with deft care. Dock Brannigan's saddlebags bulged, his stove-pipe was set purposefully, and his whole attention was for riding out of this with a whole skin.

Croft rowelled his pony through the trees, kicking eddies of rotting leaves and dodging branches. Brannigan heard him and turned. He wheeled the horse and brought up the bootleg Colt that had always seemed out of character; he was ready to use it now. It was for a time when cleverness failed, and that was now. He took aim like a marksman, his arm straight but not stiff, his rutted face set. Jim wheeled around, slipped out of the saddle on the offside, and rested the Walker across the saddle.

Brannigan took his shot. Croft saw the burst of powder fumes and felt the saddle jerk with the impact of the shot against the cantle. He steadied, seeing the contractor turn, and fired quickly. Brannigan dropped the single-shot pistol; his hands went out to clutch the horse's mane. He remained in the saddle for the first couple of bucking jumps the pony made. Then his body lost contact with the saddle and the stirrups, and he went overside loosely.

Croft came back to the road. Colonel Lightfoot, officious as a jaybird, had a handful of renegade soldiers in custody. But old Tom McCash appeared deeply shaken by the violence. He had not so much as fired the gun, but his religious heart was aghast. Yancey lay hunched where Saul Lightfoot had dropped him; Lightfoot was of half a mind to scalp him for the fine black hair with its short pigtail.

"Damn' near enough for a hair bridge," he told Jim.

Jim talked him out of it. He was for bringing shovels from the camp and burying the dead as they lay, which was the custom of the country, but McCash raised a hand in horror.

"We'll carry them back and bury them in Christian ground. Respect them for their immortal souls, if not for what they did with their lives."

Jim Croft caught up the reins of Brannigan's horse, mounted his own, and rode toward Pistol Creek.

Death and the protocol of death were for the old. Living was for the young. And there was more to life now than there had ever been. This Texas of his, this girl waiting for him, whose hair was gold and copper, and whose waist was a redbud stem—they were both full of mystery and wonderfulness, and there weren't enough days in a week or weeks in a year to do right by them. But a man could spend his life in trying, and be none the worse for it.

Whiskey Creek
Stampeders

I

Carnagey traveled overland from Arizona after selling his freight string. He was going home, and he moved fast. He had the eyes of a man who has been a lot of places and seen a lot of things, but not enough of home. He went by stage, by railroad, by steamboat, unconscious of the variety of discomforts involved, but fascinated by the mechanics of each. If he had a mistress, her name was transportation.

Carnagey had owned a small pack outfit operating from Grants Pass to Whiskey Creek before he left Oregon. In Tucson he had run a freight string. He supposed there would be a good freight road into Whiskey Creek by now, for mining towns either grew up fast or died.

But when he left the stage at Grants Pass, he found there was still only one pack outfit into the downriver country—the line he'd named and sold—the Southern Oregon Freight Company. But it had expanded. No one around the office and corrals knew him. The freight agent quoted him a rate of two-bits a pound on his luggage without blinking.

Carnagey growled in his throat. "What do they eat down there, with a rate like that? Popcorn?"

It was a hot day, and the agent was bored and

ill-tempered. "You can ride the river if you don't like the rates. Saddle horse will be three dollars a day."

Carnagey hoisted his two cowhide bags onto the scales, noted the weight, and watched what the man put down. Then he went out.

Here was an odd thing. If the town were alive, why weren't there a dozen pack strings, or one good freight road? He went to stand on the bridge at the foot of town. The Rogue was clear and deep. A few miles down, it crumpled into torrents of green and white, fanged with boulders.

Carnagey felt the challenge the river sent up to him. He was like a bronco-stomper outside a corral, sizing up a bad horse. Glenn Carnagey knew the river, knew where you could boat it, and where you had to line. The Rogue was his boyhood and his youth. He'd trapped and fished it, had boated down it all the way to the ocean, 100 miles away. He had half a notion to buy a boat and take the river road down.

He thought: *Why doesn't Hugh Badger or somebody start another pack string and bring that rate down?* That was the way with him. He thought in terms of rates, of the proper stock, of slugging it out with competition and coming out on top. But lately he thought of gentler things, too. Of home hills and rivers, and of a girl named Christy, who lived near Whiskey Creek. There was a tingle involved in his thoughts of her. A tingle and a worry, for she had stopped writing eighteen months ago.

There was a string of freight going out that afternoon. Carnagey rode with it. He counted forty-six mules. Somebody, probably Charlie Hammaker, to whom he'd sold out, had the world by the tail. Those mules were packing $2,000 of freight under their diamond hitches.

Suddenly he knew which way his compass pointed now. He was going into competition with Hammaker. The squall that would go up when he announced a new line was going to be started! But it was all down in the agreement. Glenn had agreed not to operate a freight company of any description out of Whiskey Creek for a year. It had been two and a half years now.

He camped that night at the Bear Mountain corrals. There were four large corrals here. Carnagey had operated with one. In the morning he went on, through scented forests of pine and fir, then across a ridge and onto a mountainside that shelved down to the river, the brawling, tempestuous, disdainful Rogue. The trail, from here, followed the headlong progress of the stream down cañons and gorges to the sea. Below Rainy Falls he found his eyes questing through the thick *madroña* tangles along the river. He didn't see the cabin right away, but he caught a feathery lift of smoke.

He pulled his horse off the trail and spoke to a

packer. "I'm going down to say howdy to Hugh Badger. . . ."

Badger's place was at the point where Fish Creek tumbled down a granite falls into the river. It was five acres of the flattest land in all this tumbled wilderness. Badger had an acre of fruit trees and a truck garden. Behind the log cabin were a springhouse where he kept stone jugs of whiskey and crocks of butter, and a smokehouse where he smoked salmon and steelhead.

Hugh had come with the first of the miners, nearly a generation ago. But he was a man more to the woods than to the mines. He found more money in selling meat than in panning gold. He had been married to a Basque woman who died when her daughter was ten.

Carnagey heard Hugh's shout as he came down the trail. The hunter was stacking laurel branches at the smokehouse. Badger was a lean, undersize, and profane man with a warped mouth and a nose like a skinning knife.

"Told them you'd be back before the steelhead ran again," Badger said as he shook hands. "Which did you come back to see . . . the women or the rivers? Hear tell they don't know how to grow neither down there."

"Both," Glenn admitted. "Hugh . . . dammit, this is good! That smoke brings the tears to my eyes."

"So will a cup of corn."

He fished a jug from the numbing coldness of

the springhouse. Talk came from Hugh Badger as water came from a spring, endlessly, spiritedly, disconnectedly. Then he glanced at Carnagey's horse and stopped.

"What the hell! Ridin' a rented hoss! Where's all them stagecoaches you bragged on? Thought you'd come back in an honest-to-god Troy wagon."

"They were freight wagons," Glenn said. "I thought of bringing them, but it's a good thing I didn't. When is this country going to have a freight road? Have the mines folded up?"

Badger shrugged. "Oh, the mines are all right." He put a special emphasis on it. Then he took another poke at Carnagey. "Well, what about Arizony? Going back?"

"Not if I can make a living here. And I reckon I can. I'll underbid Hammaker twelve cents a pound."

"What are you going to do? Swim the river with the freight on your back?"

"I can still throw a diamond hitch with anybody in Oregon. I'll have a string of mules inside of a month."

"But will you have a franchise?"

"What do I want with a franchise?"

"Gilliam and Ott tried to operate without one. Hammaker busted them. Got an injunction against them and then took to dumping their pack trains in the river. He owns this town, brother. Charlie

Hammaker's the boy says whether we eat spuds or chew roots. He owns it, and you sold it to him."

Carnagey's eyes were level and gray as old lead. "Are they still hashing that over? It was my line to sell. If you didn't like his rates, it was somebody's chance to elbow in on him."

"That's what the others thought. But by the time they thought of it, Charlie had the whole thing skinned and butchered. He knows somebody in the capital. He's got a franchise that cuts competition off at the shoelaces for five years."

Carnagey tossed off the whiskey. He was a large man, rough and big-jointed, and, when he moved, it was with a slow aggressiveness. There had been bad blood about his selling the line. In the hills there was little enough to talk about that the distance across the river at a given point had been known to end in a killing. So now they had all got together and decided he was at fault in selling out. Particularly since Hammaker had proved to be a wrong one.

"The hell with them," he said. "Hammaker's not so tough."

"Some of us would like to see that proved."

"I'll prove it myself."

Badger raised a finger. "Cover yourself, brother. Leave a hole to wriggle out of, because you'll want it."

Carnagey's temper surged up. He chopped it

off. "Reckon it's not hurting you any. Bet you're getting top prices for your meat."

"I'm getting exactly what I got before. Tell you the difference between me and Charlie Hammaker. He's got faith in Charlie. I've got faith in Oregon. If one town blows up because they kept the lid on it too tight, that's too bad. It was just one town. But to me it's a part of Oregon that's blowed up."

Apparently Badger had been at the whiskey before Carnagey arrived. He had the pink loops of moist skin beneath his eyes that drinking on a warm day gave him.

"Came here twenty-five years ago, just me and the Umpquas. Fought my share of 'em, too, to stay. Why? I don't know. Maybe the sap of the trees has gone into my veins. Whatever it is, I can get drunk on it. I can get drunk enough to kill a man like Hammaker."

He stabbed Carnagey twice with his forefinger. "Glenn, this town is set to grow! It's a seed we've planted, but Hammaker keeps it in a bottle. Someday it'll break the bottle. But maybe the gold will be gone, then, and it'll be too late. Because we still need gold to underwrite the rest . . . the lumber mill they've built, the truck farms, the bank, the saloons. The mill sells 'em timbering, the farms feed the miners, and the saloons keep 'em drunk. But if we could just get out with wagons, there'd be some point in building other mills and clearing land for farms."

The raw sound of his voice died. Carnagey's guilt, lying there for two and a half years, rose and began to shake off the dust. He'd known the kind Hammaker was when he sold out. But the profit had been too good to miss, and he told himself a mining town ought to be able to take care of itself.

"I'd walk a little light in town, Glenn. Don't claim no more than your rightful space at the bar. And look out when you pass Tay Pike's place today."

"Hasn't anybody shot him yet?" Pike was the unfiltered dregs of a rough society, the wilderness outcast and the town pariah. Woodsmen hated him because he shot doe, fawn, and buck in or out of season, because he shot bear for the hell of making them crawl. Townsmen disliked his manner of picking up whatever was not nailed down. But he could outhunt and outdrink anyone in the hills, and held his own with them. Tay Pike was tough.

"You know Tay," Badger said. "Got to have something to feud over. At first he was going to kill Hammaker. Then it was you. It's been you for quite a spell now. If he happened to be drunk when you went by . . ."

Carnagey glanced at the sun and saw that it had worked down into the notch of the river. "Better ride," he said. He mounted, but as if in afterthought he asked: "How's Christy?"

"Fine."

"She around?"

102

Hugh grinned. "The hell with you. Come to see me and then chatter about her. She's in town. Got a little caf-fay. Prices nobody but a miner can pay."

You could generally smell Tay Pike's place 500 yards off. Pike was careless about such things as spoiled carcasses and refuse. His cabin was a ruined miner's shack at Poverty Bar. Huckleberry tangles, crowding in about the shack, provided a good part of Pike's diet. Game provided the rest. He was given to disappearing for days at a time, but it had been noticed that, if anyone approached the cabin during one of his absences, he was wont to appear suddenly from behind a tree.

Carnagey was not a man who hunted trouble, but he had learned that a good way to avoid it was to recognize it early. He rode down to the cabin and shouted. Then he sighted Pike downriver 100 yards, rowing with quick, strong stroke against a riffle. He swiftly cut through the roiled water handily, skirting foam-crested boulders without seeming to look at them. He beached the boat, slung a sack over his shoulder, and came up the rocks, lugging his old Burgess in his free hand. Some wild instinct gave him the warning. He stopped and his head snapped up.

Carnagey waved. "Howdy, Tay!"

Pike's thin face studied him. Then he shifted the sack and came on. "Whereat you from, Glenn? Dammit, we missed you."

"Figured you might, so I came home. How's the fishing?"

Pike's mouth, thin and downcurving as the mouth of a cut-throat trout, swore. "Starving to death for a mess of trout. But they've wrecked it. The dredgers up at Grave Creek wrecked it."

He got a hunk of smoked bear meat from the cabin and insisted on Glenn's chewing some with him. It was rancid and dirty. Glenn said: "Thanks anyway. I ate at Badger's."

"How is old Hugh?"

"Talkative."

After an instant, Pike got it. Color roused through his face. Carnagey went on: "He said I'd better steer clear of you, Tay, or I was apt to run into trouble. How about it?"

Pike made a show of resentment. "Well, I been pretty much on the butt about Hammaker. I blame you for that."

"I hear a lot of other people do. I'm going to tell you the same thing I'll tell them. Go to hell. If you've got a carcass to skin, skin it on Hammaker's doorstep."

The other's eyes were shallow and pale as a fish hawk's. "Who brought him in? Who do we thank for that?"

"He didn't have to have my line. He'd have bought his own stock if I hadn't sold him mine."

Pike's temper was rising but he wouldn't meet Carnagey's eyes. He stared about with quick glances, breathing hard through his nose. Carnagey knew that what was driving through him was a shame that he had not the guts to make good all his brags.

"If you've got anything to say," Carnagey remarked, "say it now."

Pike shook his head. All his furtive courage disintegrated in a showdown. But he was nonetheless dangerous for that. As Glenn turned back to his pony, he was watchful. Pike suddenly said: "Say, you going to do anything about Hammaker?"

"Sure. I'm going into competition with him."

"Well, by God!" Pike laughed. "Don't forget old Tay, ever you need a job done. Quick and clean, Glenn . . . a horse, a packer . . . a whole damn' pack string if you say so." Carnagey stared at him until he added: "Forget it, then. But if you go up against Charlie Hammaker, you're going to want help."

"Not your kind. When I fight a man, he's going to know who he's fighting, not wonder what tree the shot came from behind."

Glenn rode out of the yard. As he reached the trees, he heard a movement, a clean whisper of oiled steel. His hand was already on the butt of his carbine, and he pulled it and wheeled the horse. He fired a snap shot that thundered across the river and back in an avalanche of shattered echoes. The bullet hit the tree beside Pike. Pike still held the loading lever of his rifle down, hunching over it. "Drop it!" Carnagey shouted.

Pike dropped it. He backed away. Glenn put a shot through the stock of the gun. It was akin to spitting in the hunter's face. "The next time I pass here," he said, "you'd better be in sight. I'll shoot anything that moves. Pike, those woods talk, and plenty of us around here can understand them. Think about that, any time you feel like smoking any two-legged venison."

Standing at the foot of Whiskey Creek's main street, you could see the unhealed red wounds of the hard-rock mines in the shoulder of a mountain. Standing at the head of the street, you could see the river, across it a neat acreage of farms. Smoke from the small lumber mill drifted over the town, tangy and warm. Whiskey Creek poured its roiled red waters into the Rogue; upstream were the placers. A dull stroke in the earth told of a shot in the hard-rock mines.

Carnagey went into the freight office. An argument was going on outside the back door. "If that horse don't come in," a man said, "it'll come out of your pay. After this, they stay with the string. Hear?"

"OK, Mister Quade."

A heavy-set man of forty came into the office with a sheaf of papers in his hand. He frowned at Carnagey. His hair had been red, but was going gray, crisp with tight waves; the long sideburns slanting toward the corners of his mouth were already grizzled. He had aggressive good looks, his mouth firm, and the eyes steady and deep-set. He wore dusty black trousers and a wrinkled shirt with lavender sleeve garters.

"The horse is out front," Glenn said.

Quade slung the two cowhide bags up. He glanced at the tags. "Carnagey?" he said, his mind feeling for a link.

"Maybe you saw it on a letterhead. I used to own this outfit."

Quade struck his fist against his palm. "By God! Where you from, Carnagey?"

"Tucson."

"Staying a while?" Quade's manner was hearty, yet the edge of an anxiety showed in his eyes.

"I'm on the loose. No telling what I'll do." He turned away.

"Hold on! Mister Hammaker would cut my throat if I let you get away without shaking hands with him. He's out back."

They went into the yard. Corrals were fogged with the dust of mules rolling out the soreness of pack saddles. A last mule was being unloaded at the loading platform, snubbed down between the rings. Carnagey picked out the bearish form of Charlie Hammaker among crates on the platform. He saw him turn as Quade called. Hammaker was slow to recognize the long-coupled, blunt-jawed man in the brown suit and flat-crowned gray Stetson. After a moment he jumped from the platform and came across the tawny strip of ground.

Hammaker had not changed. He must have made $20,000 here, but he still needed a shave; he still wore the seedy gray suit, the greasy, loose-knotted black stock, the paper sleeve protectors, the expression of harassment. He always looked as though he had just received bad news.

They shook hands. Hammaker turned to look over the system of corrals with their milling animals and sweating hostlers. "How's she look to you? Few changes, eh?"

"Never saw anything like it," Carnagey said.

Hammaker received it gratefully. "I've four times the number of animals I started with. It's the biggest pack train in Oregon."

"That's what I meant. You're like a gent making the biggest collection of privies in the world, instead of getting one water closet."

Quade and Hammaker compared frowns. "What are you getting at, brother?" Quade asked.

"When a line gets this big, it usually switches to wagons."

Hammaker snorted, his wide mouth grinning. "Over that trail?"

"Hell, no. Build a road."

Hammaker sadly shook his head. "Do you know what it would cost to enlarge that trail into a road?"

"About ten thousand. I had an estimate made before I sold to you. I couldn't swing it then, and I wasn't sure the town was going to keep on growing."

Hammaker lowered his voice. "Confidentially I'm not quite sure of it yet."

"Then you ought to sell out to somebody who is."

Hammaker kept his sharp black eyes on him. He was nearly bald, with just a fuzz of hair within a garland-like fringe; perspiration beaded his scalp. "I've got a theory that when a boat is riding well, it's foolish to shift cargo."

"You seem to have a theory about keeping your sails furled, too. This town's ready to move, if somebody would give it half a chance." He turned from scrutinizing the corrals. "Do you want me as a competitor, or do you want to sell the line back to me?"

Hammaker took him thoughtfully by the arm and steered him into the office. Carnagey watched him take a card from a pigeon hole and write on it. WALTER A. MILLIS, ATTY. AT LAW was the legend on the card. Hammaker had written: *Mr. Carnagey is interested in competing with us. C.H.*

"Millis is my lawyer," Hammaker said. "He'll tell you about the legal side of it. Mister Quade will tell you about the . . . other side of competing with me. Why don't you see what's doing in Grants Pass?"

Then Carnagey saw that his lips were trembling, that the heavy countenance was shaking with fury. But the man's formal nature compelled him to put his threats and his rage into undramatic language. He said only that and went into his office and shut the door.

Glenn could picture him sitting alone, staring blindly at a wall. For him, dollars had the tender power that daughters had for other men. Someone was trying to seduce his dollars away from him. Carnagey wondered how far he would go to keep them home. . . .

Quade stood rubbing his palms slowly together, frowning, his lips pressed into a firm line. His attitude was patronizing but threatening, quiet but heavy as a clenched fist. "Carnagey . . . ," he began.

"If you're the other side of it, let's have it so I can understand it. And if I'm going to understand it, be sure it's not going to make me sore."

Quade looked over the other man. "We're about of a size, if it ever comes to that," he reflected. "But Hammaker's bigger than four of me or ten of you. People go into business to make money. What he wanted me to get across was that you're not going to make any money in Whiskey Creek, not in the freight business. Do you understand that?"

"No."

Quade was annoyed. He cleared his throat; his

eyes kept measuring Glenn. "I won't try to make it any clearer until I know there's some point in it. Talk to Millis, talk to Gilliam and Ott, if he can't convince you. The point is . . . we're the only legal carriers this town will have for the next five years."

"I think you've almost got yourselves convinced of it. Keep an eye on me, Quade. I may be able to teach you some tricks."

II

A theory of Carnagey's about women was beginning to totter. Leave them alone long enough and their need of you increased. Let the girl know she required you before you bought the diamond. But from the day he left, a cooling process seemed to commence in this particular girl. The cooler her letters got, the more he was drawn back to Whiskey Creek. Suddenly he had decided to sell out and move back. She and Oregon had won. And now he was looking up and down the street for her restaurant, and feeling an odd sense of panic— Badger's Café was across the street from a wood yard, a small restaurant with a counter and two tables. There were blue-and-white curtains in the windows.

Coming from the sunlight of early evening into the dim interior left him groping. Then he saw the girl and the man at the end of the counter. She made an exclamation. "Glenn!"

Christy came to the front and gave him her hand, but somehow it seemed to have no more significance than a man's handshake. "Why didn't you tell us?" she said.

"Spur of the moment," Glenn told her. "I'd have been here before the letter."

She wore the same blue-and-white material with which the room was set off. It brought out the clean copper highlights of her hair. Like the town, she had changed—completed the act of growing up. Her breast was fuller, her waist more slender, and her lips rounder. Carnagey had a desperate thought: *She's the one, all right . . . but am I?* There was definitely a wall between them.

Christy's hand drew from his. "Glenn, this is Sam Gilliam," she told him. "Sam, you've heard them speak of Glenn Carnagey?"

Gilliam shook hands with him. He was a hard-jawed, brown-skinned young fellow with a look of slow force, pleasant but not aggressive. "Glad to know you, Glenn."

Carnagey asked abruptly: "You're one of the men who went up against Hammaker?"

Gilliam looked sheepish. "Well, it was worth a fling."

Christy sounded like a mother defending a son. "It was two against twenty. But Sam's going to have it back before he's through. He's raising hay

112

now, and squeezing eighty dollars a ton out of Hammaker for it."

She laughed. She had the poise and sureness with which a woman sets at zero a man's physical superiority. She left him feeling off balance. In an excess of heartiness, he took a seat and slapped his hand down on the counter. "How's the chuck, Gilliam?"

"Best in town."

"Hash, pie, and coffee," Christy announced. "Bear steak on Saturday. If I could afford the freight on a good stove, I'd have a choice every day."

Carnagey's food was served with that casual politeness a bachelor gets used to, but it deepened his sense of frustration. Other customers began to arrive. Christy was too busy to talk.

"So Hammaker gave you a run?" Glenn asked Gilliam.

"It was coming down to gun play. He had to back out. He happened to have the law on his side. He dumped our last train in the river, mules and all. That cleaned us."

"Wonder what he's going to do to me."

Christy, passing with a plate of hash, stopped. "Glenn, you're not going to . . . ?"

He shrugged. "I've got a living to make."

For the first time Christy's cool veneer was scratched. Frowning, she hurried on.

Gilliam shook his head. "Look out for him.

Maybe he's not so tough himself, but Red Quade is a killer in fancy clothes."

Glenn pondered. "If I go into business, will you sell all your hay to me? Ninety a ton?"

Gilliam's reaction was slow. Then a grin lightened the squareness of his face. "Why not? But I can tell you right now you won't need it."

"If I don't, I can turn it over quick enough. I'll give you some money down and a check for the rest on delivery."

Gilliam finished his coffee. "Want me to hold off telling Charlie a while?"

"Why bother? Let his blood pressure blow his hat off."

Gilliam paid for his meal and went out. Carnagey finished and took his hat from a hook.

Christy followed him onto the walk. "Glenn, I can't talk, but . . . did you know Tay Pike is in town? They say he's looking for you. Whatever happened between you?"

Glenn smiled. "Thought you didn't know I was in town?"

Her chin went up a bit, but she ignored the remark. "You can do what you like, but I'd watch out for him."

"I called his bluff once, and I'll do it again." He drew his hand from his pocket with a small, smudged package he had brought all the way from Mexico. "I saw these in Hermosillo and . . . they're just gimcracks, but . . ."

The gray-blue eyes were cool. She did not put her hand up to take the package. "It would be under false pretenses if I took it, Glenn. You see, I learned about freighters long ago."

Carnagey's hand clamped on the box. He made a half gesture, as if to throw it in the street. Then he tossed it on his palm. His grin was quick and cocky, a little adolescent, but he would look anything but hurt. He said: "Well, I suppose I can rustle somebody else. Start pounding one of those bear steaks for me. I'll be around again Saturday."

The Oregon twilight was deepening on the mountains as he walked back up the street. The cañons were darkening, and a midnight gloom had entered a cañon in his mind. She had pinned the jackass' tail on him. His impulse was to make some large gesture, such as getting drunk and whipping half the men in town, and depart. But a core of wisdom in him kept drawing his mind back to sanity. All the grief he had, he had made himself. He had put Whiskey Creek under Hammaker's thumb; he had an obligation to make some effort to liberate it. His leaving Christy almost without warning was at least as blunt as the treatment she was giving him. Swapping punches with Charlie Hammaker might turn out to be the easy part of it. But just now the man looked about as vulnerable as a stone blockhouse. Whoever challenged him would be a fool for lickings.

He stood at the head of the street, gazing a long

115

while at the river. It had lost the sunset tints and was now a wide reach of quiet water merging into the far shore. There was a sandy bar, and then fields someone had cleared and put into vegetables, and farther still a ridge sown thickly with laurel, spruce, and rhododendron thickets. Near the bend, where Whiskey Creek flowed into the Rogue, a blue haze of smoke rose from the mill.

A boat pulled into shore. A man stopped to fill a pipe, then he dragged a canvas-shrouded roll from the stern of the boat, got his shoulder under it, and struggled up the street. Must weigh 100 pounds, Carnagey thought with a professional eye, 100 pounds at two-bits a pound. . . . Someone had saved himself twenty-five bucks by boating his load down. A small bell tinkled in his mind. Well, by God. It *could* be done!

It hit him like a fist. It gave him gooseflesh. He was standing that way, hands on hips and his Stetson on the back of his head, when someone came up behind him. Hugh Badger, limping on his game leg, looked flushed and hurried.

"Where you been at? Thought I could ketch you before you et."

Carnagey took Hugh's arm. "See that fellow coming up the road?"

"That's Milo Dufur. Owns the farm acrost the river. Bringing a load of truck over, I reckon."

It deflated Glenn a trifle, but the principle was

the same. The load *might* have come from Grants Pass. It *might* have been one load the Southern Oregon did not carry. He asked: "Do you remember the way you taught me to bring a boat down the river?"

Badger gave his raw laugh, his eyes squinting. "Shoved you off in a leaky rowboat and told you to miss the big ones and look out for the whirlpools. And you bridged in the Coffee Pot and broke the boat to hell."

"But I made it next time, didn't I? From your place clear to Gold Beach. How many men do you think we could teach the same way?"

"Not many. But take them down one trip with a second set of locks to pull them out of trouble, and they'd catch on. You going to start a boating school?"

Carnagey took a breath so deep it stretched his vest across the buttons. "A school for boatmen," he said. "And you're going to be the professor. Write your own ticket. I'll have the boats built. You break them up. Think you could handle an eighteen-foot boat? With eight hundred pounds of freight?"

Hugh inspected him carefully, spat, tapped him on the chest. "You've got money. You're young and healthy. Now, why do you want to go broke and get a behind full of Thirty-Thirty slugs? Just because they said you couldn't do it?"

"I've got to do it, Hugh, if I want to stay."

"I think you've gone plumb crazy. Tonight you buy all of Sam Gilliam's hay. Red Quade, according to what I hear, is out to ram it all down your throat. Then you decide to use boats. Now, what are you going to do with all that there hay?"

"Store it under Hammaker's nose and watch him slobber. After I soften him, I'll buy that franchise away from him or force him into a partnership. That's one partnership he'll come out of with one change of underwear. Hugh, I'm going to leave him with twenty corrals full of jackasses and not a pound of freight to carry. Charlie Hammaker will be cadging drinks in Whiskey Bar before I'm through with him."

"But in the meantime Tay Pike is waiting for a shot at your back and Quade is hunting you to rip you up and down the front. And you ask me to work for you." He spat again, and scratched his neck. "OK, when do I start?"

The Pound Diggings Bar was halfway down the block and across the street. They were about fifty feet from it when Red Quade and two of his packers turned in without seeing them. Badger hesitated. "Say, there's a new saloon down in the next block. I got credit there."

"What's the matter with this one? I'd like to hear what Quade has to say about me."

They went into the saloon and stood ankle deep in fresh pine sawdust. The saloon showed evidence of corner cutting to save on freight. The walls were unpainted but fumed by smoke. There was no mirror to reflect the line of bottles and decanters, no marble facing for the beer pumps. All the furniture was locally made. Hammaker men occupied most of this furniture, bringing the scent of their calling to the room. Carnagey felt the old tingle that preceded action.

Red Quade, hands tucked in coat pockets, was talking to Tay Pike. Pike sat on a box at the far end of the bar. Quade asked him: "What you making there, Pike?"

Pike held a foot-and-a-half length of close-grained laurel wood. His knife drew a long sliver from it and he raised the wood and squinted at it against the light. "Gun stock," he said.

"What you going to do with it when you're finished?"

"Kill me a skunk."

Quade winked at one of the packers. "When'd you lose your taste for bear?"

"I ain't going to eat this skunk. Just skin it."

Quade chuckled, but from where Glenn stood he looked puzzled. "What's the trouble?" he asked. "Did I overcharge you on that Dutch oven?"

"You ain't the skunk I was talking about."

Quade leaned toward him. The saloon was waiting for the question: *Who is?* Then the freighter saw Carnagey. He straightened slowly. After a moment he turned away and took a chair at the faro table. Tay Pike stared at Carnagey. A disciplined hatred dwelt in the lean countenance; the slack, unshaven jaw and pale eyes had a deep animation. He raised the knife and sliced another thin strip of wood from the gun stock. Carnagey went to the bar. He had had some practice at taking the temperature of towns, and this one was cold. This one had a bellyache and blamed him for it. He and Hugh had two whiskies over an interval of ten minutes, but the saloon did not notice them. Then Milo Dufur came in, the farmer from across the river. He saw Quade and said: "I just left a load of snap beans and corn on the dock, Red. Try to keep the mules from rolling on it this time, will you? It's fer Gold Beach."

"That's a mistake," someone said. It was Carnagey.

Dufur turned, a stocky, gray-bearded man with ruddy cheeks. "What's a mistake?"

"Paying two-bits a pound when you can ship for fifteen."

"Where can I ship for fifteen?"

"Nowhere, yet. But in a couple of weeks you can ship by Rogue River Express. Grants Pass to Whiskey Creek, fifteen cents. Whiskey Creek to Gold Beach, the same. No upriver navigation until I figure out how to take boats up waterfalls."

Dufur received his beer, salted it, and came to stand beside Carnagey. "You're Carnagey, ain't you?"

"Right."

"Are you drunk?"

"Too sober to be having any fun. I'm handling freight as soon as I can build the boats. That means work for the mill, cutting me clear-grain cedar planking. Work for anybody who likes to row a boat. If the business warrants it, I'll double the number of boats I start with and cut the rate as fast as I can."

Hugh punched him. Glenn saw Quade coming down the floor, his boots muffled by sawdust. Quade stopped there and looked him over with his gray, measuring eyes. "Rogue River Express," he repeated. "I've got an idea for you, Carnagey. Train steelhead to carry packs on their back, and you can haul freight to Grants Pass, too."

"I've already got some cut-throats training for the job."

Quade said: "Boats!" It was a denunciation of all such blockheaded schemes. "Reckon you won't be needing that hay, then, eh?"

Carnagey squinted. "You never know. I may buy a horse and buggy."

"If you do, I'll stable it free. But I want that hay, mister. It's the only hay on the middle route. You bought it for a quick dollar. OK, I'll pay five dollars a bale more than it cost you. But you won't catch me again."

"Nobody was trying to catch you. I may need that hay. It's not for sale."

Red Quade was a patient man, but this tried the seams of his temper. He set his whiskey glass down. "I'd like to talk some more about this . . . outside."

"Lead the way."

Glenn heard Tay Pike's clasp knife snap shut as they started out.

Sooner or later, it had had to come. Carnagey and Quade were too close to being alike. Both were vigorous men who resented being blocked. Quade parted the slatted doors and casually passed into the street. But Carnagey was watchful; he saw his feet pivot as the half door closed. It was an old trick. Catch a man in a doorway and nail him fast. Carnagey parted the doors quickly; Quade lunged in. He tried to catch his balance, but stumbled and grabbed at the door. Carnagey smashed at his face and cut him solidly under the eye. Quade reeled. As Glenn lunged into him, he recovered and closed savagely. They went down in the street, struggling, grunting curses, and broke apart and came up separately.

Hugh Badger led the crowd outside. Tay Pike came next, and then a swarm of packers and miners to ring the fighters. Carnagey, sparring, saw Pike and feared him more than Quade. The hill man moved about with quick, nervous gestures as though looking for a back to leave his knife in. Quade's eye was swelling and his face was choked with color. But he was not hurt, and Carnagey knew that he would be a hard man to knock down. Hitting his cheek bone had been like slugging a bull's head.

Quade's temperament had altered since it had come to violence. Patience had run out of him. He had himself under the slimmest of control; as Carnagey made a trial stab at his head, he slammed the blow aside and plowed in with a high, right-hand overhead punch. It exploded on Glenn's forehead. He went back two steps and sat down. Instantly Quade was there to grasp his shirt front and drag him to his feet. A fog seemed to thicken Carnagey's perceptions. He half parried the freight man's jab and felt a new pain on the side of his jaw.

Quade's crowd shouted. He grinned, thrust Carnagey back a pace, and chopped at his jaw. Glenn ducked it and closed again, hanging on as Quade wrestled him about, hunting for an opening. But the fog was clearing. Carnagey was able to notice that Quade was wide open, from jaw to crotch, concentrating on getting a hammerlock on Glenn's neck. He let him. But as the freighter began to put on pressure, he pulled back his right arm and slammed a long driving jab into the man's belly. Quade gasped. He staggered back. He tried to hold Carnagey off as he bored in, but a fist took him on the mouth and another found the soft wedge below his ribs. Quade looked white and sick. His big arms felt numbly for a hold. Carnagey threw one in from the right, brought another from the left. He swung again, but Red Quade was not there. He was going down heavily, like a tired bull dropping to its knees and lunging wearily against the earth.

He was finished. Carnagey looked up. There was no cheering. Badger said: "You can put the toad-sticker away, Pike."

Pike started, glanced down at the open knife lying on his palm, and snapped it shut. He walked down the hill with his long-jointed stride.

For a week, Carnagey had the feeling that he was on a stage. Whiskey Creek was watching him. There was not even a rumor from the Southern Oregon camp of what big Charlie Hammaker intended to do about him. But every day, men would stop to read the placard in the window of the office he had taken at the bottom of the street. They read his rates and promises—and walked on. They were not ready to talk business until he had something tangible to show them.

He got into stride fast. He and Hugh designed an eighteen-foot boat with a wide beam and plenty of rake. One man could handle her, but she would hold 800 pounds of freight. "And what good will she be after we reach Gold Beach?" Badger demanded.

"We'll dismantle the boats and bring them back on mules. It won't be any violation of Hammaker's franchise if we don't carry outside freight. We can build a boat for sixty dollars. For thirty, we can haul it back to Grants Pass, so we'll be money ahead for the trouble. At fifteen cents a pound for each half of the run, the boats will net a hundred and fifty a trip."

Carnagey built a long wharf paralleling the river. He erected a shed for storage of freight. When the first ten boats were ready, Badger took ten men to Grants Pass and brought them down the river, taking each man and boat through the fast water individually. They reached Whiskey Creek one day, sunburned, wet, and scarred. Rainy Falls had smashed a boat when a man broke an oar. But Badger thought he could make boatmen out of them all.

Carnagey had an organization. He had his boats. He still lacked two things: friends and business. Nobody came to see him. He ran into old friends, bought them a drink, and found himself with two empty glasses inside of ten minutes. This was a town that could pack a grudge. The grudge carried over into the second lack—business. Dufur, the farmer, brought in a load of truck the night before the first run was to start for Gold Beach. A trapper brought in some pelts, and there was an order for an airtight stove to be brought down from Grants Pass. But the big accounts, the stores and mines, did not show up.

For the time being, Whiskey Creek was playing its cards close to its chest. As much as men hated

Charley Hammaker, they were staying on his good side until they knew whether the Rogue River Express was a flash in the pan.

The hell with that, Carnagey thought. If the business wouldn't come to him, he'd go out and corral the business. That afternoon he went up Whiskey Creek a mile to the big Lucky Piece Mine. For all its prosperity, it was still a baling-wire outfit. Hammaker occupied the only feasible freight route. Heavy machinery was out of the question. More or less primitive arrastres reduced the rock to metal. Placering still produced a few ounces of gold a day in the creeks, but most of the business was going underground.

A.K. Sawyer, president of the company, was in his office in the big log building when Carnagey arrived. He looked like a man with a headache. His homemade desk was festooned with papers held down by chunks of mineral; a nugget dangled from his watch chain, a $1,000 bill framed on the wall was labeled: OUR FIRST THOUSAND. But Sawyer had his troubles, that was in the grooves of his face and the red ink in the journal before him.

Carnagey offered his hand. "Mister Sawyer," he said, "I'm Carnagey."

"How are you, Carnagey?" Sawyer shook his hand without much enthusiasm.

"How's the mining business, Mister Sawyer?"

A man of sixty, Sawyer had mastiff-like jowls and thorny gray brows. He picked up a chunk of ore. "Seventy dollars a ton, Carnagey, and I can hardly afford to dig it out."

"That's why I'm here." Carnagey struck the desk. "I'm back in business. It's boats, this time. Until I can break this franchise swindle of Hammaker's, I'm hauling freight in boats. Anything that can be dismantled into, say, thousand-pound chunks, I can bring down for you. My regular rate is fifteen cents a pound. For heavy freight, I can quote a figure of ten cents. But one of these days I'll build that wagon road, and it'll drop like a plummet."

Sawyer smiled sadly and said nothing.

". . . You wouldn't care to order anything just now?"

"I'm tied up with Hammaker until the first of next month. I get a twenty-two-cent rate through yearly contracts."

"After the first, then. You can cut your freight bill in half right now."

Sawyer shrugged. "I guess not."

"You guess not?" Carnagey echoed. "What the hell's wrong with you, man?"

"Let's say it's something wrong with you. You're the man who put these leg irons onto me. How can I warm up over any scheme of yours to saw them off? You'd probably sell me back to Hammaker or walk out with the contract half fulfilled. *Then* I'd be in a tight."

Carnagey's face reddened. He did not try to

127

defend his selling to Hammaker. It was his vulnerable point. "It's your funeral," he said. "But if you want that wagon road, this is the best way I know to promote it."

Sawyer rose, indicating the door. "We'll see. If you last out the first month, perhaps we can talk again."

An hour after dawn the next morning, Hugh came down to the wharf. Carnagey was already there. There was less than a ton of freight. A mood of depression prevailed. The pair of them could handle it in two boats, without help. They loaded. Badger stepped into the wide, clumsy-appearing craft. He cast off, but hung a moment in the backwash of the current.

"Going to line Big Windy gorge, aren't we?" Carnagey asked.

"What for? I was down a month ago and yawned the whole way through." He took three full strokes, let the current bring the boat about, stern first, so that he faced downriver, and shot away. Rocking easily, the boat rushed down a churning stairway of water. Carnagey got his oars. He was about to step into the boat when he heard brisk footfalls in the early morning street and looked up. Christy was coming across the wharf.

She stood there a moment above him, slender and cool, a shawl about her shoulders and her hair done up in a bandanna. Her hands were on her hips in an unreassuring gesture. "Mister Carnagey," she said, "I want to compliment you on being such a smooth worker. A week in town and you've had two fights, swindled Southern Oregon out of a load of hay, and now you're dragging an old man into a gamble he may not come out of alive."

"I didn't force him into it."

"But this is no fight of his. If you're willing to risk your life for a few dollars, there's no reason you should risk his."

Carnagey bridled. "I could invest my money anywhere and get nine per cent," he snapped. "But I sink it here, where I'm not sure of getting anything. Why? Because I feel a sense of loyalty to a town that holds its nose when I go by. I ought to leave all of you for Hammaker to pick like a buzzard. But I'm sore enough now to want to break him more than I want to make money."

"That's typical," she said.

Carnagey stepped out of the boat. He strode over to her. "Why did you wait until this morning to crab?"

"I gave you credit for more integrity than you seem to have. I kept thinking that at the last moment you'd tell Pop you didn't want him. But you need him, so you'll milk him dry of his strength, maybe let him go."

Carnagey held her by the shoulders. "I don't *need* anybody," he said. "I'll can him when we reach the end of the run. I haven't needed anybody so far but Glenn Carnagey, and you can write that on your menu."

Her lips, pale and even, smiled. "Is that true? Haven't you ever needed anyone? I had an idea you must have when you came back to town. . . ."

Anger and desire mingled perversely in him. All at once he pulled her against him; his arms claimed her roughly. Christy was unresisting and unresponsive. She was a slim flame that scorched him, that he tried to hurt by holding closer, but that only hurt him worse without taking part in the embrace. He crushed her with the full strength of his arms, his mouth on hers, and, when he released her at last, she slipped from him with a face that was white but eyes that laughed.

"It would be wonderful to be a man," she whispered, "and not need anyone. Just to be in love with mules and freight and money. Isn't that the way it is with you, Glenn?"

Carnagey turned and jumped down into the boat. He fitted oars into locks and shoved into the current without looking back. He thought it was one of the least impressive exits he had ever made.

Carnagey's schedule called for making Wildcat Riffle by the first night. This meant pulling through all the quiet water instead of drifting. The following night they were to dock at Toler's Camp, from which an old Swede ran a steam launch regularly to Gold Beach, at the mouth of the

Rogue. Through the morning they rode the fast water, skinning through rocky squeezes where a tenderfoot would have lost his boat.

It was like re-reading an old loved book for Carnagey. Pages he had forgotten flashed entire in his mind—the way the water peeled in green and white shavings from the knife edge of a hidden boulder, enticing the boatman; the trick of entering a trough, sidewise, letting the current straighten you and rush you down a sunless gorge and out into a placid vista of greenery. The lift and drop of the boat—the high-straked stern—always going first, so that a man could study each riffle— digging deep into a trough, shipping water breathtakingly and plowing up and out of it until the boat stood on end and see-sawed across. The river of ravenous water and broken boats and men—the Rogue.

By noon, Carnagey's back and shoulder muscles were tender. He stopped to bail, examining the oiled tarp that covered his load of baled furs. The load was still dry, although his shirt and trousers were plastered to his skin. He rested, while the river swept them broadly down a forested avenue where ferns and rhododendron overhung the water and the rocks lay deep. But a half mile ahead it snarled into the chaos of granite called Big Windy Gorge. He wanted his strength for this quarter mile shot.

To his ears came the boil and roar of fast water.

The hills squeezed together; the gorge compressed 150 feet of water into a gut twelve feet wide. A damp gloom hung between the walls and the water was capped with foam. A man had to sense the rocks rather than see them.

Badger's back acquired an alertness. He let the boat come around broadside to the first riffle, which crumpled against a rock as big as a freight wagon and sluiced away at right angles into the gorge. One moment he was there, tugging at an oar—the next his boat was sucked down a long, glass-green trough and rocketed out of sight. Glenn felt the weight of his cargo when the boat slewed in toward the rock. The long ashen oar pulled slowly through the water and the boat veered away so closely the other oar had to be shipped. That was all a boatman asked—to clear rather than to founder.

He thought he heard a shout. He listened but it was not repeated. He made the elbow kink into the slot and saw Badger standing up to stare over the high prow of his boat, drawing with all his strength on his oars as the boat lunged at a hopeless turmoil of rocks and foam. If there were a way through it, Carnagey could not see it. He remembered Hugh's boast: *Came through last week and yawned the whole way!* Immediately he was trying to draw his own boat into a back-water, closet-sized refuge where a boat might be rammed for a moment. He might have been rowing with laths. The heavy craft fired on ahead like a runaway wagon.

Badger's boat flung up with a crash of spray and sound. It rolled and struck the wall with a cannonade of cracking wood. Milo Dufur's vegetables were the river's. The boat plowed wetly out of the caldron and lunged against another rock. A strake tore loose. The thwarts were gone. The remains of the craft bridged. Glenn was bearing down on a splintered cedar barrier hung between two wet black boulders. He was standing, searching for the hunter and making profane shouts that were a species of prayer.

An arm and shoulder came out of the foam, a head showed briefly and sank, although the hand remained clawing. Carnagey thrust an oar against the drowning man's arm and Hugh's hands clamped on it. He came hand over hand up the oar and seized the side of the boat. Then he let himself slip around to the stern, to be as little drag as possible.

Carnagey was braced for the shock of striking the derelict. Abruptly it stirred, rolled from the rocks, and was swept away. Then it was a battle to get through a trap hardly wider than the boat. Green water hurtled against the bank and cascaded back in snow spray. The effort to keep the boat away tore at Carnagey's muscles. Yet he knew he had lost. The oar struck, twisted him off the seat, and came out of the lock. With shattering impact, the boat went broadside into the rock and shipped. Green water poured in on him. The boat wallowed away down the long, boiling stairway of the rapids. Carnagey got the oar back, but exerting his will on the boat was like rowing the river itself. The craft was more of the river than against it. His head began to swim.

He sat there, fighting and praying and tearing at the oars until he heard Hugh gasp: "Well . . . beach her, dammit!"

The gorge was behind. They drifted down a long corridor of quiet water. Carnagey brought the boat up on a bar and lay on the oars until the lights stopped swimming in his head.

III

Half the furs were soaked. They pressed them out and placed them to dry on the sand. With pegs and canvas, they put the remaining boat back into shape. But there would be no boats to freight back from this trip. Badger hiked back up the trail to the point above where he had foundered. He worked around until he found what he was looking for—a portion of a powder hole drilled into one of the cliffs, still marked with the scorch of black powder.

Carnagey looked at it, too. "Tay Pike, for meanness, or Hammaker, for profit. I wouldn't know which. Choked the gorge with rocks to trap us."

"I'd say Pike, for meanness and profit. Him and Hammaker have been clubby as buzzards ever since you hit town. Pike done it and Hammaker bought the powder."

It was another four days before they delivered the furs to the wharf master at Gold Beach and returned to Whiskey Creek. Carnagey squared his account with the fur trapper. Then he walked up to the Southern Oregon depot to square his account with Charlie Hammaker.

It was nine o'clock in the evening. The freight office was closed, but from the street he saw splinters of light around the curtained rear window. Hammaker must be still there, trying to squeeze another nickel out of the books. Carnagey had strapped on a revolver. He went under the corral gate and quietly strode down the yard. The dust was deep; he walked silently. The curtain had been tugged all the way down, but the cracked green fabric gave him fragmentary views of the room.

Hammaker was at his desk, a big, balding spider spinning webs night and day. In the hot night, he wore only pants and undershirt. Glenn went up the steps and tried the side door. It was not locked. He advanced confidently across the floor toward Hammaker's office. He heard the freighter's half-apprehensive voice.

"Red?"

Carnagey pushed the door open and stood in the entrance. Hammaker did not seem to recognize him. He had not shaved in a week; he was sunburned and dirty; his pants had shrunk from the dousings he had had. He looked like the sort of man that men who draw the shades at night dread.

"Well for God's sake!" Hammaker said. He moved to stand up, but kept his seat as the other waved the gun at him.

"Too bad about Hugh Badger, wasn't it?" Carnagey said.

"Hugh? What . . . what happened to Hugh?" Hammaker's manhood was leaking out the soles of his boots.

"We had trouble in the gorge. Hugh bridged."

In the dusk of the lamplight, Hammaker's eyes looked yellow. He sat there, staring at the gun. "Glenn, you're not saying he . . . ?"

"That's the roughest passage on the river. The foam was three feet deep. How long do you think a man would last, even if the rocks didn't tear him to pieces?"

The freighter rallied feebly. "Glenn, that's hell! But why the gun? Why bust in here like this to tell me?"

Carnagey crossed the floor. Hammaker's hands moved slightly over the papers in a covering gesture.

"You're sweating like a pig," Glenn said.

Hammaker pushed back from the desk angrily.

A drawer was open; his hand lay on the edge of it. "I'm sorry about your partner, if it's true, but I'll be damned if I'll have you badgering me over it. If he was a poor enough boatman to bridge, it was no fault of mine."

"Whose fault was it that a rock was dynamited into the gorge since he was through last?" Carnagey's thumb came back across the fretted hammer of the Colt.

The depth of Hammaker's terror was plumbed. At the bottom of it, a vein of desperate courage was struck. His left hand darted and knocked the Colt from Carnagey's hand. His other hand rummaged through the drawer. Carnagey had foreseen the move; he had not attempted to forestall it. He had brought Hammaker the tortures by fear and by hope and had made him eat both.

Hammaker's hand found the gun. As he looked up, he tried to duck. Carnagey's fist was traveling fast. It exploded in the middle of the freight man's face. It bloodied his nose and smashed his lips. Hammaker dropped into the chair and sprawled sideways from it. He was in a snoring half-consciousness when he struck the floor.

Carnagey recovered his gun. He glanced at the papers on the desk. One was a rough pencil sketch. It showed a sectional and top view of a boat, apparently a McKenzie boat by the high strakes of the bow. It could have been a replica of one of Carnagey's boats.

The other was a partial list of materials. *Planking, cedar, at? Bottom stripping—Misc.— screws, paint, etc. Salaries: Tay Pike. Addn'l. boatmen . . .*

It appeared that someone else was going into the boat business. Across the bottom of the list, Carnagey wrote: *Flowers for Tay Pike: Fifteen cents.*

Carnagey passed a restful hour in a barber's chair next morning. He had himself shaved and shorn, bathed in the warm, soap-scummed barrel, and walked from the shop a new man. Badger was already at the office, wearing buckskins and studying bills of lading assembled by the clerk during their absence.

He tossed him the slim fold of bills. With disappointment, Carnagey read them. A few hundred pounds of food to be brought down from Grants Pass. The same dreary run of vegetables and household goods, but none of the gravy. The same miserly trickle of cautious ordering and buying.

"Damn them," he grunted. "Wash out the man metal of this town and you'd have your riffles full of tin. There ain't the guts here to outfit one honest-to-god man. They're scared of somebody putting the town on wheels for them. Even A.K. Sawyer. If I spend three months breaking up boats and paying wages for a stinking trade like this, I'll go broke."

"Why don't you quit while you can?"

It was the voicing of his own thoughts. And because he was afraid of it, afraid he would not have the guts to risk his money in a gamble that drew out beyond his patience, he threw the papers angrily on the floor and walked out.

Badger followed him to the door. "I'm going down to shoot some of them rocks. You want to go up to Grants Pass for that bedspring and airtight stove? We got six boats waiting to be used up yonder."

Carnagey grunted and went on. He found himself heading down the side street in the early daylight, approaching Christy's. He had not seen her since their encounter on the dock.

He walked into the warm fragrance of yeast bread and coffee. The café was populated only by a few early-rising merchants and mining men. Carnagey started past the tables and hesitated; the men at the table were A.K. Sawyer of Lucky Piece Mine, Charlie Hammaker, and Red Quade. They were having ham and eggs. Hammaker, with tape across his nose and upper lip, was conversing sourly.

". . . I'll dicker with you, Sawyer, but I won't haggle. I don't care what anybody else is doing. We're the only licensed carriers in this region, and we'll act on that basis." Then he saw Carnagey.

"That's a nasty-looking nose you've got," Glenn said.

Quade gave him a level stare of hostility. "A sneak thief broke in last night. Mister Hammaker surprised him."

Hammaker, too, kept a steady gaze on Carnagey. Glenn was willing to leave it their way. He was still one up. Sawyer looked interested. The mining man had an envelope by his plate, scribbled on and smudged. "Sit down, Carnagey," he said warmly. "Want a little talk with you." Hammaker scowled and opened his mouth. Then he shut it like a trap and attacked his fried eggs. Christy came and went, crisp and fresh in blue and white, but with a reproving glance for Glenn.

Sawyer stirred his coffee thoughtfully. "Ten cents a pound," he mused. "That certainly beats twenty."

"How long would it beat it?" Quade retorted.

"As long as Glenn's in business."

"That's the point."

Carnagey sensed something. It was coming close to the 1st, and Hammaker was sweating over the contract renewal. For the first time he perceived genuine interest in Sawyer. "I might be able to shave that ten cents after the first few months, A.K.," he remarked.

Hammaker's fist struck the table. "Damn it, Sawyer, I told you I won't haggle! You want your bullion to get where it starts for. We're the only ones who can do that for you."

"In a reasonable length of time?"

"Five days from here to the coast isn't bad," Quade contended. "That's rough country."

"We did it in two," Carnagey remarked.

Hammaker's big, unhappy face soured. "I call this forcing a man's hand, but . . . well, in a few days I'll be in a position to offer express service myself. I've got boats being built right now. I've engaged the best man on the Rogue to pilot them through. I'll match anybody's rate. That's for small shipments. I don't hold any such notion as Carnagey that freight can be moved by rowboat."

"Who's your boatman?"

"Tay Pike. He's spent all his life on this river."

Carnagey kept his eyes on Sawyer. The miner had been slyly building to something.

"Tell you what," Sawyer said. "I've got a little bullion coming up soon. I'll let each of you carry half. Now, I figure that an outfit that's fit to operate will be ready to move any time. So I'll just walk down someday and say . . . 'Here it is. Put it on a schooner at Gold Beach.' And the man who gets it there for me first will carry my freight until I'm convinced he isn't fit to."

Charlie Hammaker got up stiffly. "I don't have to submit bids or cut rates with anybody. You can go to hell!"

Sawyer watched the pair go out. He grinned at Glenn. "But he'll have those boats in the water next week, all the same."

Carnagey was elated. When he was through, he

went back into the kitchen and caught Christy around the waist.

"So it's going to be the Rogue River Express, after all!"

The gray eyes searched his face. "What are you talking about?"

"Tay Pike's going to boss a string of boats for Hammaker. Sawyer's going to try us out. The fastest boat wins."

"You aren't going to fight Pike!"

"He'll know he's been some place if he noses us out! It's going to be the Rogue River Express, and then the Carnagey Freight Lines . . . and then it's going to be Missus Glenn Carnagey in the biggest house in Whiskey Creek."

"Some Umpqua squaw, I suppose. I've always known you were bull-headed and domineering, but now I know the rest of it. You're stupid. Anyone who would attack a grizzly bear with a slingshot and a handful of corn is crazy. That's you, Glenn Carnagey, and, if you drag Pop into it again, get out of my kitchen!"

"All right. But just to prove I don't hold grudges, you can come into mine any time."

IV

Around Whiskey Creek, the word was that Tay Pike had at last finished the laurel-wood stock for his rifle. He had fitted it to the tangs and tested it on a spotted fawn, and it shot truer than ever. But he had little time to prove it, for in a few days big Charlie Hammaker brought him down to the wharf where he had three boats ready. Sawyer was right. He was still in the fight.

Pike sniffed, pushed them around, and finally took one through the riffle below town. Carnagey was on hand to watch. Hugh was down at Big Windy Gorge shooting some rocks. He observed the ease with which Pike handled the boat. He saw him bend the oars in a strong pull upstream. Pike brought the boat slowly back through the roiled water. He handled it like a canoe, craftily, making the river work for him, utilizing every little backwash and trough. He docked it and stepped out, sardonic and taciturn.

The 1st of the month came, and Badger was not back. Carnagey began to stew. He wanted him along for the trip. They could spell each other on the oars, for he contemplated little drifting. He didn't see Hammaker, but Quade was down at the wharf a couple of times, and Pike roamed the town restlessly, lugging the old Burgess rifle with the new laurel-wood stock. Night came, and back from the river came Hugh Badger. "She's reamed out like a smooth-bore Sharps," he announced.

About eight o'clock, in the first gloom of evening, Sawyer appeared. He wore a shiny alpaca coat, gray trousers, and a stovepipe beaver hat. "That shipment will be crated and sealed, if you care to pick it up in the morning."

Carnagey rigged up a long rope-and-float arrangement to affix to the crate; in case of a spill, it could be found readily. For hours he was too excited to sleep. He stood at the window of his boarding house room, gazing out on the sleeping town. *Is it worth it?* he wondered. Worth risking a ball from Pike's gun, the gun he'd violated once? For one of these days it had to come, the clash between him and the river man. He could still get out with little loss. He had seen little to make him feel obligated to the town, and yet there was that specter of guilt at the back of his mind, that he must play for good.

At 5:30 Carnagey rose, dressed, buckled on his Colt, and hiked up the trail to the mine office. Lamps already burned in the long building. Sawyer was there to deliver the crate personally. It weighed about fifty pounds. Balancing it on his shoulder, Glenn hurried back down the trail. He had gone about 100 feet when he passed Pike and Quade lunging along up to the mines.

Quade gave him a hard, studying look. He wore

a red flannel shirt, linsey-woolsey pants, and had discarded his lace boots for shoes. About him there was something more than earnest, something last-ditch and desperate. He was a man who liked his job, and it might be at stake in the next two days.

Badger already had the extra oars aboard, locks fitted, food stored. Carnagey took a last look at the awakening town. To the last, he had hoped Christy would show up, would make some response to his overture of last week. But the street was empty of anyone with red hair and a gingham apron, and now he heard Badger snarl: "Git in, dammit! Yonder they come!"

Quade and Pike were hurrying down the steep roadway to the river. Carnagey cast off the painter, gave the boat a shove, and jumped in. Just before the current caught them, Hugh pulled a paper from his shirt pocket. "Christy sent this."

Carnagey read:

Glenn,
A good kitchen should be about ten-by-twelve feet, and should contain a cast-iron stove and a man who can be counted on to wash dishes at least eleven months of the year. Can you?

That day they took all the minor riffles and bars without slacking on the oars. They shot Tyee Bar recklessly. Wildcat Rapids nearly swamped them.

But they never lost sight of a gray boat riding the foam and the falls in their wake, a fox-faced oarsman peering after them as he thrust and pulled. And Glenn never forgot a browned Burgess rifle with a new stock. Yet Pike made no effort to pass.

The sun dived behind the mountains. A final pond-like reach was suddenly funneled into a trough choked with rocks. Rocks studded the gloom, stark and wet. Hugh was at the oars, knowing every boulder in the channel, but Glenn sat tautly. Glancing back, he saw the dim shape of Quade's boat as it entered the trough. It was like a trailing shadow, like a timber wolf, soundless and menacing.

They plunged through the channel. It was nearly dark when they raced from the mouth. Badger headed the boat for a gravelly beach.

Pike's boat flashed into sight. They watched him drift on a few hundred feet and veer to the far shore. Ahead was the Devil's Stairway, where they would want plenty of daylight. After a while the light of his fire glowed in the night. Carnagey ate heavily and fell asleep.

He woke while it was still dark. They ate cold biscuits and waited for the gloom to break. What was ahead was some of the roughest water on the river. The Stairway twisted and kinked for two miles; after that, it was a long slide through more open water. Yet there were no passing places for a full hour, so that the leading boat might pile up a lead that would hold through the pond water below, and on to Toler's Camp. A crafty boatman could fret a man to death, holding back at all the wrong spots to lure him into backdrafts and whirlpools.

Dawn seeped into the sky, wet and gray. In the leaden light, they saw Tay Pike shoving the big McKenzie boat into the stream. Quade was already in the stern with a rifle across his knees.

Carnagey yelled at Hugh, slung his duffle into the boat, and started it grating across the pebbles into the water. Glenn poled them into the current and dropped onto the thwart. Pike was 100 yards ahead. He had an almost unbreakable lead into the Stairway.

Carnagey let the boat swing about, bow down. He began to row like a madman. A man could always pull harder than he could push, but in this river it was nice to know where he was heading. He would have to swing her about before they entered the chaos of rocks of the Devil's Stairway.

Badger began to get on his nerves. Sitting there, puffing his pipe while Carnagey rowed his guts out! Once he glanced ahead and said: "That fella, Pike, reminds me of a fish hawk. Yella eyes, a beak for spearing salmon, and a mouth to tear it to pieces. I can see the barrel of his gun above his starboard strake. He shore as hell has a lead on us. And we hit the Stairway in ten minutes."

Carnagey glared. At last he dug an oar deeply

147

into the dark water and let the boat swing on it. The stern swung down. Ahead, the hills tumbled in upon one another. They heard the roar of the falls. A shaft of golden light speared down through a high pass. Carnagey laid all his weight on the oars, thrust and draw, thrust and draw, and yonder Pike was fighting to maintain his lead. But the McKenzie boat was not the boat Badger had built. It was wider and had less rake. It had been built when Hammaker was thinking of cargo rather than of speed. In still water, it dragged. Exultation surged up in Glenn as he saw the boat drawing closer. Quade turned in the bow to stare tensely at them, so close the heavy brows were a bar above his eyes. Now they could feel the suck of fast water pulling at the boat. Carnagey's craft shot ahead like a trout. Suddenly it was apparent that he was going to pass. Pike was unable to maintain his lead.

They came alongside. Pike shipped oars, and something was in his hands. There was a roar that the cañon walls picked up. Water went up in a high jet beside the other craft.

"Keep yer distance!" Pike screamed. "Pass us and I'll kill you both!"

"Let 'em go," Badger rapped. "I was hoping you couldn't pass anyhow."

Carnagey let the oars drag. "You were . . . *what?*"

Pike saw him hesitate; Quade raised his gun and

148

held it on them while the river man began to thrust frantically at the long sweeps.

Badger's grin came, thin and wolfish. "I took out all the old rocks, but I put a couple of new ones in. You know where that Eagle Beak rock overhangs the river, where you come up ag'in' the wall and then pull like hell? Well, you'll pull like hell before you come up to the wall this time. There's a rock there, too thin and sharp to make a ripple. Let Pike have it. But hang back a bit so the wreckage will drift clear."

Tautness went out of Glenn. He sat back, and in the next moment the McKenzie boat was firing into the slot.

The Devil's Stairway enfolded them. Long and winding, a gloomy granite flume, it dropped over falls, cut back and forth on itself, sent up its shouting and its spray. Under the planking they heard the singing of gravel along the streambed. For a while, Glenn was too busy to watch Pike. He was standing on an oar to swing about a dangerous rock, rowing like a fool to hold back until the current sucked them away from a shag and shot them down a long, green-glass race. Feeling the cold drench of spray on his face and wincing as the high bow dipped like a trowel and flung up again, shaking off green water.

Then they dropped into a series of falls that crashed against a far cliff and flung itself in a turmoil of spray down a new trough. Carnagey's eyes raised. Pike was slithering down this devil's gutter toward the trap Badger had set for him. He was following the old, tried route. Abruptly the boat faltered, rose painfully in the stern, and began to swing over. Pike and Quade lurched up.

The boat was about to go under, but in that moment Tay Pike did a strange thing. He flung a wild look up to the cliff at the right and screamed something Glenn fumbled over a moment before he got it.

"Charlie! No!"

Carnagey looked up. He saw a man running down the river trail fifty feet above the water. Behind him, he left something that burned with clean white smoke in a cleft of the rocks. . . .

Pike was hung up. The boat was caught on that buried rock so that it would neither sink nor float. It wallowed in the torrent. Pike and Quade fought with it. They rammed oars against the cliff and failed to pry it loose. They stared into the water and were afraid to jump.

Now Glenn understood the river man's hurry to beat him into the slot. He knew Hammaker was waiting to give him the race, Big Charlie Hammaker, who knew how long it took a fuse to burn six inches and how fast a boat traveled down the Devil's Stairway. He would let one pass and dump a mountain on the other.

Carnagey's hands trembled on the oars. He could no more hold back in such a torrent than he could swim upstream. They were being borne on to where Pike and Quade still fought their boat.

Badger's gun flashed up. He pulled a bead on Hammaker, but then he held it. "The damn' fool!" he panted. Carnagey saw the freight boss start back to the fuse, hesitate when he saw how far it had burned. And there he stood. Afraid to advance. Afraid to run and be caught in the explosion, now that he had already lingered too long.

A shot roared. Wood splinters slashed Glenn's hand. The oar was gone. Pike, balancing in the rocking boat, had brought the Burgess up. He was levering another shot into the breech.

Carnagey knelt on the false bottom and let the broken oar go. He seized his carbine and brought the lanky form of Tay Pike under the weaving sights. The gun set him back. Pike lurched back and Quade caught him and set him on the thwart. Quade stood and brought up his Colt. He fired three times. Two of the shots were lost. The final one tore a ragged chunk out of a splashboard.

Up on the cliff, another gun crashed spasmodically. Hammaker was taking 100-foot pot shots at the fizzing length of fuse. Carnagey held his shot an instant. The river was hurling them on, cutting the range down to 100 feet, to seventy-five, to fifty. Pike, resting the barrel of his gun on a splashboard, the vengeance-stock against his cheek, was taking his last shot. Glenn squeezed the trigger. He saw the pale flash of Pike's shot and heard the solid *chock* of a bullet against an oar-lock. But Pike was done. He was on his feet without his rifle, holding his hands over his face.

Suddenly the boat twisted off the rock. Stove in, it sank immediately. Quade could be seen for a moment in the foam, gesturing at them, waving the gun, and then a downdraft sucked him under and it was the last anyone would see of Red Quade this side of Gold Beach.

Glenn dived for an extra oar. He fitted it, and sat there pulling strongly against the river, just as though the sky were not about to be snuffed out like a candle, as though it were not over for him and Hugh Badger and Charlie Hammaker. And the person he was most sorry for was Christy. Little red-headed Christy, who wanted a kitchen ten-by-twelve with a cast-iron stove, and a husband who was tired of knocking around. She could have had them all, too. But the husband had challenged the Rogue and was about to take his licking.

There was a clap of thunder, a blanket of flame overhead, a cascade of the utmost sound and fury a man could imagine. Stones as big as the boat were in the air. Something else was aloft, too, a thing that looked like a man half made and discarded by his Maker. Rocks were falling now, churning the river madly, and the thunderous echoes were enough to reduce a mountain to powder. But Carnagey sat there and rowed, because a man in trouble sometimes automatically does the right thing, his brain turned off but his muscles still in operation. The boat was a cork on an ocean, bobbing, swapping ends.

For a long time it was that way. They were in the shining heart of a maëlstrom. Then Carnagey knew that something had struck him on the head. Just that sharp, red impact, then the day was gone, all days were gone; they were fused with the lost years, and Carnagey was lost in the dark corridor all men must tread.

There was this sense of peace for a while, and then someone was shaking him and talking in his face and cursing. The sun was hot on his shirt. His head slogged painfully. Hugh Badger brought him up against the side of the boat. They were beached on the sand. Carnagey closed his eyes against the pain. "God!"

"You get a headache," Badger snorted, "and you crab because you wasn't drowned. We licked it, you hear? Them rocks went so high they didn't fall for half a minute. You kept on rowing and we licked it!"

Carnagey breathed the warm, sweet air.

"No," he said, "we didn't lick it. What if we'd been sucked into a whirlpool or hit a rock? Nobody licks it, but sometimes the river lets a man win. It held up the sky till it'd pulled us out from under, that's all. Don't you ever sell it short."

"You got something there," Badger agreed.

"You bet I have. In fact, I'm about through

bucking it. I'm going to build that road. The hell with thousand-pound runs when you can haul a couple of tons at a crack. Know what I'm going to bring over that road first of all?"

Badger, trying to dry his gun with a wet handkerchief, waited.

"A cast-iron stove. With a hot-water coil built in. The best."

Bonanza Railroad

I

It was a bad town to be poor in. Fried eggs were 50¢ apiece, pies $1 a cut; you could mortgage a T-bone steak for enough to sink a mine shaft. Inflation discounted, it was not good to be poor in any town, at Sam Haddon's age. It was humiliating to have the room clerk's eyes pick at his clothing like a pawnbroker's fingers as he stood with the suitcases at his feet and Allie holding his arm.

"Fifteen dollars a night, sir," the clerk said.

Sam's mind consulted with his wallet. Five years ago he would have said: *Is that the best you've got?* Nothing was too good for Allie. A gold-plated wash basin wasn't good enough for Allie to wash her hands in. He cleared his throat. "A room over the street would be all right for tonight," he remarked.

The clerk's mouth did not quite smile. "That *was* for a room over the street."

Sam said: "Oh!" You couldn't fool anybody when you were wearing a suit you'd choused steers in, worked like a fool in, gone broke in. Allie's fingers squeezed his arm, but Sam kept his eyes on the clerk's face. They had been to four hotels already, and the story was the same everywhere. Allie was tired, and she was going to have a decent place to sleep in tonight, and to hell with Virginia City prices.

"Maybe," Sam said, "you've got a smaller room. Tomorrow I'll get around and . . . er . . . establish my credit."

"Sorry." The clerk abandoned his professional good nature. "We only cater to the higher-class trade, mister."

Sam put the suitcase down and leaned his elbows on the counter. "I didn't quite get that one," he said.

Color came into the clerk's face. He repeated it sullenly, like a man who would rather abandon his guns but cannot do it gracefully. "I said we don't give credit, and we haven't anything cheaper than fifteen dollars. A Chinaman at the foot of C Street has a tent. . . ."

Sam picked up the rusty steel pen, dipped it, and signed the register—bold and black: *Mr. and Mrs. Samuel J. Haddon, Los Angeles, Cal.*

"Thinking it over," he remarked, "I reckon we'll stay. Give us the quietest room you've got, and don't quote prices. Bring your bill around in two weeks."

He could look ugly; he had the kind of jaw that takes the shape of determination, and, unshaven as it was, it was not a jaw you argued with. Sam's forty-five years kept their distance.

"Yes, sir," said the clerk, his jaw muscles working. He started for the stairs with a key, but Sam snapped his fingers.

"My wife don't like stairs. And on second thought, I think we'd like a settin' room, to boot."

Allie looked timidly about the room after the clerk had left, as though she were an interloper. "It wasn't right, Sam," she protested. "We can't pay for even one night here. Why, it must be forty dollars a day!"

Sam took off her cloak and made her lie on the bed, by the window. She sighed deeply, giving way at last to fatigue. Ten days in hotels and on the railroad. It was no life for a woman. The rails of the jerrybuilt Central Pacific weren't even properly settled yet. They were like a corduroy wagon road, pounding and bruising the passengers. Sam looked at Allie, seeing a story of weariness and futility in her face, and he wanted to get down on his knees and ask forgiveness. If Allie had aged twenty years in the last ten, it was his fault.

But God knew he had tried! It had cost $3,000 of his money and the $5,000 that Allie had brought when he married her to convince him that he was no rancher. It seemed that all his life he had been planning toward a ranch in California— but in five years loan-sharks and taxes had taught him that because a man has been a success at staging and railroading he is not necessarily going to make a pile in cattle ranching.

Sam Haddon's chief prides were in the men he had known—the strong men of the stage trails and the railroads. But the great days of staging were over; the transcontinental iron was laid down. This was 1874, and nobody in Virginia City looked twice at him, and, if anyone had, it wouldn't have been in friendship, because everybody was too busy making millions in the silver mines. Sam had $1,200 that he had salvaged out of his fiasco in cattle. Every penny of that he was going to need. Somewhere there must be a run-down mine someone would sell an interest in. With $1,200, all he could do was back the double zero and hope it came up. . . .

Allie was sleeping when he left the room. He stood under the balcony of the hotel, mentally taking the town in his teeth to test it. He found it solid. Virginia City was no boom camp. Church steeples testified to that. They were the cement that kept a town from collapsing overnight.

A circle of ruddy desert hills held the town like cupped hands. From this waste of sage-covered hills men had dug silver and translated it into mansions and shacks, streets and alleys, churches, brothels, and saloons. And from where Sam stood, all of them who were not sweating their guts out in the mines on the day shift appeared to be fanning the fire to its ultimate brightness.

In a drugstore he found a town directory and looked under PROPERTY, MINING. He memorized an address and went in search of the Capital Clearing Company. He found it near the railroad station, on E Street, a small office upstairs in a brick building. Under the title of the company, on the small door, was the name J.J. Raab, President.

Mr. Raab himself admitted him, a lean and elderly man with a face of the color and texture of wrinkled chamois. The hand he gave Sam on introduction was cold and hard. Mr. Raab turned a chair and resumed his seat. He leaned forward, smiling and linking his fingers. He reminded Sam of a doctor.

"Now, then," Mr. Raab said.

Sam gave him the story. He showed him his balance in a Los Angeles banking house. "What I'm looking for," he declared, "is an interest in some outfit that maybe needs operating cash. Something a man could put a little capital and a lot of work into, with a chance of taking out something worthwhile."

"Small money, large expectations." Raab smiled. "Well, as a matter of fact, you fall into a rather restricted class. Up here everyone either has a million or he hasn't anything. The small-production mines go begging when they're offered. The millionaires won't fool with them, the others can't afford them."

He took some filing cards out of a box and riffled through them. He read off, as if to himself: "Gopher Hole Number Two . . . Red Dog . . . Six Bit . . . Six Bit," he repeated. "I wonder if you'd be interested in that?"

He sat frowning at the card, and Sam tried to

help him by saying: "Sounds like it might be about my size."

Raab's fingertips roamed the edges of the card. "It was owned by an Irishman named Sheedy. Sheedy borrowed a thousand dollars from me, and I dare say he'd have paid it back if he hadn't got caught in a cave-in. Sad thing. Of course I took the property. Here's an assayer's report . . . the last one Sheedy had made."

"Eighty-two to the ton," Sam read. "Is that good?"

"That's average. I'm not counting the ones that scale a thousand or better. The mine needs a little work. I trust you aren't afraid of that?"

Sam stood up. "Let's look at it."

Horses were procured at a stable; they rode out of town, up a forgotten road in a dusty cañon. Here the heat was greater, the hot desert air packing down without a breeze to disturb it. The walls of the cañon presented broken facings of crumbling rock.

Presently the cañon widened, the walls becoming less precipitous. A number of deserted mines were passed. They drew rein under a sagging grizzly, above which the slope was scarred with old stopes and the rusting remnants of mining equipment.

Raab showed Sam around, but he exhibited no eagerness to go into the tunnel. "Sheedy was a scrounging sort," he declared in his slow, rather sad voice. "He wouldn't spend the money to shore properly, so in the end . . ." He shrugged, turning to the machinery littering the slope. "It might cost you forty or fifty dollars to put it back in shape, not counting your labor. Everything's here you'd need for small-scale production."

"How do production costs stack up against the price of ore?" Sam asked.

"Thirty percent might be an average," said the agent. "At that rate, one thousand is cheap for the mine. Mind you," he added, "I'm not trying to force a sale. But this is as good a buy as I know of."

Most of the way into town Sam pondered it. When they reached the office, he was ready. "Reckon I'll take it," he said.

In the morning Sam, with part of the $200 he had left, bought a battered ore wagon and a team of mules. Allie rode with him, bright and optimistic after the night's rest. Sam pointed at a hill dominating the city.

"Right up there," he declared, "Sam Haddon is going to build a marble house one of these days. You and me are going to set on the gold-plated gallery and watch our ore wagons trundle to the mill . . . with nothin' harder for us to do than clip coupons."

"First thing," Allie countered, "will be the hotel bill. After that the marble mansions."

For a week Sam worked like a pit mule, hauling machinery around and getting the grizzly into workable shape, and every day the hotel added another $25 to their bill. Out of the original stake he had $75 with the hotel bill unpaid.

After a fashion he got the main tunnel shored up. He hitched one of the mules to the train of five small ore cars and cleaned the trash out of the main drift. Then he set his first charge.

On a hot Friday morning, with the sun blazing on the back of his sweating neck, he drove the big ore wagon into town. He hadn't given much thought to the milling end of the business as yet. Most of the stamp mills and concentrators, he understood, were down on the Carson River. There were a few mills in Virginia City, but none was operating. Sam wondered about that, with all the mines going full blast. He asked a man on the sidewalk how far it was to the smelters.

"Sixteen miles," the man told him. "It's a day's trip. Or you can dump that han'ful of dust in the corner of a railroad car and save time."

Sam drove to the railroad station, a worry pulling through his mind. Raab had forgotten to mention how far away the mills were. The rate clerk regarded Sam's single wagon of ore with a smile.

"That'll be four dollars a ton, mister," he replied. "But I can't move a thing till tomorrow."

Sam did not have to do much figuring to know that the freight charge was going to devour most of the cash he had in his pocket. "I suppose it's cash on the barrel head," he said.

"Yes and no. It's cash when you pick up your mill ticket. Same outfit owns the mills and the railroad."

Sam said slowly—"Write it up."—and the clerk was just reaching for the pencil over his ear, when the hearty belch of a locomotive came up the tracks.

II

The freight clerk, standing on the platform at the edge of the tracks, shaded his eyes against the brilliant glare of the sun. "Ain't anybody due up today," he stated. "Shoot, that ain't nothing but a loco."

A series of whistle blasts multiplied themselves against the hills. The engine came charging up the tracks, a small but gorgeous thing of black-and-red paint and brass. Her funnel would have swallowed four bales of hay without a straw spilling over; a pair of gilded antlers topped the headlight.

"Number Sixty-Nine," the freight man said, frowning. "That shore ain't one of ours."

They could see, as the locomotive stopped before the station, that only one man occupied the cab. He swung down, a large young man in overalls. He approached the agent, casually unfolding a letter.

"Mister Huntington," he said, "hoped you could

165

find a siding for my locomotive. I'll be in town a few days."

The freight agent's expression could have been tagged consternation. His natural impulse was to laugh, but set against it was the sheet of stationery he held with the letterhead of the Central Pacific Railroad engraved thereon. Sam could read three lines of script requesting that certain courtesies be shown John R. Ryan. He could make out a clogged rubric at the bottom that might have been translated: *C.P. Huntington.*

"Did you say . . . your engine?" the agent queried.

Ryan said—"Uhn-huh."—as though it were no more unusual for a man to own a locomotive than a horse. "I've got business in these parts. If you can put us up, I'll be mighty grateful."

He stood there, drawing off his greasy overalls with fine casualness.

The agent took his sanity in both hands. "Mister Ryan," he said, "you may or may not be crazy, and this may or may not be a stolen loco, but I can't let you stay without a written order from A.J. Rigdon. This is the Nevada Union . . . not the Central Pacific. Headquarters is down at Carson."

Ryan said: "Damn! And I just came by there an hour ago."

It was at this point that Sam spoke up. "As long as you're going back, mister, maybe the boss here will let you haul a car of ore down for me."

Ryan swung back to the cab. "You can hitch on if you want, pardner."

Sam waited while the freight agent wrote up the bill of lading and the yardmen transferred his ore to a car. He climbed aboard, feeling secretly proud that he was to ride in the cab with this cocky young buck. Instinctively he was drawn to him, perhaps because he reminded Sam of himself twenty years ago.

The Boston did not fold her drive rods and coast on the down trip. Not with John Ryan at the throttle. She charged through cañons and bored through tunnels. On the turns, she all but stripped the fish-joint rails off the ties.

Sam finally shouted: "You want me to lean inside, on the turns?"

Ryan laughed, but all the same he slacked off on the steam. They got around to introductions. When Ryan heard Sam's name, he stared hard.

"Sam Haddon?" he repeated. "Not Haddon of the Union Pacific?"

A little fire kindled in Sam's bosom.

"Why," he said, "I did a few little jobs for General Dodge, yes. But I don't reckon you'll find me in the history books."

Ryan put out his hand. "You're in mine, Sam, on Page One! I was with the Big Four, building west to beat you to Salt Lake City. If it wasn't for you, Sam Haddon, Promontory Point would have been ten miles out of Omaha. I'd like it," he added, and the cockiness in him was far below the surface now, "if you'd call me Johnny."

Sam said—"Why, sure, Johnny."—as casually as he could, but gratitude went over him like a warm shower. Johnny Ryan had given him back a patch of the pride he had worn in the big days, the golden days, the days of the transcontinental iron. And somehow it gave back a faith he had almost lost, that time and hard luck had no claim on a man who wasn't afraid of them.

All the way down the grade they talked, swapping anecdotes of the construction camps.

"What I'd like to know," said Sam finally, "is how come you to own a locomotive?"

Johnny Ryan wiped the face of a gauge with a grease rag. Sam noticed that the interior of the cab was as immaculate as a Dutch housewife's kitchen. All the brass was polished, the gray paint slicked down, the floor clean.

"It's like asking a man how he came to marry his wife," said Johnny. "Mostly you sort of drift into it. The Boston was one of the first locos we had on the Central. She hauled a million tons of ties and rails, and 'most a million Chinamen. I was a sort of assistant construction engineer, you might say. I got pretty attached to the old Boston when she'd come buckin' through the drifts with chow and reliefs, or bring out a new tank o' water on the desert stretches when the old one was full of polliwogs." He patted the window sill. "Yes, sir, she's my wife, Sam. She's sort of my brother, too, and in a way she's me. We talk to each other. She ain't one of these unreliable iron hussies, always flauntin' a leaky flue or slidin' off the iron. But the Central switched over to Two-Six-Ohs . . . that's the Mogul, all power and no flash . . . so I talked the Huntington crowd into letting me take her for a thousand down and five years to pay."

He grinned, and in that quick, devilish lighting up of his face Sam read much. He read weakness and strength, recklessness and cold-eyed judgment, and most of all a need for things to be doing around this man.

They pulled into the Carson City yards about noon. The grimy, shouting stamp mills and reducers on the bank of the Carson River gave off clouds of sulphurous smoke that poisoned the air for miles around, blighting every touch of green. Smoking slag piles ran up against the hills; cars ran out upon these mounds and dumped glowing streams of slag that quickly grayed and crumbled.

A hopper took Sam's carload of ore in one gulp. An employee gave him a bill with a number. "Your check will be ready tomorrow," he said.

They located the mill headquarters in a grove of dead cottonwood trees. Wide cement steps led to the entrance of a three-story brick structure. A clerk took Johnny Ryan's letter into Rigdon's private office.

In a moment he returned, leaving the door open. "Go on in."

Fortified behind a big oak desk, Andrew Rigdon stared at them. He was a powerful-looking man of fifty, bald, heavy-browed, with a neatly trimmed beard and a broad flat nose. He handed the letter back to Ryan, saying: "Why the devil should I furnish storage for Central's rolling stock, young fellow?"

"Central's got nothing to do with it," said Johnny. "I own it. Huntington gave me the letter as a personal favor."

"What made him think," inquired Rigdon, "that I would be handing favors to friends of his?"

"I reckon it was my idea," said Johnny, and, moving to the window, he surveyed the scene of smoke and clamor with hands clasped behind him. "Busy little place," he remarked. "Occurs to me it might pay the Central to run a line in here someday. Huntington was talking about it when I left. 'John,' he said, 'figurin' all the timber those mines use, and the forests our line passes through, I don't know why in hell we don't cash in on it.' Another angle," Johnny added, "would be for him to build a new set o' mills closer to Virginia City."

"May I ask," Rigdon put in coldly, "exactly what you are doing up here?"

"Just getting my breath between jobs. The Central is looking around for a new bear to fight, now that they've clawed all the hide off the old

170

one. You might call me a scout. I don't know whether to recommend that they cut in on your pie or start reaching for Oregon."

Sam stood back, missing nothing. He loved a fight. He liked to see two men, who hated each other's guts, politely cut each other up and down the back.

Rigdon's hand, stout-fingered and hairy, closed about a marble paperweight. "If I let you use a siding," he proposed, "will you promise to leave it inside of a week?"

"If you don't"—Johnny smiled—"I'll promise to go back and start forty-five engineers humping over their drafting boards."

Rigdon wrote four lines on a letterhead. He shoved it across the desk. He said: "Get out of here."

Johnny glanced at the note, folded it twice, and slipped it inside his coat. He smiled at Sam. "Didn't I tell you A.J. was a prince among men?" he said.

III

As they were eating lunch in a chophouse near the river, Sam could not get it out of his head that an intelligent, high-flying sort like Johnny Ryan did not drift around causing trouble without a reason.

"That was quite a yarn you gave Rigdon," he

said. "I got the notion before, that you and the Huntington crowd were all washed up."

"Sure we are. I told Rigdon the truth. I'm just catching my breath between jobs. The other side of the story is that I'm looking for a railroad to build. I think maybe I've found it, too. You take a set-up like this, where one outfit runs the whole shootin' match . . . well, I figure there's room for another. Rigdon's freight and mill charges are double what they should be. He got control of all the steam-driven mills in Virginia City and then shut them down. It's to his advantage to charge freight to get the ore to the mills down here, where he can operate by waterpower and raise the percentage of profit. That's why I'm here, Sam," he said, "waiting for a railroad to tap me on the shoulder and ask to be built. A man with capital. That's what I'm looking for."

Johnny decided to stay overnight in Carson and take Sam up with him in the morning. They spread blankets on the floor of the cab. By midnight it was cool enough to sleep.

After breakfast Sam reported for his mill check. He was half drunk on optimism. Twenty-three tons of ore at eighty dollars a ton—less $25 a ton milling charge, and $4 for haulage.

But one look at the check a clerk handed him convinced him something was wrong. He called the clerk back.

"You've got the wrong customer, son," he

172

pointed out. "This is for a hundred and thirty-eight dollars. Mine should run somewhere around twelve hundred."

The clerk was young and spectacled and in a hurry. He glanced at the mill ticket.

"That's you, all right," he stated.

"But the Six Bits mine runs eighty . . . ," Sam began.

The clerk said: "I'm sorry, we don't take complaints here. You'll have to see Mister Rigdon or Mister Engler."

Sam went out and sat on the steps. Johnny Ryan found him there ten minutes later, when he came over from stoking the Boston. He saw shock written plainly on Sam's countenance. He took the check out of his hand and glanced at it.

"What are you mining up there, partner?" he asked. "Cast iron?"

Sam stood up. "Johnny," he said dully, "I've been took. A man in Virginia City sold me a mine that was supposed to run eighty to the ton. It runs thirty-five."

"J.J. Raab?" Johnny inquired, and clucked sympathetically. "You ran into a door in the dark that time, partner. Raab is Rigdon's lawyer and land agent. They've got a string of second-rate mines they've taken over for freight and milling charges. When they can find a sucker to sell to, it's so much gravy. I don't know what the tarnation you can do about it, either."

The blood was beginning to thicken in Sam's face. He was commencing to breathe heavily through his nose. "I can run a bare-fist assay on J.J. Raab for one thing. And maybe I'll just warm up by tearing a couple of chuck roasts off your Mister Rigdon while we're here."

Johnny rubbed his hands, falling in beside him. "I might just go along and watch." He grinned.

Sam said stonily: "If you're thinking I'll need help, I could beat him to death with a paper bag full of feathers. I'll see you in fifteen minutes."

It took a prideful man to understand one. Johnny Ryan understood that Sam did not want or need assistance. He stopped by the tracks, while Sam went on to the red brick building above the river.

Sam passed the reception clerk without looking at him. He walked into the elegant paneled office, where Rigdon was talking to a big-bellied man with the face of a dissipated Indian, who stood beside the desk. His face showed a quick resentment.

He said frigidly: "Would you mind waiting outside? Did the clerk say you could come in?"

Sam Haddon walked across the carpet to the desk and threw the check in Rigdon's face. "Maybe you'd like to frame that," he said. "Someday it will remind you of the worst fifteen minutes you ever passed."

The swarthy man was coming around the desk. Rigdon said: "Wait a minute!" He studied Sam.

"You're the man who came in with Ryan, aren't you? What's on your mind?"

"I bought a mine from J.J. Raab," Sam stated, "that was supposed to run eighty to the ton. It runs thirty-five. Now, you can find a thousand dollars in a hurry, or you can wait and see what happens."

"We're not responsible for the hazards of mining," Rigdon declared. "One week a mine may run a hundred, and the next ten, or the other way around. If you don't like the mine you bought, sell it to somebody else."

Sam nodded. "I'll sell all right . . . to you. And right now!"

Rigdon settled back in his armchair. "I think," he said to the man beside him, "that this is in your department, after all, Engler."

"Yes sir," said Engler, "I think maybe it is. I'll put it to you this way, Haddon. Around here I'm sort of a grease man for Mister Rigdon. I keep things running smooth. Naturally I don't let grousers like you get in the way of business. The door over yonder works by turning the knob. Or do you want me to show you out?"

He came around to Sam, and he took hold of his elbow almost gently. But there was nothing gentle about Sam Haddon's reaction. His hand moved in a swift hatchet motion, the side of it coming solidly against the bridge of Engler's nose. Engler gave a yell, covering his face with his hands. When he took them away, his nose had an oblique cant. He snorted, spraying blood over his shirt. Then he went after Sam.

Age was suddenly something that had no brand on Sam Haddon. He was like an old cavalry horse hearing, after a long winter, the cry of the bugle. He went to meet Rigdon's trouble-shooter with his eyes squinted and his head tucked down. He got both hands around the other's neck and ran him back against the wall. A map of Nevada Territory melodramatically crashed to the floor. Twice Sam banged the head of the railroad man against the wall before he flung him aside. Engler went to his knees. He lumbered up again, a strong and wrathful man.

They came up against each other savagely, trading half a dozen blows, and then they closed, Sam pumping hard to Engler's belly. Engler grunted, gave ground, and became cautious. Frenzy had only given him bruises and taken his wind. He began to weave and stab and feint. But Sam could play that way, too. He hunched his shoulders, bear-like, chopping at Engler's face.

What he had not counted on was Rigdon. He might not be a fighter, but he knew how to swing a chair. The shadow of it was the first warning Sam had. He took a step sideways, throwing his arms up to shield his head; the chair hit him on the shoulder. Engler threw a punch that landed over his eye.

Sam found himself on the floor. It seemed that all

his nerves had been disconnected; he had no consciousness of pain—he was merely looking out on the scene through a small window in his befuddlement. He saw Engler's boot raised over his head, and it was pure reflex action that caused him to roll aside.

Now his senses came back, riding on a wave of pain. Rigdon had done his shoulder no good. Sam got to his feet just as Engler came in. He raised his knee; Engler's groin rammed into it. He cuffed the man over the ear with a left, and split his lip with a right.

Engler's face, bruised and bloody, somehow enraged Sam. The more he looked at it, the more he wanted to smash it. He kept on slugging until abruptly it was no longer there. He looked down and there it was looking up at him from the floor.

Sam turned, but when he looked around for Andrew Rigdon, he had vanished. The outer office was quiet as a church when Sam walked out.

Johnny Ryan had the sagacity not to ask questions. He shot the loco onto the main iron, and they started up the grade to Virginia City. Sam Haddon did some thinking. With the $1,200 gone, there was only one thing left—a job, wielding a pick or a muck stick. He could make more money working in someone else's mine than he could trying to operate his own.

Presently Johnny could stand it no longer. "Don't

tell me," he said, "that Rigdon's got that much scrap behind his whiskers."

Sam poured a dipper of water over his head. His right eye was nearly buried in puffy, purplish flesh. "A fellow named Engler was there," he said. "He kept me a little busy."

"Engler! Oh, my God!" Johnny exclaimed. "I knew I should have gone with you! That 'possum cut his teeth on Irish section bosses on the U.P."

"Must have been the Eastern section," Sam snorted. "Up front, you had to be able to eat two section bosses at one sitting before they'd let you sign the payroll."

"What did Rigdon say?" Johnny wanted to know.

"What he said don't matter," Sam grunted. "What does matter is that he ain't one man, but a thousand. I came five hundred miles just to lose my stake in a day."

Johnny lit a cigar, but he had no answer. There *was* no answer; it was tough jerky, and, when you had said that, you'd said it all.

That night Sam told Allie, straight out, what had happened.

"I'll leave it up to you, Allie," he told her. "I can take a job in the mines at eight dollars a day, or we can go down to Texas and I'll drum up a job on some jerk-line stage outfit. Small potatoes either way, but a living."

Allie Haddon didn't have red hair for nothing. Time hadn't managed to get much silver to stick to it, nor had the years worked any alloy into her spirit. "Small potatoes and the Haddons," she declared, "are like oil and water. They never mixed before, and they aren't going to mix now. The details are up to you, but I was promised a marble house on the hill, and I'm not settling for any adobe hut on the flats."

While Sam was trying to decide, next morning, whether to start out by getting drunk or hunting a job, there was a knock at the door. It was a young woman who stood in the hallway, an unusually pretty young woman.

"Mister Haddon?" she asked.

Sam nodded.

"If you aren't busy," she said, "I'd like to talk to you and Missus Haddon for a few minutes."

Allie was always delighted to have a lady caller, especially in a hard-luck town like this. She had Sam bring up the best chair for the girl.

She was Laurie Briggs, she said. They talked about small things—the heat, and the flies—for a few minutes, and then there was a pause.

"I'm sure the name of Briggs means nothing to you," the girl declared, "but it was pretty well known a year ago, because of my father's mill. Things change fast in a mining town. Dad's dead now, and I guess nobody ever heard of the Briggs Refining Company."

"I'm wondering," Sam said, "where *you* heard of *me*."

Laurie Briggs smiled. She sat with golden sunlight slanting across her gray skirt. She wore a thin white blouse, with a red ribbon worked through the neck of it. Her hair was ash-blonde, combed high; Sam could see Allie trying to figure out how the crown effect of her hair-do was achieved.

"I'll tell you how I heard of you, Mister Haddon," she said. "And I'll tell you some other things, too, and then, if you aren't interested, we'll have had a nice little visit, anyway. I was going up Red Rock Cañon the other day to look at the mill . . . I just came back from San Francisco last week . . . and I saw the work you'd been doing at the Six Bit Mine. I knew that United had taken it over after Sheedy went broke, so I got your name from Raab."

Sam leaned forward, his hands on his knees. "Raab told me Sheedy died in a cave-in."

The girl shook her head. "No. Rigdon wrecked him and he left town. Like all the rest, he couldn't pay forty dollars' freight and milling charges on low-grade ore. It cost ten dollars to get the ore by wagon to the railroad. Then the real charges began. I'm wondering," she said thoughtfully, "how you have arranged to take care of the hauling yourself."

Sam rubbed his eye. "Rigdon and I were talking about that yesterday," he admitted. "It looks like I'm hooked."

Laurie shook her head. "It's happened to scores of other mine operators since the bonanza ores died out. Virginia City is still on a hill of silver, but it costs more to get it out than it did in the old days. After Dad went out of business, Rigdon moved half of the mills down to Carson, where he could run them by waterpower. He built the railroad, and now everything has to be moved sixteen miles before it can be reduced. That has run all but the richest mines out of business."

"Where's it getting Rigdon?" Sam demanded. "When the mines all go under, he's finished, too."

"Not if he owns them. He's taken over thousands of dollars' worth of fair mining property. When he wants to, he can start mining them. But he doesn't need to, while he can run at capacity for profits."

Allie linked her fingers in her lap. Laurie Briggs's story had not cheered her; it had only shown her how big a thing they were bucking. "Then I don't see what people like you and Sam and I can do," she declared.

Laurie Briggs said: "I've come to see you because I want to open up my father's mill again. I'm going to fight A.J. Rigdon. And I think you can help me."

IV

Someone pounded twice on the door; someone called: "How you feelin', pardner?"

Sam let Johnny Ryan in. "Meet Laurie Briggs," he said, "of Briggs Refining Company."

Johnny looked at the girl, sitting by the window with Allie. The sun was doing things with the girl's hair; the warm touch of it lay on her cheek. Her eyes, blue with flecks of gray, had a shine. These matters were not lost on Johnny Ryan. His derby came off; his cigar came out of his mouth.

"Pleased, ma'am," he declared.

"Miss Briggs," Sam said, "was just telling us something interesting. She wants to open up the mill again . . . give Rigdon a run for his money."

"We've had enough piracy," Laurie cut in. "With the help of the small mine owners, I don't know why I couldn't reopen. I'll improve the road to the mill and work out a co-operative hauling outfit. What I need is someone to help organize it."

Johnny said flatly: "It won't work."

Everyone stared and Laurie asked shortly: "Why won't it?"

"Transportation," asserted Johnny. "Freighting costs money. It's slow. It's a great idea, but it won't work."

Laurie flushed. "I didn't ask for your opinion,

Mister Ryan. I've got it all figured out, on paper. I know exactly what I'm up against."

"Do you know you're up against a million-dollar outfit?"

"Yes, and I'm not afraid of it. I'll bet a hundred dollars that Briggs Refining is solvent a year from now."

Johnny sat down; he tilted back in the chair with his cigar in his teeth and his derby set back on his head. "Transportation," he told her, "has whipped the biggest of them. But people will still try to squeeze by with ox carts when they could have a railroad to serve them. Sure," he said, suddenly brisk, "you could make half a million dollars out there, Laurie. Easy! But you'd need a railroad."

Sam began to get the picture. "Do you know anybody," he asked, "who could build that railroad?"

Johnny grinned. "Give me just a month," he said, "and I'll lay 'er down. I'm looking for a job, Laurie Briggs. Will you hire me?"

"But railroads cost a fortune!" Laurie objected. "We couldn't begin . . ."

"We've got ten thousand ties just waitin' to be laid," Johnny said. "Right now they're serving as timbers in played-out mines. I'll guarantee to get rails on credit. Central Pacific's got a stockyard full of them, at Reno. C.P. Huntington would give his shirt to put a knife in a competitor's back. I'll take care of the materials, and Sam and I can lay 'er down. You do the milling. We'll be the Big Two of Nevada." He asked eagerly: "How about it, Sam?"

Allie Haddon answered for her husband, who was without speech: "He'll be glad to oblige, John. You just tell him what you want, and Sam will get it done."

Johnny bounded up to secure from the desk paper, pen, and ink. He drew up a rough outline on the spot. They named the railroad the Nevada Shortline. President, John Ryan. Vice-President, Samuel J. Haddon.

It was the vice-president who presently ventured a dubious glance at the prospects. "I don't exactly see," he remarked, "where the money is going to come from to get under way, Johnny. . . ."

"Stock! Gilt-edged stock!" Johnny exclaimed. "I'll have fifty thousand dollars' worth printed up tomorrow. We'll sell it to operators who can understand that the railroad will double the value of their claims. No phony promises, either. I'll give it to 'em straight out . . . that the stock ain't worth a dime today, but six months from now a hundred dollars' worth will get a thousand. There ain't a man in Virginia City who won't take a gamble like that."

Johnny and his enthusiasm had completely taken over. Everyone else was silent, watching him stride up and down, dropping cigar ash and giving off optimism as the sun emits warmth. A button had been pressed; a dynamo had begun to hum.

Johnny turned to Laurie. "You look hungry," he said. "Let's go have some lunch and talk this over."

Laurie Briggs hesitated, glancing at Allie and Sam. "Perhaps Mister and Missus Haddon . . ."

"They've already eaten," Johnny said. From the door, with Laurie's hand on his arm, he gave Sam a wink.

In the morning, Sam went down to Miner's Hall, where Johnny was selling stock. He listened to his pitch. Johnny was better than any side-show barker he had ever heard. Johnny made the Nevada Shortline sound like the successor to the Union Pacific. He held the prism of his enthusiasm to a scant ten miles of track until it looked like a thousand.

The buying spirit ignited. The line lengthened, with Johnny personally taking the money in, issuing the stock, and shaking the purchasers' hands.

There was a grim, dried-out individual at the table beside him who had been making entries in a ledger. "Public accountant," Johnny explained to Sam after the meeting. The stock was all sold. "Nobody's going to sling mud at this outfit. We don't draw a dime out of the bank without him writing in that book. Now, then," he declared, "we need a crew. There ought to be enough hard-up miners in this town. . . ."

Sam said: "I'll get you a crew."

In two days he assembled a gang of fifty hard-rockers, men he lured from the tunnels with the promise of good wages. He got a list of defunct mines in Red Rock Cañon, along the ten-mile stretch to the mill in Round Valley. He put half of them to pulling out stulls and timbers. The rest attacked the freight road with pick and shovel.

Sam sent a dozen workmen out to the stamp mill. Clogged boilers had to be scraped, rusted parts freed and greased. The mill buildings, a small city of sheet-metal structures, wooden settling tanks, and dismal slag piles, occupied the eastern end of Round Valley. It was here that A.J. Rigdon and Hap Engler came one day, looking for the partners.

Rigdon rode a large bay with three white stockings, stout-limbed in keeping with its rider's bulk. Engler gave Sam a stony stare. The mementoes of their recent unpleasantness were still upon him. There was, this time, no contempt in his eyes.

Rigdon kept slapping his boot with a black leather quirt ornamented with gold wire. "Do you men know what you're doing here?" he demanded.

"We've got a pretty good idea," Sam told him. "We think we're building a railroad." He stood with his hands clasped behind him, rocking on his feet.

"Good luck to you," Rigdon said dryly. He let his eyes roam among the work gangs sledging boilers

186

and swabbing oil on rusted machinery, and then he glanced back at the cañon. "That's a good road-bed you're laying," he remarked. "But I can't help wondering what you're going to use for rails."

Caution whispered in Sam's ear. "We've got that worked out, too," he stated. "When the time comes, we'll have them."

When Rigdon smiled, it was not good nature that turned his lips, but a cold sense of superiority. "Don't be mysterious with me, Haddon," he advised. "I was playing high finance when you were still tooling jackasses along a freight trail. You're counting on the Central Pacific shoving a knife in my back, aren't you? They'll sell you all the rails you want, of course. But how do you plan to get them in?"

Sam said, straight out: "On your flatcars. You're going to haul them for us, Rigdon . . . at your usual rates."

Hap Engler laughed. "Never one to write to Santy Claus, were you?"

"You're going to haul them," retorted Sam, "because you've got to. You're public servants, even if damned poor ones. You can't say what freight you're going to accept and what you aren't, as long as the toll is paid."

A.J. Rigdon tucked his hands under his belt, nodding. His whole manner was that of a man in command; it disturbed Sam just a little. "We're public servants, as you say," Rigdon agreed. "But

I hope you'll let me know in plenty of time when you want these rails moved, because we book pretty far ahead. First come, first served. I don't think we can touch a thing for about fifteen months, can we, Engler?"

Engler cocked an eye. "I'd say that was about it."

"So you see," Rigdon summed up, letting a smile disturb his short-cropped gray beard, "you'll have to figure on marking time a while before the profits come in. But you'll probably make out." He tapped his horse with the quirt.

Sam sat on a rock and watched them ride away. He was confused, befuddled. Finance! Stock! Public servants! He'd said what he and Johnny had decided was right, and Rigdon had moved right into the king row. Were they licked before they started?

He thought about the $50,000 dollars they owed. He thought about fraud, and he wished he'd stuck to staging, where he knew his weapons. He wished to hell Johnny Ryan would come back.

V

There was a conference at the hotel that night. Sam told of Rigdon's visit, and Laurie added another touch of gray to the picture.

"Something else to worry about," she said, "is

money for the mill. I've got to hire a crew. I've got equipment to buy. I thought you might advance me some from the railroad fund."

Sam grunted. "We can't transfer a dime from the Shortline to Briggs Refining, Laurie. It ain't legal. What about issuing stock?"

Laurie shook her head. "It was all right for you to sell stock, because United didn't know what was going on. If I try it, they'll buy all they can, under other names. I'd lose control of the firm. All you'd have then would be a railroad running to nowhere. I suppose," she said, "you've heard of Colonel Tom Morgan. He's worth over a million dollars. Colonel Tom was a great friend of Dad's. He'll lend me the money. I'll see him."

Johnny said: "Be careful. If you can trust him not to sell your note to Rigdon, all right."

After Laurie went to her room, Johnny maneuvered Sam into the hall. He said: "Get your hat, pardner. We're going for a little train ride."

The night was black, full of stars and clamor from the saloons as they left the hotel. Up among the mines, donkey engines puffed and clanked, windlasses clattered, ore rattled down wooden grizzlies. They proceeded in the direction of the railroad yards.

Johnny said: "You didn't think Rigdon would haul our iron without throwing his weight around a little, did you? I've had rails on Steamboat

Siding for two weeks, just waiting for the right time to haul them. I'd say this was it."

Sam's flesh began to tingle. After all the days of shadow boxing, they were going to throw a few Sunday punches! He threw the switch while Johnny mounted to the cab of the Boston on the siding and quietly let the brakes off. The locomotive moved silently onto the main iron. Sam caught the grab iron and swung aboard. They passed the barns and in ten minutes, the town behind them, started the fires.

About nine they neared Carson City. Here they went cautiously. There was considerable activity about the mills and smelters. Slag cars dumped waterfalls of scarlet that crawled slowly down the hill. They passed unobserved through the yards. Ahead, now, lay the comfort of the desert, black and empty.

Out here Johnny let her roll. Just short of Steamboat Siding, the engine's iron pulse began to slacken. They halted beside a barren clutch of tool sheds and material; a water tank balanced on stilts beside the tracks; piles of ties and rusting ranks of rails flanked the road. On the siding were ten flatcars ready to be picked up. Johnny backed in and made the hitch. From now on, the Boston would earn her pitch pine!

The road was level north of Carson, enabling them to gather speed before hitting the grade, but between them and the grade was the city, and many watchful eyes. Sam kept watch as the rails clattered under them, wondering if it would be as clear sailing as Johnny Ryan anticipated.

Suddenly Sam heard him yell: "Hold your hat, pardner! Here they come!"

A locomotive on a parallel track was running alongside the Boston. She was coming tender first; Sam's eyes picked up half a dozen men atop the cordwood. There was no chance that she could beat the freight train to the switch and get ahead of her, but there was likewise no doubt that a party had been planned for the Boston.

They passed through the yards and hit the grade. All of the little locomotive's speed was spent prodigally in the first mile. Her drivers began to slip; she got down on her hands and knees and bludgeoned the rails; she panted and chuffed and dug. When they won the first straight section, Sam looked back and saw the other loco directly behind.

Johnny was grimly sober. "This is where you start earning your money," he told Sam. "Ever pulled a rivet?"

Sam had not spent a year with the U.P. with his eyes closed. "Show me a drawbar!" he said. "You want a car cut loose if they board us?"

Johnny grinned, and Sam clambered over the tender and began to climb across the flatcars to the rear. He went on hands and knees, for the stacked rails, with the buckling cars beneath, made a poor platform. When he reached the next to the last car, he stood a moment on the coupling, watching, over the long ranks of iron, the men on the tender of the other loco. They were not behaving precisely as he had expected. They seemed to be striking matches, which the wind immediately snuffed out.

The tracks curved into a shallow, winding wash, where the moonlight sifted down upon them. The figures of the other train men came into sudden, sharp focus. Right then Sam realized what they were doing. It was enough to send him scrambling ahead on all fours. Just as he reached the clattering coupling separating the last cars, he caught the sputtering red trail of sparks arch from the tender to land among the rails. Dynamite! Dynamite to upset the car and dump the whole line into the cañon!

For five seconds he hesitated. He said a prayer for a long fuse and vaulted to the top of the rails. He had taken only one stride when he heard Hap Engler's voice, an inarticulate bawl that told him he had been discovered. The sharp *pop* of a revolver confirmed this. Sam went down, flat. Another shot sounded and a chunk of lead wailed off the flatcar.

Sam Haddon knew when to retreat. Other guns would come out in a moment, and what was his one .44 against all of theirs? He slid back into the windy gorge between the cars. Sweat was cold on his face and palms. He was tensed against the expected flash and roar behind him, and this tension made every movement stiff. Engler must be sitting on coals back there, too. Engler knew he was trying to pitch the explosive off, and he didn't intend to let him, but at the same time the Nevada Union loco would pile right into thirty tons of cold iron if she didn't slack off pretty soon.

Sam bent over the drawbar. What he couldn't do by hand, he might be able to manage by cutting the rear car loose. But the pin was frozen by the pull against it. He strained until his back ached. Gray with fear, he stood up. He could see Johnny looking back at him; in a last, "please, God" effort he waved the washout signal. Johnny Ryan almost piled the tender on top of the loco by applying the brakes. It threw Sam to his knees on the platform. He seized the drawbar again, and in the split second that the coupling was loose he felt the iron grind, turn, and rise free. He dropped the pin; he crouched there, hearing the *clatter* of the trucks under him, seeing the flatcar swiftly drop back. Johnny knew his stuff; he threw the Boston on full throttle the instant the slack came. Without losing speed, she labored on.

There was turmoil aboard the other engine. Engler went in a scuttling crawl across the wood. Other men crouched in frozen expectancy of the explosion. A man jumped off the tender and rolled down the bank. The timing was all off. At the last instant the engineer threw the Johnson bar. The drivers screamed into reverse. A cylinder head went out with a roar of liberated steam.

Then a vast flaming mushroom bloomed over the flatcar. The whole scene stood out in black and orange—the derailed flatcar stumbling down the ties, the locomotive behind it on the point of collision. Sam saw men piling off the tender as it crumpled against the now stalled flatcar. Just before the flame died, the locomotive began to lurch. He heard the thunder of its overturning a moment later.

VI

It was almost dawn when the Boston finished her run. Johnny Ryan ran the flatcars onto a siding; 100 feet from this point, beyond the Nevada Union's right of way, they would begin to lay track. He told Sam to go back to the hotel; he would stand guard over the rails himself until they could get the crew down in the morning.

Sam was back, shaved, bathed, and ready for action by eleven. Johnny had his crew of track layers already at work. The Boston stood on her own ground—200 feet of iron had been spiked to the waiting ties; the engine stood panting at the mouth of Red Rock Cañon.

Johnny ran the outfit like an army. Timing—that was what he constantly preached to Sam. Bring your rails out fast. Don't let the maul men coast and keep the next rail waiting. Climb all over an iron peddler if he's ten seconds late distributing bolts and spikes. That was the way they did it on the Central, and it was how they laid down ten miles of track in a single day.

The Virginia City stationmaster drifted over during the noon lay-off. He had a letter in his hand that he handed to Johnny.

"A.J. sent it up this morning," he explained. "Mail come in two hours late. Seems there was a little trouble down the line."

Sam read the letter with Johnny.

Mr. Ryan, Rigdon had written in a hand all up-and-down strokes and feathery crosses, *as it is not the intention of the Nevada Union Railroad to work hardship on any competitor, we are prepared to carry your rails on delivery at Carson City. Cordially, A.J. Rigdon.*

Johnny slapped his thigh. "Damned if he ain't a barracks hero, Sam! He talks a great fight . . . but shake a little gunpowder on him and he crawfishes! Andy Rigdon ain't sure but what the Central would back our play. So we get our iron."

Sam was the pessimistic one. "I peg him for more guts than that, Johnny," he said. "Put him in the ring with a checkbook and a couple of ideas, and he'll keep anybody stepping. He's stacking the deck for the next deal."

Laurie Briggs stopped by in the middle of the

afternoon. "I'm going up to see Colonel Tom Morgan about the loan," she told Sam. "I thought you might like to come along and meet him. You two will find plenty to talk about. Colonel Tom used to run a stage line out of San Anton'."

Morgan's office was in his home, a two-story mansion of native sandstone. The house stood against the barren foothills, without a blade of grass or a tree to break the sharpness of its outlines.

As they pulled up in the buggy, Sam saw a horse tied to an iron hitching post. He studied it a moment.

"That's Rigdon's three-stockinged bay," he said. "I thought you said Morgan was one you could trust."

"I don't understand it!" Laurie exclaimed. "Rigdon and Colonel Tom have never been friendly. . . ."

"Maybe Rigdon is a jump ahead of us. Maybe he's here to buy Morgan off."

Laurie scoffed at this.

A Chinese let them in. He led them to a town hall of a parlor, furnished with all the overdone elegance of a Pullman car.

"Colonel Tom busy, please." He smiled. "You waitee here, please." Windows were open; flies floated in and out on the warm air. None of them spoke.

Somewhere a door opened and they could hear

a man's voice, gruff and nasal. Someone else spoke angrily and slammed a door, and this speaker was Rigdon. When he came into the parlor, he held his stride for one second while he stared at them. Then, without a word, he marched out of the house.

Colonel Tom Morgan met them at the door to his office. To be so important, he was a small man indeed. He was frail and bald, but these failings were offset by challenging eyes with the thrust of a fist. Colonel Tom was old and tough and weathered; he had the appearance of a man who has worked hard all his life, and for all these things Sam liked him.

They shook hands. Morgan, asking leave of Laurie, set out whiskey and cigars. They talked. It was good talk, leaving the taste of Texas on their tongues. Again, in that small untidy office, Concords rattled and dust boiled and Comanches made their blindingly swift attacks! Had they been women, Sam and the colonel would have been calling each other "dear" in the first five minutes.

In the pause that had to come, Laurie stated her business. "Just a few thousand will get me by," she declared. "I should think five thousand, and I'll pay you back five hundred a month after I get in operation."

The colonel passed a cigar under his nose, moistened it all over with his tongue, and leisurely set fire to it before replying. "Somebody," he said then, "has got word out that I've got all the money in this town. Second time today I've been tackled for funds."

"Was the other party Rigdon?" Sam asked.

Morgan's bald, brown head nodded several times.

"Rigdon," he stated, "wanted seventy-five thousand dollars . . . cash."

Laurie caught her breath. "But, good heavens . . . he's already wealthy!"

"That depends," said Colonel Tom, "on what you call wealthy. If you call owning a couple of million dollars on paper wealthy, then he's your boy. I'd rather have a few hundred thousand stuck in the sock myself. Mister Rigdon," he added, "stands to take one hell of a beating on the market one of these days . . . and he knows it."

He was in a mood to talk. Sensing it, they were silent. Colonel Tom played with a small pearl-handled belly gun that lay on his desk. It was empty; he kept squinting across the sights and snapping imaginary shots at a lynx crouching above the hearth.

"Someday," he said, "paper fortunes will be the ruination of a lot of men. Pyramiding! It's worse'n drink. Take Rigdon. He owned one mill clear, and he borrowed against it to buy another. He kept that up until he could get credit to build a railroad. By that time he owned everything in sight . . . on paper. He's safe enough now, because, if any of his creditors demand payment on one mill, he can sell another to pay off. But what happens if they all demand payment at once?"

"They wouldn't," said Sam. "Things ain't done that way."

Colonel Tom's eye was hard and knowing. "They are in a panic. I had a letter from my banker in San Francisco last month. Things haven't been right on Wall Street since the Jay Cooke thing. It's earthquake weather, Haddon."

Sam stirred. "For seventy-five thousand," he grunted, "Rigdon can do a lot of fighting."

Morgan said: "Well, he didn't get it. I'll give you a check for the five thousand right now. Call loan all right?"

"Call loan's fine," said Laurie.

Colonel Tom Morgan gave her the check. He told Sam: "Come back soon. We'll fight a couple of wars up here. By hell, there was nothing like the old stage days."

With money to spend, Laurie Briggs refurbished the mill. Everything was accomplished that could speed up the work, once the ore began to roar down the hoppers. She put a large sign on the bulletin board before Miner's Hall, advertising the new milling rate of $14 a ton. The Nevada Shortline added a notation that freight charges would amount to $2.

Laurie had an office fixed up for herself and the partners in the stamp mill. She showed them their desks one day, each with its silver nameplate.

Johnny Ryan put an end to her gaiety. "The desk's fine," he said dryly, "but the name on it is wrong. It should read . . . Samuel J. Haddon, President. And there'll be somebody else at the vice-president's desk."

"I don't understand," Laurie said, frowning.

"Point is," said Johnny, "I'm a builder, not an operator. Anybody can run a railroad, but not every man can build one. I'll be moving along in a few months."

"That's not fair, Johnny," said Laurie. "The fight won't be over when the road is finished. You know that."

Johnny shrugged. "Oh, I ain't leaving tomorrow. But I thought I'd let you know."

Sam caught him outside. "Now, then," he said, "let's have the straight of it."

Johnny kept walking with his head down. The hardness he had shown in the office was gone from him. He looked sad; he looked discouraged.

"What do you think of Laurie?" he asked at last.

Sam, with the heart of an adventurer himself, began to understand. "The question is," he countered, "what do *you* think of her?"

"A whole lot," said Johnny frankly. "She's the kind you dream about when you're out in the desert five hundred miles from nowhere, and you haven't seen a white woman in six months. She's beautiful, and she's gentle . . . dammit, Sam," he blurted, "I keep thinking about marrying . . . !"

"There's worse things to think about."

"Not for me. I'm already married."

Sam's heart compressed, and then jumped. "Married?"

"To a lady I can't divorce . . . the high iron. It would be bigamy if I married Laurie. I'd be trying to be faithful to her and to railroading, and you know as well as I do that it can't be done. I'd be forever hankering after roads to build, and, where those roads take you, you can't be dragging a wife and family."

They walked down the raised roadbed, the dust rising under their heels, the August sun burning their necks. Johnny said: "You're a smart man, Sam. What am I going to do?"

Sam sighed. "I'm too smart a man," he replied, "to give advice to the lovelorn. All I can give you is sympathy."

VII

A month after the meeting with Colonel Tom Morgan, the Nevada Shortline had its coming-out party. There was beer for everybody. The mayor was invited to drive the silver spike. Laurie Briggs broke champagne over the cowcatcher of the Boston.

In the excitement, few miners discovered the new notice alongside that of the Shortline, on the bulletin board. Under the letterhead of the United Mill and Mining Company, it was announced:

Effective this day, ore will be hauled to United Mills for *one dollar per ton,* and will be refined thereat for thirteen dollars.

News got around by the next day. Rigdon had shown his hand. Rigdon was going to attempt to wreck the new outfit by underbidding. The partners spent one haggard week waiting for Virginia City to desert the colors, but by the end of that week it was plain that a saving of two dollars a ton was not enough to proselyte her.

"What A.J. clear forgot," Johnny chuckled, "is that Virginia City has got fifty thousand dollars sunk in us. She's got to cover her bets."

"We haven't got much over fifty stockholders," Sam reminded him. "We can't stay in business for that many. But that's all the business we'll have if he goes much lower."

In Round Valley, the stamp mill pounded and bellowed. Every day the Boston hauled in a full line of cars, and every day a few ingots of silver went out. Sam's Six Bit Mine got into production. He began to bank some money, profits from both his mining and railroad investments. He paid the hotel its bill and began to look around for an architect to whip up some plans for a little place on the hill, of about two stories.

Down on the Carson, only a few of A.J. Rigdon's mills continued to turn rock into powder, and powder into soup, and soup into silver, and, for every ton that went through, United lost money. United was fighting overhead, a fifteen-mile grade, and a paucity of business.

Rigdon was desperate. The fact came out when it became known that he was selling most of his coyote-hole mines for operating money. Secretly Sam and Johnny began to put all their cash into mines. They took Colonel Tom's advice and dealt strictly in cash.

An invitation came from Rigdon one day to visit him at his Carson City office for a talk of mutual benefit to all concerned. Partly out of curiosity, the Shortline partners went down.

Rigdon did not extend himself to be pleasant. Engler was with him, sitting back in the gloom of the big office, Rigdon's ever-present shadow. They were both smoking cigars, both sour-faced.

Rigdon shuffled papers on his desk. Finally he drew from the top drawer three fat envelopes that he thumped down before him. "I'm getting tired of this sand-lot war," he announced. "Neither of us is making money. But United can hold out for a long time, and you can't . . ."

"Sure about that?" interrupted Johnny.

Rigdon did not answer. He paused a moment after the interruption, frowning at the envelopes. He said: "There's fifty thousand dollars' worth of

United stock in each of those envelopes . . . fifty thousand for each of you, the same for the Briggs girl. You'll turn over the railroad and mill for it. All you men have wanted from the start was to hold me up for some easy money. It's worth it to me now to get rid of you."

"You wouldn't want to make that cash, would you?" Sam inquired.

Rigdon cleared his throat. "In the long run," he said, "you'll be getting substantially more by taking stock."

"If it came to a choice," said Johnny, "I'd rather have Confederate money. There's a rumor that United stock isn't worth a match to burn it."

"You've been listening to too many of my competitors," said Rigdon dryly. "When the show-down comes, you'll find I'm solvent enough to whip a dozen bonanza railroads."

Sam was grinning as he rose. "We'll think it over."

"You'll think it over before you leave this office," Rigdon snapped. "Because whether I own the Nevada Shortline or not, I'm going to close it up."

"Then," Johnny said, "we'll just have to forget it's closed up, and keep right on operating it."

They walked out in a stunned, frozen silence.

They stepped down from the afternoon mail train shortly after 3:00. Already the sun had dropped behind the looming red hill that cut the city's day almost in half. The heat was going out of the pebbly earth. Sam went up to the hotel and changed his sweat-soaked shirt for a fresh one; afterward they boarded the ore train for the trip to the mill.

There were checks and papers to sign, which kept them busy until nearly dark. It was as they were preparing to leave the office that the explosion rocked the stamp mill.

Sam found himself hanging to the desk, waiting for the ceiling to fall in. The explosion had come like the boost of a monstrous hand beneath the building. Later the noise came, a muted clap of thunder.

Sam ran outside. From the hillside he could see the great hole in the side of the main building housing the stamps. The hoppers that swallowed the ore and fed it under the tireless hammers had been blown into a tangle of sheet-net metal and broken wood. The stamps were silent for the first time in days.

Workmen were assembling, shouting and getting in each other's way. Sam reached the scene as they began carrying out the injured. Six men had received broken bones; one workman had been killed.

The foreman came up to Sam, scared green. "Damned if I know what happened!" he declared. "I've had sixteen years in stamp mills, but I've never known one to blow up."

Sam was looking over the wreckage through the hanging fog of dust. "Was that this afternoon's ore you were milling?" he asked.

"Just went down the hoppers."

"Somebody," Sam said, "tucked a stick of Hercules into one of the loads, with a percussion cap and no fuse. The stamps might have exploded it, or just the rocks. Somebody around here is too free with his dynamite." He looked at the tangle of wreckage. "How long will it take to get back into production?"

"If the whole outfit ain't out of plumb," the other said, "she can be operating again in a week."

It was late when Sam and Johnny returned to Virginia City. Walking up E Street, they sensed a quiet foreign to the town. They were used to twenty-four hours a day of headlong activity, but Virginia City, all in a moment, had slowed to a walk. Men were gathered in the streets and on the stair-step boardwalks, unnaturally subdued. The saloons were quiet as churches. It reminded Sam of a night in St. Louis, when word had come that Fort Sumter had been fired upon.

He asked a man before Miner's Hall: "What's up, brother? Town run out of liquor?"

"What's *up?*" the miner grunted. "Ain't you seen the *Enterprise*? Wall Street's gone to hell! It came over the telegraph this afternoon . . . the exchange ain't going to open tomorrow. Old Raab," he added, "must 'a' been in pretty deep. He shot himself."

Sam and Johnny did not speak all the way back to the hotel. At the entrance, Sam hesitated.

"This is it, Johnny," he said. "We're settin' on top of the pile. Rigdon's whipped. I'm going up and have a drink with Colonel Tom over it."

It was a hard walk, all uphill, into the outskirts of town, where abandoned mine stopes made puddles of shadow on the hillsides and the few houses stood, large and gaunt, in their barren surroundings. Morgan's office and parlor were lighted, but no one answered Sam's knock. He waited, at intervals sending the echoes of his fist through the house. He heard movement in the back; at last he decided that Ah Ling, Morgan's Chinese servant, was out and that Colonel Tom was puttering around in the kitchen.

The back door was unlocked. Somewhere in the brush, Sam imagined, he heard movement. He went in, calling: "Hey! Colonel Tom!"

He passed through a succession of small rooms to the hall, following it to the office. The door stood open. Sam went in—then he stood perfectly still, looking down at the body of Colonel Tom.

Morgan had been shot through the head. His office had been rifled; papers were slung about in wild confusion, a cabinet overturned. Sam stood above him for nearly a minute. Then somewhere beyond the wall, he again fancied that he heard sounds up on the hillside. He went out, his gun in his hand. He stood beside the back door for a moment before he started into the brush.

He had not moved far when a gun weaved a red thread into the black fabric of the night. Sam dived for the ground. He lay there until he heard them moving again, up in the mine stopes, deep in the shadows. He rose to his knees. He picked out a light patch that moved; he fired and went down again. Two more shots answered him, snapping twigs yards away, and after this men ran blunderingly across the rough ground to the mouth of a barranca. Again he fired, but when his eyes cleared from the powder flare, both men were gone. A moment later he heard horses. He ran stumblingly up the slope until he stood in the barranca, but he was alone now with the night and the shadows. . . .

VIII

The city marshal and a dozen policemen came up and poked around and swore, but got no place. Sam sat disconsolately in the parlor. There weren't few enough of the old-timers left, the men who had wiped the frontier's nose and taught it some manners when it was an ornery kid; they had to murder the best of the ones who were left.

And Sam Haddon knew who had done it, even if the city marshal said there wasn't a footprint or any other lead that anything but a bloodhound could follow. Morgan was the man with the brains and the money, and A.J. Rigdon was the one who needed both, and Rigdon had come here in terror and in desperation—and killed Tom Morgan to save himself.

The next morning Virginia City shambled around like a barfly, trying to comprehend too many things at once. The stock market crash had automatically padlocked a few doors, and it would close some more when the banks began calling in unsecured paper. Only the saloons prospered. Here men mulled over the murder of Colonel Tom and the suicide of Raab. They mixed with their drinks the rumor that United Mill and Mining Corporation was tottering, and found the taste good. Pyramiding—this was the key that unlocked every puzzle that morning of September 20, 1873. Raab had been pyramiding without Rigdon's knowledge; Rigdon had been pyramiding his profits, but the pyramid had been built upside down, so that now it was about to topple.

Sam got his proofs about Rigdon's guilt later that day. It was Hap Engler who came to the door of the hotel room with his pearl-gray Stetson pulled down on his brow. He stood there, looking the room over for a moment after Sam opened the door. Dissipation had its brown thumbprints under his eyes, and there were deep channels in his face put there by a resentful stomach.

Engler said gruffly: "The Briggs girl here?"

"What do you want?" Sam asked.

"Did she know Morgan sold her note last week?" Engler inquired.

It began to come to Sam now, like ice water creeping down his back. "Morgan wouldn't have sold her out," he declared, and then he waited.

"You never know," Engler remarked. "I reckon he was unloading. He sold a five-thousand-dollar note of hers to A.J. for four thousand cash. It was too good to pass up. It's a six-week note, and it's due in five days."

Sam was after him with a roar, and Engler, startled, slammed the door in his face. He was halfway down the hall when Sam got it open.

Laurie Briggs took the news with composure. "If it hadn't been for the dynamiting," she said, "it wouldn't have mattered. I could still have paid. But now I'll have to use everything I've got left to repair the mill. And there won't be anything coming in while it's out of commission, either." She shook her head. "Colonel Tom wouldn't have sold me out, Sam. I *know* he wouldn't! If they've got his endorsement on my note, it must be a forgery."

"Then how do you suppose they got the note?" Sam asked pointedly. Something in his tone brought her eyes around to his. Suddenly the realization came to her, the knowledge of why Colonel Tom had died, and Laurie's eyes filled with tears. Sam sat at a table, pouring new loads into his old Dragoon, carefully dropping each ball into the chamber and ramming it home. He loaded an extra cylinder and rolled it with his fingers.

Laurie looked up. "Sam . . ."

Sam grunted and put the gun away. "Don't worry," he told her. "I won't hang for such as them. But I'll never be much farther behind Rigdon than his shadow, until I see him hang."

"I suppose," Laurie ventured, "I'll have to borrow the money from you boys to pay him. It won't be for long. But no one else will loan a dime until this blows over."

Sam's voice was wry. "Johnny and I," he said, "haven't got enough cash to finance a beer bust, honey. We put everything into mines as fast as it came in, on Morgan's advice."

Sam consorted with whiskey that night and, as usual, found no wisdom in it. It merely took the teeth out of his misery. He thought about the murder soberly the next day and saw what a beautiful case they would have against Rigdon—if they only could prove that he was the murderer. The motive was solid as oak.

And Rigdon, bold as damn, stomped about town, visiting banks and stock companies. Word got around that he had stalled off his San Francisco bank until he could attach the Shortline and mill.

It was four days after the murder when Sam remembered Ah Ling, Morgan's Chinese servant.

It was funny about the Chinaman, thought Sam. Nobody suspected him of murdering the old man, but on the other hand nobody had seen him since. It was assumed that somebody had thrown a scare into him and put him on a horse, thus getting him out of the way.

But Sam was remembering the affection between Colonel Tom and Ah Ling. They were both old in years and in the ways of the West. Ah Ling had panned gold in 1849. Ah Ling had loved Colonel Tom, and Ah Ling would have stuck by him in a scrap.

He went up to the deserted mansion and looked it over again. He poked into the cellar. He beat the brush about the house. He found where he had lain on the ground that night to escape the murderers' fire.

When he sighted in the direction he had fired, he discovered the black mouth of a glory hole on the hill. Sam climbed the hill, stopping once to mop his red face. He reached the mine dump and looked about. Not far from the main drift he found dried brown stains on a rock. He located more near the tunnel. He went inside. He discovered a rusty lamp with a little coal oil in it.

A little way down the tunnel he noticed increasingly large bloodstains. There was no doubt as to their being blood now, for the cool air had not dehydrated them completely. And then he caught a sickening smell. He retched. For a minute he had to go back to the sunlight and fresh air and then, fortified, he returned.

Ah Ling had crawled to the extreme end of a side drift where, crouched against the wall, he had gone to join his ancestors. He had been shot in the chest.

Sam subdued his queasy stomach long enough to discover the black quirt, laced with gold wire, clutched tightly in the right hand of Ah Ling. The hand gave it up readily enough, the bony yellow hand that once had doubtless defied all efforts of a panicky killer to wrest it free.

Sam went back to the open air, the sweet air, the warm air of the desert. He inspected the quirt, trying to remember where he had seen one like it. The tassel was of white rawhide, the rest shiny black, with thin gold wire woven through it. It had a gold head, like that of a cane. On the head was the monogram: A.J.R.

He hung the quirt under his coat, alongside his gun; he did not want to walk back to town carrying this thing. He tried in his mind to reconstruct the double murder. Perhaps Ah Ling had broken in when he heard the shot. Perhaps, wounded, he had run up the slope to the mine. Rigdon and Engler might have followed him to where the Chinese had come out of the shadows to grapple with Rigdon and seize the quirt. Sam's guess was that he himself had come along during this fracas and broken it up. Those were the sounds he had heard on the hill. But Ah Ling had escaped into the tunnel and his murderers had fled.

There were still two days left before Rigdon came to take over the mill. Sam did not propose to tip his hand by overeagerness. Johnny moped, beating his head against the problem. Johnny pointedly avoided Laurie these days. He had worries; any man with two sweethearts had worries, but this was only half of his trouble.

"I don't understand Johnny," Laurie told Sam one day. "He acts as though he were angry with me. And yet I've done nothing . . ."

"What you've done," Sam said gently, "is just to be Laurie. You ain't exactly homely, Laurie Briggs, and there's some other things about you that a young buck like Johnny would be noticing."

Laurie's face began to color. She said: "I . . . it didn't even occur to me . . ."

"The thing is," said Sam, "if you're interested in Johnny, you've got a rival. The Boston is Johnny Ryan's sweetheart. And for the life of me, I don't know whether he'd be truer to a woman or a railroad engine."

Laurie ran her fingertips into her hair, trying to think, and then without a word she hurried out of the office.

It was on this day that the note came from A.J. Rigdon: *Please be prepared to turn over the books on the refinery tomorrow. Foreclosure papers have been filed with the county clerk.*

IX

The morning was cool, with a light haze to turn the edge of the sun. In the office of Briggs Refining, the only sounds were the *clatter* of workmen repairing damaged stamps. Sunlight filled the room, but gloom cast shadows of its own.

Horses *clopped* up the railroad right of way. Suddenly Laurie stood up at her desk, her fists clenched. "I won't take it like this!" she cried. "They killed Colonel Tom, and now they're going to use his death to steal the mill!"

Johnny moved uncomfortably on his chair, but he did not raise his eyes. Sam glanced at the ceiling. "Maybe something will turn up," he suggested.

Footfalls sounded in the silent stamp mill. Boots ascended the long run of wooden steps to the office in the top of the building. Someone brought his fist smartly against the door. Men could be heard breathing on the landing.

Sam admitted Engler and Rigdon. They both smelled of liquor; they had the ruddy, talcumed look of men who have killed a nervous hour in the barber's chair. Sam indicated chairs.

Rigdon stood. "If the books are ready . . . ," he stated.

"On the desk."

Rigdon sat down and humped over the books.

He scanned them expertly, bringing most of his attention to the final entries, apparently afraid someone might have jettisoned all the capital from the sinking ship. He banged the tan cowhide ledger closed.

"Everything seems to be in order," he grunted. He frowned at the desk; industry was creeping back into his bones; the marble front was about to go up again. "I've given some thought to your position, Miss Briggs," he remarked. "It would be a shame to leave you with nothing whatever to show for your efforts here. . . ."

Laurie stood looking out the window, her arms crossed, silent.

"Accordingly, I've arranged to put fifty shares of stock in trust for you, the stock to remain in our possession, but the dividends to go to you. It seems only fair."

Drums were rolling in Sam Haddon's brain. Trumpets were sounding and the warhorses were beginning to snort. "How big a cut," he inquired, "will you give her for this?"

He laid the quirt on the desk.

Andrew Rigdon's cheeks grayed. The years mounted in his face until Sam began to have gooseflesh, just watching the transformation. His features were loosening. His hands shook as he touched the quirt, and quickly they drew back.

Deep in his throat, Engler made an inarticulate sound. Rigdon rose and leaned on the desk by one hand. "I'd like to see you in my office some time, Haddon," he said, hardly audible. "Have you . . . discussed this generally?"

Sam shook his head. "Set a day."

"Tomorrow. In the morning."

Rigdon forgot his hat when he left.

Johnny bounded up. "What the hell! What have you been holding out on us, Sam?"

Sam tucked his thumbs under his belt, watching the visitors depart on their horses. "It was a secret between me and the quirt and Colonel Tom Morgan," he told them. "I found it in Ah Ling's hand, in an old mine stope. Rigdon's initials are on the head of it. Everybody in Virginia City has seen him with it."

"Then why," Johnny demanded, "did you let them get away?"

"They won't go far. Rigdon's too old and too well known to make a getaway. He really thinks he can buy me off. He doesn't realize that everybody isn't an industrial ghoul, like he is."

Laurie began to sniffle. "It's wonderful, Sam. But I can't believe it."

"You bet it's wonderful," Sam agreed. He put on his Stetson. "I'm going back and tell Allie about it now. You kids stir up those workmen. We've got ore to mill."

Johnny followed him to the landing. "You'd better let me go with you," he said. "You can't tell . . . they might . . ."

"Might?" And Sam chuckled. "But, Johnny, this is between me and the colonel. You go back and see what you can work out with Laurie."

He jogged across the barren diameter of the valley to the mouth of Red Rock Cañon. Out here he felt freer, uninhibited, ready for action.

He rode a couple of miles, scanning the cañon's crowding walls, studying the horse tracks beside the rails. It was some time before he reached a section where the red sandstone cliffs were sufficiently broken to afford ambuscade. Now his vigilance sharpened. He was watching everything, and thus he noticed in one stroke the jungle of rocks to his left and the way the distinct hoof prints broke abruptly into the deep cup marks of running horses. Here they had dismounted and choused the horses on upcañon, out of the way.

Sam's eye caught the blue polish of sunlight on steel. He left his horse in a sprawling dive for the ground. He heard the shot carom off a rock, and a second later a tumbling avalanche of echoes tolled down the cañon. He lay there until Engler's head appeared amid the giant rubble of broken rocks. Sam's Dragoon was already against his cheek, making it as simple as the flick of a wrist to bring the gunman under his sights. The gun rocked. Engler stood a moment with his face a scarlet ruin, then he sank back.

Sam ran forward fifty feet and sprawled. Rigdon gave away his position, at Engler's left, by firing three jittery shots that a ten-foot circle could not have corralled. Sam changed direction. He did not fire again. He kept working through the rocks. Again Rigdon's revolver roared.

Sam's mind kept tally: *Four shots. Two to go.* Rigdon stood up, searching for him, only half concealed. Sam raised his gun and, reluctantly, deliberately fired a shot a yard above the railroad man's head. Rigdon ducked.

At Rigdon's back was an angle in the cliff, fencing him in. Before him were a dozen porous red boulders through which Sam was slowly working. Sam could picture him crouching against the rock, the nice barber's talcum on his face and neck washed away by sweat. He could taste the panic of this man who liked nothing more violent than the scratch of a pen on a foreclosure notice.

He would be trying to decide whether or not he had time to reload. He would start to scratch open the ejection piece, and then close it again when he heard the stalker move forward. Now he popped up, saw Sam within twenty-five feet of him, and fired his fifth shot. This one was close. Sam was running low when it *spat* wickedly against the ground under his feet.

And now Sam was on the opposite side of the same boulder that sheltered A.J. Rigdon. He took two steps to his right and heard Rigdon also move—the other way.

Sam began to talk to himself. "Don't know

whether I ought to take time for a smoke now, or not," he muttered. "Of course, if I did, it would give that feller time to reload. Reckon I'll work around to the left. . . ."

He shuffled off that way, and again Rigdon's terrified feet moved him counter-wise. Sam muttered: "Although, if I come around from the right, I'll have my gun in better position. . . ."

He moved in that direction. He heard Rigdon start. He heard a choked gasp.

"Still," he grumbled, "the way this rock slopes, I could climb right over the top of it and take him from above. By God, I think I'll do it."

Now he ran with all his speed to the right, away from the rock.

The report of Rigdon's gun was flat. Sam pulled up short. He swore. Andrew Rigdon had cheated him. He lay crumpled at the foot of the rock. Suicide ran in the firm, it appeared. Sam Haddon had talked him to death. . . .

It was only a few minutes later when Johnny Ryan came along in the Boston. Sam had caught his horse and dragged the bodies to the road. They loaded them into the tender in silence, and in silence they chugged toward town.

"Think you could get along without me and the Boston?" Johnny asked suddenly.

"What am I going to do?" Sam frowned. "Pull the cars myself?"

Johnny was gloomy. "You can buy locos and ore cars from United's receivers for nothing by next month. I'll stick around that long. But I reckon I'll be rolling pretty soon."

Sam watched his face. "Let's have it," he said.

"Women," Johnny groaned. "The Lord made 'em just to make jackasses out of men. I thought it over till I knew I had to have Laurie. So after you left, I asked her. 'Johnny,' she says, 'it's good of you to ask me. I admire you ever so much. But, you see . . . there's a boy in San Francisco. . . .'"

Sam said: "Bah! Follow her back. When she stands you up against him, you get the girl."

Johnny shook his head. "It ain't that simple, Sam. This boy lost an arm in the war. He's got a little law business . . . just gettin' by . . . and she's going to try to talk him into managing the mill for her. You can see where that puts me. I don't know," he said thoughtfully, and he paused, ". . . maybe it's all for the best."

His hand caressed the throttle, inching it forward now and then, and every time he shot some fog into the cylinders the little locomotive spun her drivers. "Remember that night on the grade?" he said reminiscently. "The old girl sure brought us through. Yes, sir! She's quite a gal."

Yes, sir, Sam thought, *everything's going to be all right with Johnny Ryan.* It would be nothing less than bigamy if Johnny ever married. He had taken railroading to love and to cherish, and he'd never divorce her while there were railroads to build and the Boston to run on them.

But as for Sam, he had Allie to go back to, and a marble house to build, and he was glad for his part that his wife didn't run on wheels.

Cowman-on-the-Spot

I

Hardesty stood on the boardwalk before the Cheyenne House in the cool dusk of the Wyoming summer. Down from the bold granite heights of the mountains west of Caballo River settled a cold breeze flavored with pine and spruce. The town was small and quiet. Hardesty liked small, quiet towns. That was why he'd moved up from Colorado when they began passing too many rules. But there was something wrong with this town of Antelope. People acted as if he were trying to sell them something.

The men in this place wouldn't let him get close enough to say howdy. In the Lodgepole Saloon there had been twenty or thirty men from the lumber camps up in the hills. He had moseyed around, trying to put himself across and had got nothing but the cold eye. Finally he went over to the Cheyenne House. There were businessmen and cowboys there. He had been received with the enthusiasm usually accorded a mortician passing out cards. You couldn't say they were unfriendly. But you'd have been crazy if you called them friendly.

There remained the Elkhorn Bar. He tucked his hands in the tight pockets of his washed-out overall pants and crossed the street. He was not a tall man but he was about as wide as he was tall. As he walked, he looked about him. Antelope was one of those towns where you could see open country at each end of the main street. You saw meadows and hills, and beyond those hills the Wind River Mountains rose up like giants from the earth.

There was a fair crowd in the Elkhorn Bar for summer, made up of cowboys in work clothes: denim pants, woolen shirts, and the high Stetsons they affected up here. They were making a lot of noise, playing Indian dice, cards, and just drinking. Hardesty's spirit stretched itself like a cat to be petted. He was home. This was the cowboys' bar. He stood beside a yellow-haired man in a pony-skin jacket and ordered whiskey.

He got the sting of the liquor on his tongue. In a lull in the conversation between the yellow-haired man and his friends, Hardesty remarked: "Yes, sir, this is a nice little town you've got here, mister. A first-rate town."

He had the cowpuncher's attention for an instant. "We like it," the man said. He turned back to his friends.

Hardesty raised his voice a shade, gripping the glass tighter. "You don't know me, mister, so I'll introduce myself. Glen Hardesty's the way you spell it. I'm from Colorado. I bought the Jake Spinner place six months ago and I've just come up to take over."

The cowboy's glance returned, an annoyed glance with a pinch in it. "Is that right?" he said. He moved so that Hardesty's view was of his back. He and his companions had been talking before, but now they were just looking at one another.

One glanced into his glass and said: "I got one of them leaky glasses again. This thing's gone plumb empty. Baldy!"

Hardesty set his own glass down with a slam that brought heads up all over the saloon. His patience had given out like a frazzled rope. He put his voice out so they could all hear it. "If somebody in this place ain't too damned uppity to drink with a stranger, I'll buy him a drink. Not counting the character in the pony-skin vest."

Yellow-Hair straightened before he turned. Hardesty remained leaning on the bar by his elbow. He hoped the man would ask for a fight. There were some towns where the only way to show people you were worth knowing was to whip somebody. He saw in the pull of the man's lips that he was going to get it.

"You seem pretty sure a Colorado man's worth drinking with," the cowpuncher said, and his eyes made an inventory of Hardesty from Stetson to spurs that said he would give about four bits for the lot.

"I don't remember anybody ever telling me I wasn't," Glen Hardesty said. "Maybe you'd like to be the first."

The yellow-haired cowpuncher pulled up his pants with a movement reminiscent of a big dog beginning to circle a little dog. He had a long, buck-toothed face, with fair skin reddened by exposure. His brows were as yellow as his hair. It was a combination Hardesty didn't like.

"I wouldn't exactly say that," the yellow-haired man remarked. "But if I had my choice between drinking with a sheeper and a Coloradoan, the man I drank with wouldn't be wearing spurs."

Hardesty straightened quietly. He said: "Ah?" Blood was stirring in his veins. And just as his shoulder hitched back, someone stepped out of line at the bar. He caught Glen's eye and shook his head. He walked along the bar and stopped between them.

"I'm going to take you up on that drink, at that," he said, smiling. "You'll have to excuse us. We're a little bit backward up here. Did you say your name was Hardesty?"

Glen nodded and repeated what he had told the other man about having bought the Spinner Ranch. Immediately he understood that he had been sponsored, for other men now left the tables to take advantage of the free liquor. The yellow-haired cowpuncher stood looking sullen and let down, and then returned to his glass. The big, heavy-browed man put a hand on the shoulder of each.

"Hardesty, this is Laramie Slade. He's been picking fights for years and never won one yet.

I've got a notion he wouldn't have won this one, either."

They shook hands with the lack of enthusiasm of men forced into it.

Hardesty paid for the round of drinks and afterward five of them took a table. Tully was the big man's name; he owned the Seven-O-Seven Ranch. Besides Tully and Laramie Slade, there were Tully's foreman, Stu Winter, and two other small ranchers. Tully was a large, confident rancher with a faculty of making you feel that what you were saying was important. He would listen keenly, his dark eyes interested under their thick brows, his whiskey glass like a thimble in that big, hair-padded paw of his.

Someone said something that reminded Hardesty of a joke. He told it, and all of them laughed and slapped their legs. Glen began to feel better. He was sitting at a table with men of his own kind. He began to be convinced that he had just had one of those dreams in which you went around trying to talk to people who couldn't see you. But still there was the recollection of the Cheyenne House and the Lodgepole.

"I can say this," he said, "now that you boys have broke down. Antelope's just about the toughest town to get acquainted in that I've come across. Somebody must have been through here selling wooden nutmegs."

Joe Tully bit the end off his cigar, and the others

looked embarrassed and waited for him to make the answer. "We don't aim to be cagey," Tully said. "But we like to look over the hand a man offers, just to be sure it ain't got a belly gun in it."

Hardesty said: "Oh, oh! Sheepers? Or grangers?"

"Loggers," Tully told him.

It came to Hardesty then. In the Lodgepole Saloon there had been dozens of loggers but not one cowman. He had been a long time catching on. Regret flashed through his mind that, of all the Wyoming cattle country, he had selected a range where trouble was ready to bust.

"You might as well have it," Tully was saying. "You're in it, now, yourself. They're logging just above your range. They've stripped the foothills. The law limits the number of trees they can cut, but they go through like a thirty-horse combine across a wheat field. Then we get a heavy rain. The water cuts gullies where there were creeks, and cañons where they were gullies. They sent out their tie hacks a year ahead to take up claims under the Stone and Timber Act . . . a hundred and sixty acres apiece. Then they bought it back for two-fifty an acre. And they're spreading onto everything within twenty miles of the river that isn't already taken up."

Laramie Slade looked up, a malicious light in his eyes. "I got squared up for that beef of mine they killed last week. By God, I shot one of their mules that was dragging logs to the river. And I told the 'skinner . . . 'Laramie Slade's the name, and Barney Carriger knows where to find me. But I don't think he'll have the guts to look.'"

Joe Tully didn't appear pleased. "That's not the way, Laramie. First you get an injunction. *Then* you shoot the mule."

They laughed but it was sour laughter. It answered a question for Glen: *Why don't you go to court?* Evidently they already had.

It was amazing the way the tongues of the naturally taciturn cowmen loosened when they got on the subject of logging. They couldn't recite the stories fast enough. The tie drives came without warning all summer, generally catching a few dozen cows in the river when the logs came down the rapids. Loggers' saws and axes would creep over a boundary into your land unless you stood there with a gun, and who could do that on 40,000 or 50,000 acres of mountain rangeland? Glen assembled the facts that Carriger and Converse operated the logging firm, that they were making ties for the railroad, floating them to Antelope River, where they put them through the treating plant outside town before freighting them east to where the Chicago and Northwestern was building toward Lander.

Eventually they ran down. Hardesty came under their collective glance. They were waiting for his response. Again he thought: *Of all the spots in Wyoming . . . !* "Well," he said, "that sounds like a hell of a situation. What's their side of the story?"

"*Their* side?" Laramie repeated, not understanding. He and the others had been making the point that they hadn't a side. Laramie's eyes narrowed.

"They must claim to have a side, anyway. They don't *admit* they're breaking the timber laws, do they?"

Tully grunted. "They do their talking in Cheyenne. They read out of law books, talk in circles, and get the right people drunk. All the satisfaction we've ever got was an injunction to prevent them from logging on proved-up land. They didn't even fight it. They just said that was perfectly agreeable to them because they wouldn't think of doing such a thing."

Again they were looking at Hardesty, waiting for him to declare himself. And again a strain of stubbornness in his nature kept his mouth closed. He didn't like to jump into a thing; especially he didn't like to be pushed. He wanted to be sure all the discard had been shuffled in before he bought chips. Somehow he didn't feel sure of Yellow-Hair.

Laramie's eyes, the color of faded denim, considered Glen thoughtfully. "We've got a league," he said. "Joe could sign you up."

For an instant, Joe Tully's eyes and Hardesty's met. Tully had a quick perception where men were concerned. He spoke quickly but casually. "Let's let him get his breath before we make him sign the pledge," he suggested. "Plenty of time after he gets settled." Hardesty felt he had a friend in Joe Tully.

Laramie's eyes were still on the target. "He's going to run cattle, ain't he? How about it, Hardesty?"

Hardesty looked up. "I kind of think Joe's right. I'm not much of a joiner. I had to move out of Colorado when it got too civilized. We had school taxes and head taxes on our cattle, and God knows what else. I reckon I'll play it alone until I know what I'm doing."

Laramie glanced at Tully with deep contempt. He said: "What I said about Coloradoans. . . ."

II

Hardesty stood up. Behind him he heard the springs of the slatted doors *creak* and a glow of late afternoon sunlight suffused the room. Then the soft whipping sound of their closing told him someone had entered. He kept his eyes on Laramie but Slade wasn't thinking about him now. He was staring at the newcomer.

A large man stood just inside the door. He was no cattleman. He wore a loose-fitting brown coat, pants tucked into lace boots, and a narrow-brimmed brown hat. His hands were in his coat pockets, in a gesture Hardesty had never observed in a cowman.

Joe Tully said: "Didn't you take a wrong turn somewhere, Carriger?"

Baldy, the bartender, set down a beer schooner he had been drying. His red-mustached Irish face was anxious. "We don't serve no loggers in here, Mister Carriger," he said.

"I don't want service," Carriger said. His eyes had found Laramie. He walked toward the table, his calked heels silent on the strewn sawdust. The men sat motionlessly. In the rear of the saloon some men were still talking; a keno goose made its soft chattering sound. Laramie came to his feet.

Glen experienced an admiration for the logging boss. He was walking into no man's land with the coolness with which he might have entered a restaurant. He was a man of forty-five, well-made but with a humorless, rutted face. Brown smudges were under his eyes and the skin about his mouth had the hard gathers of careless living.

He stopped before Laramie with his hands still in his pockets. "I thought I'd give you an opportunity to buy a mule I'm selling," he said. "It's a stout animal, worth every dollar of the seventy-five I'm asking. Not a thing wrong with it except that it's dead. I think you'll find it cheap, however. Like to buy it, Slade?"

Slade's fists were doubled. "Get out of here," he said.

"I intend to," Carriger replied. "After I get the seventy-five dollars or your note for it."

Tully cut in: "It was an even trade, Carriger. A mule for a steer. Now, get out."

"I suppose you weren't losing any stock before we started logging," Carriger said. "But now that we're around, it's convenient to blame all your grief on us. Slade," he said, "you'll find seventy-five the best deal you've ever made. Better grab it before the price goes up."

Laramie said in a strangled voice: "So help me, if you aren't out of here in thirty seconds . . ."

Carriger smiled. "You make a lot of noise, Slade, but so does a jackass on a windy ridge."

Laramie stepped in and smashed at the side of the lumberman's head. Carriger caught his wrist and held it, while he struck Slade on the mouth with a short, hard smack. Slade fell back. Carriger followed him. He let go a belly punch that doubled up the yellow-haired cowpuncher on the sawdust. A scraped chair caused him to turn quickly. A man was lunging for him in a knee tackle. Carriger caught him on the side of the head with his open palm, but at the same time two more men rushed him from the back.

Tully's voice mounted over the uproar. "Let's get him, boys!"

Hardesty watched them pile over Carriger, slugging, clawing, bearing him to the floor. Carriger went down still swinging, bellowing like an ox. Suddenly Glen was angry. Slade couldn't handle him, so the whole gang piled him. It wasn't the kind of fighting Hardesty understood. It wasn't the kind he was going to watch. He drew his Colt and fired a shot into the ceiling. The reaction was direct, as automatic as the drop of the hammer when he squeezed the trigger.

The men rolled away, hugged the floor, went scrambling under tables. Carriger sat alone in the sawdust with blood on his mouth. His hat was gone and the dark, stiff hair was roughed.

Glen said to him: "Move out, mister. The rest of you stay where you are." Carriger recovered his hat, gave Hardesty a quick, puzzled glance, and moved toward the door. Hardesty holstered his gun. "We don't seem to see eye to eye on anything, boys. Laramie shouldn't have started the fight if he wasn't ready to finish it. You'd think it was just hell if Joe Tully went into the Lodgepole after somebody and they mobbed him. But it's fair enough if you do the mobbing."

He walked to the table and finished the drink he had left. Tully, tight-mouthed and flushed, watched him. "I thought you didn't want to take sides in this, Hardesty," he said.

Hardesty shook his head. "I'm buying nobody's second-hand feud. Because I sided Carriger just now doesn't mean I'm bucking you. But if anybody tries to crowd me, I may have to."

It was nearly dark when he went out. He was not

surprised to find Carriger waiting for him at the hitch rack. Carriger was dabbing a wadded handkerchief against his lip. He put out his hand. "That was pretty, cowboy."

Glen Hardesty shook hands with him unenthusiastically. "Tully gave me the impression you were smart," he said. "I didn't get that idea in there."

"You didn't?" Carriger smiled. And something about it told Glen that even a licking could be put to advantage by a really smart man. "I'm going to make a guess," he said. "You're the owner of those cattle in the meadow south of town. You're moving onto Jake Spinner's old ranch."

Hardesty wasn't impressed by the deductions, and merely nodded. "Where can you get a meal around here?"

"You can get the toughest steaks in Wyoming Territory at Frank's place. But you'll get the best food in Antelope over at my partner's . . . E.C. Converse. If you meant what you told Tully about not taking sides, you shouldn't have any objection to hearing our side of it over a dinner table."

Hardesty knew he would be observed riding away with Carriger and that it would probably cook him for good with Tully's crowd. But the way it looked now, the honeymoon was definitely over anyway. Also, he was curious to hear what Carriger had to say, since it affected him directly.

He said: "All right. But if you bring out a petition, I'll sure as hell get sick."

The Converse home was a large white house at the north end of town. It stood in a young grove of alders and poplars, although there was little shrubbery and no lawn. A picket fence stood between it and the surrounding undeveloped land. Lamps glowed softly against the windows.

A stableman took their horses. "Don't let E.C.'s starched collar and Chinese houseboy fool you," Carriger told Hardesty. "He's just people, same as you and me."

It was a subtle form of flattery. The diamond in his necktie would have bought a third of Glen's herd. A Chinese opened the door for them. He announced them at the parlor door and vanished.

A fat old man sat in a straight chair by a table. A chess game was set up on another chair facing him. A whiskey decanter and a half-filled glass gleamed under the painted shade of the lamp. He glanced up over the tops of his spectacles, removed them, and stood up with a puzzled smile.

Carriger tried, in a few easy phrases, to give his partner the whole story. The story was that here was a man who could be valuable to them, a wedge in the enemy's wall.

"I had a run-in with some of Tully's boys, E.C.," he said. "Hardesty was good enough to see that it was a fair fight or no fight. One of their own men, at that. Do you think that rates him a square meal?"

Converse continued to shake Glen's hand

cordially, peering with dim blue eyes into Hardesty's face. "I should think so," he declared. He was an ineffectual-looking old man with long yellow front teeth and a beef-steak complexion. "What's your pleasure, Mister Hardesty? Anything you can name. Including the best Irish whiskey you ever drank."

As they drank, Converse wanted to know his background and his plans. He kept asking questions that kept Glen busy talking about himself. Glen was aware of the concentration in Carriger's eyes.

"How long have you been logging up here?" he finally asked Converse.

"Two years now. It's not strictly logging," Converse explained. "We're cutting ties for the C. and N.W. Barney really does all the work. It's not oftener than once a month I can get him down from the camp. I just sit around signing checks."

Glen heard a woman's step in the hall. A dark-haired girl of about twenty came into the room. She looked surprised when she saw Glen.

"Jean, this is Mister Hardesty," Converse said. "He's going to be a neighbor of ours. My daughter, Mister Hardesty."

She smiled, acknowledging the introduction, but she didn't offer her hand as most of the women Glen had known did. Glen had been taken by surprise, too; he felt his face growing warm. She had a nice little figure and a creamy, dark complexion. The blue crystal earrings she wore seemed to pick up the lights in her eyes.

"If anybody's hungry," she said, "I think we can find something to eat in the dining room."

Carriger flapped some papers against his leg. "Might as well get your father's John Henry on these, before I forget," he said. "You and Mister Hardesty go ahead."

This time Jean surprised Hardesty by taking his arm as they went toward the dining room. He felt completely left-handed about it. He was afraid of knocking over every piece of furniture he passed; he was conscious of not having shaved that morning and of smelling of horse sweat.

He sat down in a species of terror as he thought of trying to make conversation with her. And again she surprised him.

"Those are good-looking cattle of yours, Mister Hardesty. I was riding down the river today and I came across them. Aren't they blooded?"

"I've got some good bulls," he told her. "I'll bring them up as fast as I can."

She asked more questions, and suddenly he discovered that she had a nice sense of humor and that she knew enough about ranching to talk intelligently about it. He began to be less afraid of her.

"Is the tie business going to be a permanent proposition?" he asked her.

She didn't reply at once, and then it was a

cautious answer that told him nothing. "It's hard to say."

The men came in. Converse lowered his body heavily into a chair. He gave Glen a smile. "I suppose you've heard all sorts of things about us, Hardesty."

"A few."

Converse began absently aligning the silver beside his plate. He spoke fretfully, like an unhappy child. "They claim we're stripping the land," he said. "A little of that may have occurred at first, before it was decided exactly what percentage of the timber we were allowed to cut. They say we jump lines. That we slaughter their stock, start fires, drive cattle away from the streams. There's been none of that that I know of. And if we caught any of our men doing any of those things, we'd get rid of them. They're simply excited and scared, and frightened men will imagine anything."

"Tully claims some of his cattle have been killed by your tie drives," Glen said.

"That's happened once or twice." Barney Carriger shrugged. "We've paid for them when it did. It can't be helped, though we try to give notice when a drive is coming. If there's no one at a ranch to warn, we can't ride all over the country looking for him."

Dinner was finished almost in silence. They returned to the parlor. There was a feeling of things having missed fire. Converse made a desperate, almost bewildered effort, Glen thought, to get through to him. He couldn't seem to understand that his Irish whiskey, his affability, and his pretty daughter had failed to get Glen's name on the line in an hour and a half. Finally Glen stood up to go.

Jean went to the door with him. "I hope you won't sentence anybody until you've read all the evidence," she said, smiling.

"Count on it," Glen said.

"You'll come back whenever you're in town?"

She looked as though she meant it. Good business, he thought, but he wanted to think she hadn't been entirely scared off by the work clothes and the whisker stubble. "Thanks. I'm liable to," he said.

Carriger went out with him while his horse was brought up. "I'll send a couple of boys around to help you dig in," he said. "You've only got a few weeks before the cold weather. That old shack of Spinner's isn't fit for hogs. And it's right on the ridge, where the wind will strip the mortar out of the chimney bricks. I'd say somewhere up Rawhide Meadow would be a spot. Up against the terrace, where you've got protection."

Glen turned the stirrup. "You wouldn't know a hint if one hit you in the eye." He grinned. "If I let you build my cabin, you'd be telling me how to run my cattle next. I'm still on the fence, Carriger."

Carriger knocked his pipe against his heel.

When he looked up, he was smiling. "We're two of a kind," he said. "My guess is we'll get along all right. But I'll be damned if I don't send over some hardware. You can't buy it closer than Casper. You can dump it in the river or use it. There's no obligation."

III

In a fir-ringed meadow south of town Glen Hardesty had bedded his 1,500 beef animals. At the edge of the trees was his camp, consisting of a wagon and the bedrolls of himself and his four men—an old Mexican who drove the wagon and did the cooking, and three cowpunchers.

In the morning they started up Caballo River. Before them, the range was a broken panorama of mountain slopes, dark green with timber, pale green where parks and water meadows opened broad holes in the spruce and lodgepole.

They spent the first night at Jake Spinner's camp. The ancient, crumbling cabin was inhabited now only by chipmunks and mice. It was another five miles to Rawhide Meadow, but Glen pushed on. To the ridges there was a protective and yet a forbidding look. They soared, gaunt and frowning, above the valley while behind them, even higher, rose the glaciers where weather was made, a lost land of stone, ice, and wind.

His first look at Rawhide Meadow decided him. He picked out a spot against the cliff. He was surprised to find, on riding closer, that a half dozen crates of hardware—nails, bolts, and hinges— were stacked there. A note was tacked to one of them.

> Hope these help you out.
>
> Carriger

Hardesty grinned and decided to accept the favor. During the next week he almost wished he had accepted Carriger's free-labor offer, as well. A lot of things had to be done; up here, winter meant business. He kept one of the men cutting wood, two repairing fence and working cattle, and old Vicente, the cook, helping him to build the cabin and outhouses.

One morning Joe Tully and Laramie Slade rode in with four cowpunchers. They appeared so suddenly that Hardesty was caught by surprise. He looked at the hard-mouthed line of riders and thought of his Colt, hanging in the feed barn.

Tully dismounted. "So you still think you'll stay," he said.

Hardesty said: "Nobody's given me a good reason why I shouldn't." He glanced at Slade and the rest, trying to discover by an expression or a gesture what their business was.

Joe Tully rubbed his nose. "We're not here on a

matter of friendship. You can call it a cow-country habit, if you want. If you were Barney Carriger himself, we'd be obliged to lend a hand with his cabin. You furnish the chuck and we'll help out with manpower."

Hardesty was relieved. He was not inclined to turn it down. He said: "No strings?"

"No strings," Tully said. He looked at the stack of peeled corral poles, at the new feed barn that was serving as a bunkhouse, and at the bare start of the cabin. Then he looked up at the looming face of Granite Terrace. "Sure this is where you want it?"

"Why not?"

There was the *creak* of saddle leather as the other men dismounted.

"Just asking," Tully said.

With an eight-man crew on the job, the cabin was finished in four days' time. Corrals were strung and a barn went up. When it was done, Glen produced a half gallon of whiskey. The men accepted a couple of drinks, but they saddled when Tully did.

The first snowstorm came two weeks later. It raged over the mountains for two days. But, although there were four- and five-foot drifts in many places after it cleared off, there was only a foot of snow around the cabin.

After that came the clean up. Cattle had drifted and had to be brought back to safety. It was while he was hunting a strayed steer that Hardesty found signs of logging on his range.

Between his upper boundary and the base of the mountains, a mile-wide path of timber and underbrush forested the steeply sloping section that funneled down into Rawhide Meadow. Across a strip a quarter mile wide, at least half the trees had been cut. Tier-like piles of trimmed ties, frosted with domes of snow, jutted from the bank.

Glen sat staring at the tiers, his anger rising. They had not only cut the trees but they had torn up most of the ground cover. When the snows melted, the run-off would cut the earth like plows.

There was a wagon road to the tie camp. In the bitter afternoon air he rode along the just discernible ruts. The camp was a collection of tar-paper shacks in a large clearing. Dusk was not far off; tie hacks were arriving on wagons from the woods. From the stovepipes, blue smoke ascended perpendicularly on the motionless air. Hardesty stopped at the office to ask for Barney Carriger. A heavy-jawed Swede talked to him.

"Mister Carriger's in Antelope. Anything I can do?"

"Are you the superintendent?"

The Swede looked him over. He was a short, middle-aged man with a soup-strainer mustache; he wore the half-inch-thick woolen shirt and dark, shagged pants of the logger. "I'm the logging boss. Sig Johnson."

"Then you can give your men a message for me. Just say that, if I find anybody on my land with an axe or a saw, or even a big pocket knife, I'll quirt the ears off him. And don't try to move those ties until I reach a price for them with Carriger."

Johnson regarded him slowly. "It would help," he said, "if I knew who you was."

"Hardesty. Double Eight iron."

The Swede's mouth seemed to be smiling under the straw-hued mustache. "Pretty tough man, Mister Hardesty?"

Glen said: "Try me out."

Johnson smiled. He took a stub pencil from over his ear, and scratched his head with it. "I'll give Barney your message," he said.

In the raw, new cabin that night, a blueness smoked the room from the stove that did not draw well. Hardesty made a list of things he planned to do in Antelope. The first onslaught of winter had pointed up a number of necessities. He had these as an excuse to go into town, and he had the business with Carriger. But the remembrance of Jean Converse was drawing him, too. He understood that she would have asked a peddler to come back, automatically, as a matter of friendliness. Yet he found himself reading exaggerated meaning into the invitation. And he caught himself wishing that E.C. Converse sold steers instead of logs.

In the morning he hitched up the spring wagon

and drove down the river road. The sun-tinted vista was sharp with cold.

About a mile down he caught a *clink* of metal from the road ahead. He held the horse, searching the road that threaded in and out of the scant spruce woods. Suddenly, on the bank, he discerned three men. Their horses stood nearby. A steel cable extended from the tree beside which they were working to Tully's side of the river, a rusty streak on the frozen white surface.

Hardesty drove ahead. He had not gone far when the cowpunchers heard the grind of his tires on the tough snow and faced around. He pulled up beside them. There was Joe Tully, huge and red-faced in heavy winter clothing; Laramie Slade, his face pinched with cold and a muffler wrapped around his head, under his hat. The other man was Tully's foreman, Stu Winter.

Just what they were doing was not entirely clear. The cable had been anchored to a large tree on the opposite side of the river, on Tully's land. They were trying to anchor it now to the tree on Glen's side. Then he saw the rank of peeled logs along the opposite bank, and he understood.

"Once you start building," he said, "you don't know where to stop, do you?"

Tully pulled off his gloves to roll a smoke. There was a look of guilt in the wide-set dark eyes, but behind it was determination. He hadn't shaved in a week. With a quarter-inch black stubble on his jaws and chin, he looked like a hard customer.

"Hope you don't mind," he said. "This is something we've been meaning to put up for a long time. We're doing it now, while the river is frozen and we can work. It's a trump card, Hardesty, in case we don't reach terms with him by spring. To tell the truth, I didn't mean for you to see it, either. After the next storm, you wouldn't have. We're going to sink those logs under the ice with chains running to the cable. If he doesn't put up money against future damage, there won't be any tie drives next spring."

Hardesty said: "And when he drags you to court, you'll drag me along, is that it?"

"You can count on one thing," Slade snapped. "This thing won't be settled in a courtroom."

"And there won't be any cable anchored on my side of the river, either," Hardesty declared. "You can count on that."

Tully lit the cigarette. It trembled on his lips. Emotion was rising in him that the big, patient cattleman was having trouble to master.

"Hardesty," he said, "I want no trouble with you. But, by God, I'm not going to duck it! The cable stands."

Glen dismounted and strode to the tree. He examined the splice. A heavy clevis served as the master link. When he put his hands on it, Tully reached him almost at a stumble and tore him back from it. He shouted hoarsely—"I said it stands!"—

and he shot a blow at Glen's head. Glen ducked and took it on the ear. There was stunning power behind it. He went back two steps and struck one buckskinned fist against the other palm, his heart pounding. Slade and the others were moving in.

"I can't promise to whip you all," he said, "but I'll give you a hell of a fight. I reckon you run too much to yellow to want to make it one at a time."

Tully growled at the others: "Stay out of it. I'll handle him." He threw his gun on the snow and Glen's landed beside it a moment later.

IV

Tully moved in to fire one at Glen's chin. Glen's shoulder got in the way. Glen chopped a short, hard punch to the rancher's cheek. A white streak appeared on the ruddy skin. He followed with a jab to the belly, and then Tully slammed him on the ear with the side of his fist. Glen went to his knees, filled with the ringing pain that only cold skin can know. Tully stood back until he arose and Hardesty had a confused wish that he had tried to jump him while he was down. A fight was a fight, but this big overgrown cowhand couldn't shake his inhibitions long enough to follow up a lead.

He moved in again with the only kind of defense he knew, to crouch low and carry the fight to his opponent. Tully stabbed at his face and failed to connect. The breath of both men was heavy and white in the cold air. Hardesty brought a hook around to mash against Tully's mouth. He watched the blood appear, slow and dark and thick. Tully winced, his eyes beginning to show real anger as he wiped his mouth.

He charged into Glen and took a blow to the face. It didn't slow him. He was a stubborn indestructible man and Glen knew he had a fight on his hands. Suddenly Joe Tully's fist came from nowhere to crash against his cheek bone. For an instant, a cloud of sparks seemed to obscure everything. Glen came out of it to find himself weaving, going back with his hands still up but with the cowman slugging him with everything he had. His foot caught in the snow and he fell. This time, Tully dragged him up with a hand in the front of his jacket, to slam him three times with his right fist before Glen could tear loose.

The forest was rocking. Tully was out of focus. He was a great lumbering tree trunk falling over upon him. His voice came, high and breathless. "I say it stands! Will you quit?"

Glen didn't answer, but he kept his left arm extended and his right hand close to his chin, taking the cold air in desperately. Tully began crowding him again. Glen let himself be carried back. Strength began to return a little, but he was saving it.

Slade and Stu Winter were yelling advice,

following the men as they moved along the riverbank. Tully was catching the spirit at last. In every man a dark vein of brutality is to be found if he is probed deeply enough. Strong and unhurt, he was heaving everything he had at Glen's face and body.

He slowed, and again he said: "Will you quit?"

Glen said: "When I've finished you." All his strength was behind the fist that traveled in a savage uppercut to the stubbled chin.

Joe Tully was shaken to his spurs. He reeled back, his right leg bent, and he almost fell. When he squared off again, he was facing Laramie Slade.

Laramie pointed. "Joe! Over there!"

Tully turned heavily, his chin leading into the already traveling blow. He sagged. He made a low snoring sound in his throat and sat down. Then he went forward on his face. On the trampled snow his body was a huge dark pattern with one arm extended and one lying straight along his side.

Glen looked at the others. They were watching Tully incredulously. He didn't get up. They carried him to a tree, where they sat him against it with his chin on his chest. Slade started across the river to where his horse was tethered.

Hardesty washed his face with snow until his head was clear. He pulled the clevis pin that held the cable and watched the long, rusty cord slither across the ice. . . .

Far down the river, where the foothills reached for the valley, he made a cold lunch of dried beef and sourdough biscuits. He felt a sense of regret over the fight. Tully had been as convinced that he was right as Glen was that he was wrong. He wanted to be a fair man, but he had lost his sense of perspective somewhere along the line. But if this squabble ever reached court, Glen meant to be clear of it. He couldn't do that by letting them make a battlefield out of his land.

Out on the snowy flats Hardesty saw a horse and rider coming toward him. The horse was a sorrel shadow on the bluish afternoon snow. The rider's jacket was a deeper red. Before long he knew it was Jean.

He was conscious of the swellings on his face as she rode up. "Just in time," she declared. "I'll go back with you. It's getting too cold out here for a town girl."

The cold heightened the freshness of her coloring. Hardesty helped her dismount and put her in the wagon, spreading a buffalo robe over her lap. He knew she was looking at his bruised face, but she didn't ask about it. He tied her pony behind the wagon.

As they started off, she said: "I was hoping you'd be in before now, Glen. I meant it when I asked you to visit us."

"I meant it when I said I'd come, too. But this is

the first time I've been able to get loose. And this is business."

She sighed. "You're a very business-like man."

"You've got to be business-like with winter breathing down your neck. Not to mention a corral full of loggers. You don't happen to know where Barney Carriger is? Sig Johnson said that he was in town."

She glanced at him, and then slowly shook her head. "Trouble, already. What's happened?"

"Somebody cut a little timber on my place," Glen said. "I thought Carriger and your father might like to explain it."

"I'm sure they will. Sometimes the men get a little free with their axes when they find a nice stand of timber. But I know it wasn't done on orders."

Glen smiled to himself. She didn't like the smile. "You'd rather suspect us than not, I think. You don't take much on faith, do you?"

"Only religion. Some men would consider it good business to trespass, make their profit, and straighten things out with a few dollars and an apology."

The tires of the wagon squealed on the hard snow. She looked at him somberly. When she frowned that way, she looked like a small girl laboring over her arithmetic, and there was something small-girlish about her complete conviction that Carriger and Converse could do no wrong, when she probably knew no more about their methods than he did. She pulled the buffalo robe higher about her.

"Why don't we talk about something safe, like the weather?" she said. "Or you might explain whether it was a tree or a door you ran into."

"You're still talking about business," Glen said. They were coming into town now. That was all the explanation he gave her.

He was sorry the ride was over. There was a lift in being with her that nothing else had ever given him. There was a vividness about her that you could warm your hands before. She wasn't wearing the crystal earrings today, but he remembered how they had deepened the clear blue of her eyes, and he remembered the dark luster of her hair in the lamplight. A small voice of caution tried to get his attention. He wouldn't listen to it. Conscience was a kill-joy. It said: *You can't fall in love with this girl. She might turn out to be on the wrong side of the fence.* And Hardesty thought: *Can't I?*

V

Antelope, with its main street cut by wagon tires and the mud and snow refrozen, had a cheerless look. Wood smoke flavored the air. Horses stood at the hitch racks, humped against the cold wind. In the windy sunset they pulled up before the Converse home. A film of frost diffused the golden lamplight. E.C. Converse opened the door to peer into the twilight with his squinted, old man's eyes. "Getting worried about you, Jean," he said. Then: "Why, it's Hardesty! Come in, come in!"

Do we have to go through this again? Glen thought. They went through the same rite of deciding what it would be to drink, and Converse carefully set his chess game aside and began to question Glen on what he was doing.

Carriger came in from the office in the rear of the house. Tall and sober, he carried himself with easy self-confidence. He shook hands with Glen and poured himself three fingers of whiskey. The lamp incised the creases of his face deeply. He sat there appearing increasingly annoyed at E.C. Converse's small talk. With no preamble, he said: "I don't like that cable business, Hardesty."

Glen shrugged. "I didn't know about it myself until this morning. Tully and I had a little discussion over it."

For the first time Carriger smiled. He looked relieved. "I was wondering about the face. One of my men saw the cable and log string up there the other day. It wasn't hard to deduce what they were going to be used for. So you took a fall out of him?"

"I said the cable would have to come down. As a matter of fact," he said, "I don't think it would be out of order if I had let them put it up. Do you?"

Carriger's shadowed eyes regarded him steadily. "You know the answer to that."

"I don't know the answer to why ties are being cut on my range."

Jean looked sharply at Carriger. Her father rubbed his chin. "Hadn't heard anything about it. Had you, Barney?"

Carriger pulled a billfold from his pocket. He handed Glen a check already made out in the amount of $300. "My woods boss got a little ambitious," he admitted. "I heard you'd been up. This should pay for the timber."

"It won't stop gullies from forming when the run-off comes."

"If there's any damage done, we'll stand for it. Those things happen. I don't know whether you realize it, but you're not in a healthy spot, mister. For your own good, you ought to tie up with one side or the other before long. There's every reason why you should be in with Tully, instead of fighting him. Why don't you try to patch it up?"

Converse smiled feebly. "Stop joking, Barney." The smile wilted under Carriger's stare.

"I'm not joking. He's only making it tough for himself by bucking them. At the same time, he's not getting any help from us. In a way," he said thoughtfully, "it would be better for us, too, if he reached an agreement with Joe Tully."

Glen kept his eyes on Carriger's face. Now it began to make sense.

"There are too many firebrands in that crowd," Carriger complained. "They need a cool head for balance. Why don't you get in solidly with them? Don't let them break out in a rash without trying to stop it. I've got a hunch you could handle them. It would be worth fifty a month to us if you could. How about it?"

There was a cold emptiness in Glen, and then there was a rush of heat to his brain. He put his drink down. "I could answer that a lot better outside. You're looking for a spy, you mean."

Carriger raised his voice, and his eyes were angry. "Don't try to jack me up, mister! Fifty a month is all it's worth . . . plus a bonus for anything hot. I've heard some loose talk that they intend to burn all our winter ties before we can float them. If they attempt anything like that, I'd like a little notice that they're on the way."

"If you get it, it won't be from me." Glen stood up. "Why don't you stop by my place sometime? I'd like to return your hospitality."

Carriger's face was stormy and baffled. "You're talking like a damned fool. I'm making you a decent offer and showing you the way out of a lot of trouble."

"If I ever sell out," Glen told him, "it won't be for a free meal and a couple of crates of nuts and bolts."

He walked to the door. Converse was piping futile protests that Glen hadn't understood. Glen opened the door and stepped into the freezing darkness. Jean followed him. She pulled the door closed. Then she held the lapels of his coat so that he had to listen to her.

"He didn't mean it that way, Glen. I don't think he realized what he was asking you to do."

"Any time that monkey makes an offer, he knows what he's doing." Glen was angry and breathless. "He thought he'd put his log mark on me with a little Wyoming hospitality. If I hadn't been a greenhorn, I'd have known what was happening from the first."

He would have gone down the steps, but she held him. "He was wrong, but I do know this. In six years we've never had any trouble over our logging methods until we came to Antelope."

"Did you ever cut ties in a cattle country before, where there was someone around to squawk if you broke the timber laws?"

"I . . . I don't know. But I know Dad wouldn't permit anything rough. It's not in him."

"If he'd leave his chess game for twenty-four hours, he might find out some things about his logging methods that he doesn't know."

His anger was beginning to thin, as regret took its place. His conscience had been telling it straight. *You can't fall in love with this girl.* He couldn't, but he had. She was shivering with cold, but still she stood there, trying to think of the answer to something she didn't understand.

Glen held her by the waist. "I may not be getting back again," he said, "so if I'm ever going to do this, I'd better do it now. I keep wondering how you'd look if you were mad. Maybe this is my last chance to find out."

He pulled her against him. The cold had chilled her lips, but they were soft, and they weren't afraid of his. After a moment she pulled away. She was smiling, but there were tears in her eyes. "You won't find out that way," she whispered.

That small voice was talking to him again, telling him it was time to get out. This time, Glen took its advice.

One nice thing about cattle ranching was that there wasn't much time to get lonesome. Storms brought their particular problems, and after the storms there were other things to worry about. But with all of it, Glen found time to wish he could reshuffle the cards and start all over.

It was worst when the work was caught up and there was nothing to do but stoke the fire and listen to the pipe-organ roar of the wind ripping at the top of Granite Terrace. Life was complicated enough without some extraneous factor like a woman to confuse a man. Pretty soon she was the hub of the whole thing and he was trying to make the world revolve around her. All it accomplished for Hardesty was to make him dizzy.

He made a trip to Antelope in March, but he

didn't look her up. She had written him, friendly little letters about what was going on in town, and she hoped he was getting along all right and not to take things too seriously. The kind of letters a nice girl wrote who knew she shouldn't be writing to a man, but couldn't help it.

He didn't see her because he didn't trust himself. Evidence was piling up that Carriger and Converse were a couple of shades blacker than Tully had painted them. One day Glen rode high up into the cold country of thinning pines and craggy peaks. From timberline down, Carriger's tie hacks had sheared the range like a sheep. They left a forest of stumps and trash. Here and there, near old campsites, he found the bones of slaughtered beeves. They could have been paid for; he doubted it.

In Antelope, he saw a street fight between six loggers and half a dozen cowpunchers. He ached to get into it but stayed out because he had no business fighting.

Suddenly everything seemed waiting for the thaw. Along Caballo River, ranks of ties mounted, great piers jutting to the edge of the frozen stream. Tie hacks patrolled them casually, but with guns in the crooks of their arms. One morning the ice would crack and the sleeping river would stir. The ties would not be many minutes behind the ice.

But in Antelope, Joe Tully said the men at the treating plant might as well quit. He had hung up a boast that not one tie would reach the pond.

After a series of warm days Glen began hearing the grumble of snowslides high in the Wind River range. The time was running out. One night in April, he made up his mind.

Damn it, if he was wrong he could admit it! In the morning he would ride over to Tully's and apologize. For the first time in weeks he slept soundly.

Sometime before morning he heard a patter of rocks on the roof. He was awake instantly, piling out of bed to pull on pants and boots. He found his gun. Then he stood there, his gun in his hand, listening.

The sound resembled the vacant roar of a string of empty boxcars at a distance. It was coming closer, shaking the whole cabin with its force. Something that sounded like a pine branch landed on the roof. Another, and another fell, until he knew it could be only one thing—wet snow, falling from the top of the cliffs! The spring snowslide, and he was right in the path of it.

VI

Vicente, the cook, came in from the kitchen, where he slept, yelling in Spanish: "¡Patrón! ¡El monte se cae . . . !" A dim figure in long underwear, he ran to the door.

Hardesty was there in time to stop him. "It's a

snowslide! If you go out there, you'll be killed!"

"And what will I be in here?" Vicente yelled. But he stayed, paralyzed by the thunder of descending rocks and snow.

Hardesty lit a lamp; not that it could help, but terror feasted on darkness. He sat down and rolled a smoke. When he got through and touched a match to it, he discovered he had lost all the tobacco. With the roof visibly giving way under its load of snow and débris, his nerves were something that leaped like a snake on a griddle. He understood, now, all the rocks and deadfall about the cabin.

Something cracked, and a heavy cascade of wet snow funneled in through a hole in the roof. A rending clamor sounded from the kitchen. Snow and the broken fragments of a roof timber burst through the door. He ran to the far wall.

Vicente came with him. The old Mexican looked puzzled. "I do not understand. They say it is shelter here . . . we don' haf to worry. I do not see what . . ."

"Don't worry about it. Stand close to the wall. I think we'll have a better chance if it gives way."

Barney Carriger hadn't worried about it. Barney had helped him build his cabin right where he knew the spring avalanche would land. It was nothing he could not have explained if Glen had signed up with him. He'd have told him about it, made a joke of it, and bought him a drink on it, then he'd have sent his boys over to construct a new one.

But since he hadn't come around, Carriger had discreetly remained silent. Was it his fault if a thick-headed cowman misunderstood his advice and built his cabin under an avalanche?

The oilskin windows were all punched in, admitting white gushes of snow. The roof pole was sagging. A long splinter snapped from the smooth, peeled log. All at once the long pole was two short ones. Glen was wildly trying to back through the wall when the slide came. The candle gone, he had only his sense of hearing left. Something struck him in the shins. He closed his eyes.

After a time it was silent. Silent, except for a mumble of Spanish. Vicente was praying. "*. . . santificado sea tu nombre, venga . . .*"

The blackness was dirty gray. Above them, a triangular rent in the ceiling admitted a tepid wash of daylight. Glen breathed deeply. "Let's get out," he said.

Vicente's mumbling stopped. "*¿Patrón?*"

"Let's get out of here. It's over."

They scrambled out. The avalanche was a ragged talus a mile or two long. At the deepest point it was fifteen or twenty feet high. Broken treetops thrust from the churned snow here and there. The horses had been at the far end of the trap; they were unhurt. But somebody was going to freeze unless they found some heavy clothes pretty soon.

The east side of the cabin had received less of the slide than the other. They crawled through a window into a sort of lean-to formed by the wall and the caved-in ceiling. In the corner, they located their coats and hats.

Hardesty told the Mexican to clear away the snow in the kitchen and drag out the food. "You can shack in the feed barn for a while. It looks all right. If any of the boys come in, send them over to Joe Tully's."

He rode hard. It was four miles downstream to where a wagon bridge spanned Caballo River. He knew before he reached the stream that there would be no ice to cross on. The thaw was on. The grinding roar of broken ice was like distant thunder on the air.

Hardesty reached the river and knew it was more than that. From bank to bank, like heaped yellow matchsticks, a river of trimmed ties crept sluggishly along the eroded banks. The drive Joe Tully had said would never be held had begun.

Hardesty had been regarding himself as a cautious, broad-minded man. He saw himself now as stubborn and suspicious. He could have brought matters with Carriger to a head months ago, but he had drifted along, suspecting everyone and doing nothing about it.

Tully was a wise and forward-thinking man. He had known that by his cable trick the pressure would have been on Carriger. Nothing but guns would have served to break the cable blockade, and the side that started gun play would be the side a court would rule against. Now the positions were reversed. To stop the tie drive, the wedge would have to be applied at its source, where the endless piers of lumber along the river were being dumped into the stream. Glen didn't know how Tully felt, but he was ready to spearhead such a move.

He was about to turn downstream when he heard a shout. He turned quickly in the saddle. As he sat there, three men in plaid woolen shirts, shagged pants, and shapeless hats came into view. One of them spudded a peavey into a log nosing against the bank and got it back into the stream.

They moved quickly on, hard-looking men doing a hard job. Glen saw now that a man in the rear carried a carbine instead of a peavey. It was Sig Johnson, the big Swede with the stained yellow mustache, Carriger's woods boss. Johnson shouted over the moving rumble of ties.

"You men follow it on down! Keep 'em moving, night and day! And remember . . . all the whiskey you can drink when the drive's finished!"

The men shouted something back at him and the first turned to stride on down the bank. He stopped short, looking up at the horseman who had come out of a stand of alder. This man's rifle was held lightly in his hands and the view they had of it was of the shining ring of its muzzle.

"You can drop the gun right there, Johnson,"

Hardesty said. "You others leave your peaveys and go back with him."

Johnson's face became a strangled red. "This is armed hold-up!" he said.

"You name it," Glen told him. "I'd hate to make it murder, though. Let me see that gun drop."

Johnson did. He leveled a finger at the cowman. "Hardesty . . . !"

Glen put his cheek against the walnut. Johnson turned and walked quickly up the stream.

After they had gone, Glen recovered the gun and tied it behind his saddle. He started quickly downstream. The fat was in the fire. Whether Tully wanted it or not, Glen had turned over a card that spelled war.

He was hoping the bridge had not been damaged by the thaw. As often as not, these jerrybuilt bridges went down the river with the ice. He framed what he would say to Tully. *I was a pig-headed fool. I've put us all in a tough spot, but I'm going to try to make up for it.* There was one thing on his side. He had witnesses that Carriger had advised him to locate his cabin under the ledge. *You could call that attempted murder. Even Tully and Slade could testify to that. Even Tully . . .* It hit him like a fist. Why hadn't Tully warned him he was building in a danger spot? He should have known Rawhide Valley as well as Carriger.

It struck him that the ties were moving more sluggishly. From being a crowding, eager rush, they were welding into a sluggish mass of jammed timbers. He rounded a wooded point and saw that the drive had jammed a quarter mile below. He frowned. It was at the spot where Tully had tried to string the cable!

Hardesty put the horse to a lope. Before he reached the tree, a gun *cracked* and the echoes leaped back and forth across the wide cañon. He saw no one, but he had the good sense to raise his hands. Men moved warily from a motte of birch. Big Joe Tully spoke to them and approached Hardesty alone.

Tully was grinning. "You're a sharp customer, Hardesty, when the light's good. Too bad you don't get around at night. We put 'er back the night before the second storm hit. We've been ready for months. And no timber-lovin' son's going to pull that pin now!"

"What would you think," Glen said, "if I told you I was riding to your place to organize a raid on the lumber camp?"

"I'd think you were an ambitious liar, but a damned poor one. Get off your horse."

Hardesty dismounted. "Listen to me. I've been all winter making up my mind to apologize to you. I came to a showdown with Carriger last December over some timber cutting on my land. He tried to hire me to spy for him, on top of that. Last night I decided it was time to admit I've bungled things for fair. And what happens? Ten tons of snow and ice cave in my cabin and nearly kill me."

If he had been angling for sympathy, he didn't get it. The cowpunchers howled. In the cattle country, nothing was so funny as a man's saddle cinch breaking when he had roped a tough steer.

Only Tully kept a straight face. "I meant to warn you," he said. "I figured a bull-headed one like you deserved any trouble he got himself into. But I didn't want to see you killed. This is the earliest thaw I've seen in fourteen years. It jumped the gun on me." A scowl bunched his forehead. "What the hell am I apologizing to you for? I'm thinking I'll let just one tie go through . . . with you on top of it."

But Glen could see that the cattleman was genuinely perplexed. He wanted to trust him, but he had to be cautious, and he had five men at his back and no doubt another gang across the river watching his actions with critical eyes. Glen remembered something.

"See that carbine behind my saddle? There's another one in the boot. The second one is Sig Johnson's. I just sent him and a couple of tie hacks back up the river. Carriger's going to be down pretty soon, looking for trouble. I hope he doesn't find us standing here glaring at each other."

Tully examined the gun. He found the lumberman's initials carved in the stock. He turned to his men. "I leave it up to you, boys. Do we take him in or run him out?"

Stu Winter, his foreman, lowered his gun. "Maybe I'm getting democratic. But I reckon it'd make the odds better if he was with us."

VII

Crouching there in the wet snow was cold and monotonous. Glen's boots were soaked and his toes numbed through. He had learned from Tully that there were a dozen men across the river in addition to ten on this side. Noon came and there had been no sign of Barney Carriger.

Back of the cable the ties were a solid river of yellow sticks that completely hid the stream. Beyond the cable, the water leaped, white and roaring, into the shallow gorge of Caballo River. Glen had to strain to hear anything but the groaning of the ties and the rush of churning water. Tully had posted him in a thicket of buckbrush not far from the anchor tree. He had a clear view of the road, but there was no certainty that attack would come from there. It might come from all sides at once, or Carriger might bring his men over the solid barricade of the ties, which provided a thousand battlements for protection.

Tully whistled a short, sharp note. Above the other noises, Glen heard, now, the brisk *chunk-*

chunk of hoofs in the snow. Still he saw nothing. Then he saw Joe Tully emerge from his vantage spot into the middle of the road, facing downstream. Now he saw two riders come into view, to be confronted with the rancher's rifle. The riders were E.C. Converse and Jean.

Converse yanked his horse to a stop. He was bundled in heavy clothing and his face was red with cold. He stared at the cowman, then at the dam. His voice was high and intolerant. "I won't have this, Mister Tully! My plant foreman told me that not a dozen ties have come down. That thing's got to go!"

Tully spoke patiently. "Go on back, Mister Converse. People are going to be getting hurt around here. You've stayed pretty well out of it so far. Better keep it like that."

Jean sat there looking at the dam and Glen saw her smile. "Mister Tully," she said, "I think maybe a truce is in order. Will you go with us and talk to Barney Carriger?"

"Carriger can come here and talk to me . . . alone."

Converse's heavy body labored out of the saddle. He marched up to the tree and put his gloved hands on the clevis. Glen grinned. With a few hundred thousand tons of timber pushing the cable, pulling the clevis pin would not be quite like throwing off a log chain. The old man struggled with it. Then he looked around in desperation. Tully had come close. Glen emerged from his ambuscade and saw Converse lunge for the rancher's rifle. Tully shoved him back.

"I'm telling you to get out and take your girl with you! We're going to find Barney and see what's to be done."

Jean shook her head. She looked at Glen. "We know what's to he done, Dad. Admit we haven't played fair with them. Barney will have to talk business with them if you say so."

Converse put an outraged glance on her. "I don't know why I let you talk me into taking you. The least I could have expected was that you would keep out of something you know nothing about. . . ."

"How much do you know about it?" Jean asked him. ". . . Beyond what Carriger tells you?"

Converse said pompously: "I own a controlling interest in the company. That ought to give me some understanding into . . ."

"Doesn't seem like it does, though," Glen interrupted. "Mister Converse, you're a good chess player and a fine judge of whiskey, but you're a hell of a judge of men. You don't seem to know we mean business. We're giving you a break in assuming that you don't know what Carriger's been doing, either. That's why we're letting you get out of here under your own power. But it will have to be *pronto*."

Converse's face congested. His mood seemed to

be imparted to the horse, which tried to rear under him; he held it in roughly. He snapped at Jean: "Come along."

She still sat her pony beside Glen, her face anxious. She made one more effort to placate him. "Dad, we don't know what we'll run into up there. Maybe it's too late to cross Carriger. But you can promise these men the things they want . . . you can put up a guarantee that you'll keep your word."

Tully looked at her with respect. Here was a woman who talked better sense than most men. Converse hesitated a moment, but his nature and the pressure being put on him were dictating the only answer he could make. "My business is with Carriger," he said. "I'd advise you men to cut that cable and let the ties through."

They watched him lope on up the mushy spring road.

Glen made a sign to Tully. Tully went back to his position, and Glen led the girl's horse some distance into the trees. He looked up at her and knew immediately she was going to cry. She was unused to violence; nothing so violent as a quarrel with her father, he was sure, had ever taken place in her life before. He tried to change her mood before the tears came.

"What are you going to do next? You can't stay here."

She looked helplessly at him. "I thought you might have an idea. I can't let him ride up there,

Glen! There's no telling what Carriger will do when he starts asking questions."

"*If* he starts! He sounds pretty well satisfied with Carriger, it seems to me."

"He's stubborn. But I've caught him going over the books and reading all the correspondence, trying to find out what's been going on. He wanted to have all this out with him before it came to a showdown, but then the thaw came early and the plant foreman told him the ties weren't coming through. He was scared and angry."

"Whatever happens," Glen said, "you can't help by hanging around here."

She stared at him resentfully, as if she had counted on his knowing her better than that. "If that's how we've been making our money, riding roughshod over everyone who gets in our way, I'm not going back to it." She said with sudden decision: "I'll go back to Cheyenne. I have an aunt there."

"What kind of money is hers?" Glen asked. "I suppose she's only a stockholder."

It was a good guess. She glanced at him furiously, and then the tears came. Glen reached up to lift her down. He didn't let her go. She tried to move away, but he held her closely and tilted her face up.

"Honey, this is the quickest proposal I ever expect to make," he said, "but I can't be all spring about it this time. I've been trying to bring out the point that you need at least one honest man in the family. I can't offer much but a caved-in cabin and a tin stove, right now. Carriger let me build under an avalanche. But by fall I'll have a crop of good white-faced calves, a new cabin, and maybe a few trees left, depending on how we make out with these bull-necked loggers. I'd sure like an incentive to keep my head down today."

Jean sniffled. Her body relaxed. "It's the quickest proposal I ever expect to accept, too," she said. "You didn't even answer my letters."

"I was afraid to. I didn't know how you felt about cattlemen, and I wasn't going into lumbering for anybody."

"I feel wonderful about cattlemen . . . when they're alive. Glen," she said suddenly, "let the old ties through! Then we can hold them up until we bring Carriger to terms."

"It's a good idea"—Glen smiled—"except that I'm not making the rules. You tell it to Joe. He's only been playing that gambit for two years. All he's got to show for it is a lot of deadfall and a corral full of crippled cows."

He kissed her. This time she was the one who hung on. Glen whispered in her ear: "You're going to ride up to my place now, until I come for you. I wish I could be there to carry you across the threshold of the feed barn. It's still standing, and the stove may work. Vicente will take care of you till I come."

He went back to the buckbrush, and it was different now. He didn't notice the cold, and the little prodding fear of what was ahead kept its distance. He was convinced that he was invincible. She was waiting for him, and he was going back. It was simple, when you looked at it that way. A lot simpler than looking at the score card: 100-odd loggers on Carriger's side, all or part of whom he would bring into the fight. Twenty-two men on theirs. . . .

Crouching there in the snow, he watched Laramie Slade, across the river, appear from somewhere to examine the cable. He turned and cupped his hands to yell something, but the roar of the river whipped the sound away. From his gestures, Glen gathered that something was going wrong with the cable or the clevis. Laramie made a decision. He came gingerly across the head of packed ties.

Glen was concerned. If the cable went out, the whole thing would be blown to hell.

Slade did a strange thing. He lurched suddenly to his right, went to his knees on the slippery ties. He struggled up and took one more step. Glen heard the first shot just as the second came. Laramie caved in. He rested on hands and knees for a moment, as if trying to get his breath. His carbine slipped over the ragged bulkhead of the ties. A moment later he fell after it, to disappear in the cataract.

They couldn't tell, immediately, where the shot had come from. Then there was motion on the sand beside Caballo River. Down there under the overhanging shelter of the bank, they were working upstream. A dozen shapes in dark shirts and pants lunged over the bank into the barricade of rocks along the brink.

VIII

Glen fired one shot into the cairn of boulders where they had scattered like quail. A snarling fusillade burst through the flimsy network of brush that was his whole protection. He flattened on the trampled snow and stayed down, cursing Tully and himself. Carriger had taken the direct, elementary strategy of advancing straight to his target—from the rear. He was in a position where he could lie low until one of their shots severed the cable. There would be a rush of ties jamming the gorge, and then the river would drop and they could slip back over the bank and return the way they had come.

Tully had dispersed his men over so wide an area that only he and Glen and a couple of others had a clear shot at the rocks.

Glen lay flat on the snow with his gun extended toward the rocks. He saw another tie hack attempt to ascend the bank. For one instant he had a full-length target. He let this man have the shot in the brisket. The man dropped his gun and balanced for a moment on his toes. He stepped back and was gone.

Now Carriger's men brought the whole force of their rifles down on Hardesty. By the fact that there was a lift in the ground between brush and riverbank, Glen was saved. Lying flat, he could hear the passing of their bullets, like cloth being ripped. When he shifted his gun, it felt slippery in his grasp. He realized his hands were sweating, that perspiration was coming out on his belly and face. He had the unmanly wish that they would sever the cable and get out. Pretty soon somebody would get the idea of climbing the rocks for a shot at him.

Three times Tully's gun crashed. Each shot was followed by a fusillade that kept him silent for several minutes. Glen pictured him behind his tree, thinking of his wife and kids and wondering just how much it would advance the cattlemen's position to get himself killed. But each time his gun roared again.

From his spot, Glen could see the ragged battlement of the uppermost rocks. He thought he detected color in the gray-green of the stones. About the time he was certain he had been wrong, the yellow-mustached face of Sig Johnson showed in a narrow slot. Glen snapped up the carbine. Johnson's face disappeared. At the same instant, other loggers who had seen movement in the buckbrush poured another dozen rounds at him.

He thought: *Damn them!* Did they want him or the cable? They had a clear shot at the tree, only fifty feet from them. But instead of chopping it to pieces with steel-jacketed slugs, they were vindictively out to get him first. Johnson would pepper away at him until he exposed himself, then the rest would get him.

Yet he discerned a flaw in that strategy. Carriger, who had shown himself a good general up to now, seemed to be making a bad mistake for the sake of revenge. Nothing prevented the half dozen cowpunchers in the woods from working around below the loggers. It might take a half hour, but Barney Carriger was giving them all the time they wanted.

And suddenly Glen remembered the man who had tried to climb the bank. Something like raw, white lightning illuminated his brain. Carriger wouldn't have come with a dozen men to face what might have been fifty! He had the bulk of his force below, where they were awaiting a chance to get out.

Just to the left of the rocks stood the tree, a stout Douglas fir clear of branches for its first fifteen feet. The cable had bitten deeply into the red-brown bark. Glen wriggled up into better position. He got the dark strand of cable under his sights. He fired and saw bark fly. A strand of cable tore loose and unwound from the main body with a whip.

Glen eased the bolt back, seeing the hot cartridge as a smoking blur. He eased another shell in. When he raised his head, this time, the shooting broke loose again. His first thought was to risk it, to get the job done and to hell with them. When a slug took off his hat, he ducked.

Then once again the heavy throb of Joe Tully's gun echoed. The hot curtain of slugs over Glen's head stopped, then resumed. Again Tully's .30-30 boomed, and now the tie hacks turned their guns his way. Glen glanced and saw that Tully was half exposed behind his tree as he, too, took a shot at the cable. He had seen the bark fly and knew what was in Glen's mind.

Hardesty did not rush this shot. He might not get another. His elbow supported the barrel of the carbine; his finger carefully took up the trigger slack. The stock jolted him.

Out there another sound was audible, much like a shot itself. The cable whipped from the tree, rising on a long tangent over the stream. There was a moment in which nothing was different, the heaped-up ties still packed like matches in a box, the log jam still presenting a solid front. Then the mass stirred, groaned, and seemed to roll forward. A section of ties burst loose as though dynamite had been exploded inside the jam. The keystone was out.

Even above the muted rumble of those tons of lumber falling, the cries of Carriger's trapped gunmen were audible. Two of them sprang over the bank and ran like deer for the rocks. Glen dropped one of them. He saw the other go down and knew Tully was still in action.

He came to his knees, a fresh shell under the pin. A long two minutes passed. Then Sig Johnson came down the rocks with his hands raised. Another man trailed him.

Carriger's voice boomed. "Stick it out, you gutless devils!"

Johnson went on. Barney Carriger exposed himself for the first time. Standing upright, he took his bead on the middle of the Swede's broad back. The gun jumped, and Johnson made a little stumbling run toward the brush before he fell. Someone back in the woods got Carriger.

Joe Tully took ten prisoners from the rocks. Trussed together in a long chain, they started the hike to Antelope. Hardesty, Tully, and several others rode upstream to the lumber camp. Glen worried over Jean's father. The old man was foolish enough to have tried to stop Carriger's army single-handed, if he felt like it. On the other hand, he was probably stubborn and hot-headed enough to have ridden down with them to loose the log jam.

They found him tied flat on a bench in the mess shack. He had deflated somewhat since they saw

281

him last. As they stood over him, he said stiffly: "I've been thinking about this thing, gentlemen. Carriger has refused to work out a compromise. As senior partner, I'm in a position to force him out."

"You're not in a position to force anybody out," Hardesty said. "We're trying to decide whether to dump you in the river or leave you here. Carriger has resigned. Along with about two dozen of his men."

Converse stared at them, and then at the ceiling. After a moment he said: "He wouldn't be told. It was his way."

Glen whipped out the blade of his knife. "That's been your way, too, up to now, old-timer. These boys are ready to work out a deal with you. But all I want from you is a promise that you won't ever try to crowd me into joining the firm. I like cows, and Jean likes cows, and that's good enough for us."

"What has Jean . . . ?" E.C. Converse blinked. Then the old-time ruddiness, the geniality that was as insistent as a cat rubbing your leg, suffused his face. "Why, that's fine . . . fine!" he declared. "Caught her sending a letter to you by a cow-puncher one day, and I wondered. A shame we don't have something for a toast. Down at the house I have some excellent . . ."

"Irish whiskey," Glen cut in. "We'll get around to it, E.C. In the meantime, Jean and I may run down to Cheyenne for a few days. Things to do."

Dakota Man

I

To Mitch Atkins, Frijole looked like a remarkable town. It was remarkably small and remarkably ugly. It was remarkable that they should have bothered to name it. Finding it had been like finding a man named Kelly in Jerusalem. The Kansas City beef buyer had told him it was near Laredo, but until he hit Laredo nobody had ever heard of it. Atkins understood why now. What he didn't understand was why, of all the towns in Texas, the man had mentioned this one as a good spot for a young buck to set himself up as a cattleman.

Mitch sat his horse at the foot of a long slope up which the town rambled. The brush had begun to thin about fifteen minutes ago, until suddenly the trail broke into this clearing of perhaps 1,000 acres. Mexicans were dry-farming little irregular patches about the town. In the cold winter sunlight, thin curlings of smoke arose from the dozen-odd buildings of Frijole. All of the structures were of adobe, most of them merely rip-rapping affairs plastered with mud. It was a bleak and uninviting vista, and Mitch Atkins was sorry he hadn't stopped somewhere north of the Red. But here he was, the ink scarcely dry on his discharge papers, $5,000 in gold *clinking* dully in his saddlebags, and the frayed remnants of a dream lurking in his heart.

He was a blond, lanky man with the raw look of a Kansas farmer. He had big hands that appeared too heavy for his arms, but they were working and fighting hands. The index finger of the left hand was missing. Mitch knew approximately where it was—somewhere in the vicinity of Gaines's Mill in Virginia.

He rode past a slab-sided *jacal* and a Mexican youth grinned and called something like— "¡*Cuebolay*!"—and Mitch waved back. He had found the Mexicans friendly and a lot more plentiful than cattle. The brush was supposed to be full of cattle. He'd seen about a score so far.

There was, thank God, a saloon in town. It was called the Jeb Stuart Bar. That was ominous. Mitch still wore a faded blue shirt. Well, he could forgive, if they could.

At a horse-chawed hitch rack a dozen mounts were tailed up against the wind. Mitch's sorrel made it thirteen. The others resembled veterans of a luckless cavalry charge, scarred and beaten up. There was a collection of twigs and branches jammed under the fork of one of the wooden Mexican saddles. It looked to Mitch as though the rider had ridden through a thicket instead of bothering to ride around it.

Mitch walked through the batwing doors into a dirt-floored big room without windows but with a few lamps hung about. He stood there, his thumbs hooked under his belt, trying to get oriented. The smells were of strong tobacco and whiskey and the strange, sour odor of pulque.

Someone barked—"Tensh-hun!"—and Mitch found himself almost snapping to attention. Then there was a round of laughter, and he realized they were having fun with his Army shirt. He fell in with it, saying with a grin: "Rest!"

This time there was no laughter.

Mitch walked to the bar. Four men slouched against it. The rest were divided between two tables. The man closest to Mitch, an American with a craggy, bald face, sunburned and devoid of hair right up to the eyebrows, grinned at him. "The occupation troops have arrived, boys. What'll you have first, General . . . the women or the silver plate?"

Mitch sat stubbornly on his temper. "I'll have the best whiskey in the house. And glasses for everybody."

He could have cut the silence up into building blocks. For a while the fat bartender with his dirty flour-sack apron didn't make a move. Then he brought a bottle up. With a piece of chalk, he marked the starting level. The bald-faced man let his eyes stay with Mitch, impudent, measuring eyes. Someone spoke at one of the tables.

"What the hell? It's free."

He approached, giving Mitch a flick of his eyes,

and then pouring a shot glass so full it ran over. He was under average height and built like a mesquite root, warped by saddle and stock into rough but utilitarian angles. There was a long, ragged cut on the back of his hand, which wore a black scab. Cartilage half closed his left eye. He wore a ducking jacket and the heaviest chaps Mitch had ever seen.

He took the whiskey at one flip of his wrist, bulged his cheeks, and shuddered. He spat it across the bar. "The man said good whiskey," he said.

The bartender glanced at Mitch. Mitch laid a gold piece on the bar. The bottle was removed and a bottle of A.J. Cutter No. 1 brought up.

"Now, we're gettin' some place," the brush hand said.

Mitch raised his glass. "Atkins is my name."

"Bat Fisher."

They set their glasses down. "Atkins," Fisher repeated. "Any kin of Joe Atkins, over at Big Spring?"

Mitch shook his head. "Dakota. My old man ran stock there before the war."

The silence rolled up again, like water over a dropped pebble. Fisher had a second drink. He said to nobody in particular: "Good liquor." No one took the hint, and in a moment he turned to the big fellow who had baited Mitch. "Clabe," he said, "you're standing on the brink of gettin' a drink . . . right between the eyes. I like noise when

I drink. I don't like bein' stared at. Drink your own liquor or the man's, but drink."

The man called Clabe remarked: "The liquor may he good, but the company ain't." He walked outside.

Mitch put down his glass. Fisher was there to refill it quickly. "Get pretty cold up in Dakota?" he asked.

Mitch got the idea. It was one against twelve. "Why," he said, "it gets right snappy along about Feb'uary. One reason I'm down here. I had a tip, too, that there's money to be made in cattle. Beef's on the way up, you know."

"That a fact?"

"Thirty a head at K.C. Now, if a man could buy them for ten in these parts . . ."

Fisher's grin was surprising and brief. "They go for two-fifty. After you ketch 'em."

"That's the hard part?"

"Been called hard." Fisher glanced at the vicious thorn scratch on his hand.

Mitch Atkins had a forlorn wish that he had never heard of Frijole. It had come to the point now where he must risk the money his father had left him in a cattle gamble, or start back up the trail. It had been a fool's trick to head south in the first place. But recollection of all the months on the trail kept him from deciding too quickly to start back.

The liquor warmed him a little, giving rise to a

false self-confidence. "I was thinking," he said, "that I might settle here. Heard of any land for sale?"

All over the room men were turning their heads to look at him. Silence came back to brood over the saloon like a buzzard. Bat Fisher gave him a curious look. "Ain't there enough room in Dakota?"

"Not enough cattle. They tell me Texas is overrun with them since the war."

In a way, Fisher's deep-pocketed eyes looked pitying. "Doc Barrows sells some land now and then," he said. "Happens he's in town today. You might ask him."

The barkeeper spoke up. "He's down at Widder Satterly's store. Courtin' or buyin', I don't know which. If he's courtin', he won't talk business."

Fisher finished his drink. "Walk down with you, if you like."

Mitch said: "Why, I'd sure . . ."

There was a commotion at the hitch rack. Hoofs struck a quick, scared tune on the hard earth, and a man's voice loosed the spine-stiffening sound Mitch had heard in dreams for five years—the Rebel yell of the Southern cavalryman. He heard a horse running, and the whiskey warmth in him cooled. He thought of his $5,000 in gold pieces scattered through the brasada as his pony ran.

They were laughing as he ran out.

The big hairless cowpuncher stood there twirling

a pigging string. Down the center of the road loped Mitch's horse, the reins tied to the horn. The Texan, Clabe, grinned. "That stud of yours shore is boogery, General. I just cleared my throat and he plumb took off."

Mitch didn't know what he was going to do, until he was within three feet of him. Clabe looked less sure and began to back away, his fists making vague feinting motions. Mitch hadn't time for a knock-down-and-drag-out. He brought his long Navy gun out of the holster. The blued steel flicked in a sidewise chop. Clabe was trying to pull his Colt when the gun struck him on the cheek bone. He stopped, swayed, fell forward against Mitch in a loose, hard bundle. Mitch side-stepped him.

Men were coming out the door now. Bat Fisher was first. Mitch snapped: "Which 'un's his horse?"

"Three-stockin'ed sorrel," Fisher said.

Mitch grabbed up the reins and mounted the pony. The sorrel tried to fight. Mitch didn't fool around. He let it feel the bit and at the same time spurred it heavily on the shoulders. When the horse endeavored to pitch, he pulled it off balance with one rein, spurring at the same time. The horse shook its head angrily. Mitch spurred again and let it have some slack. Outmaneuvered, the pony began to run. Mitch kept it in hand as they went across a dead chile field after his own horse.

The pony had reached the brush and plunged into a twisting aisle in the *huisache* tangles. Mitch heard it squeal and knew it had been raked by a thorn. He ducked low under a branch, lost his hat, and felt a long cactus barb rip his shoulder. Immediately a stinging ache pervaded his whole arm. He flipped Clabe's rope from the tie and tried to make a loop; the rope was short, but even so he didn't find room to swing it.

Ahead was his own horse, fighting the brush in panic. Another thorn found Mitch's cheek. The elbow of a chaparral branch slugged his knee. A kind of panic took hold of him. He had to get that horse, but the brush would slash his eyeballs out and cut him to ribbons before he ever did it.

He came into a hole in the brush and there stood the sorrel pony, head high, nostrils sucking air, limbs shivering. Mitch rode up beside it, talking. "Sho', now. Sho', boy." He changed horses. The saddlebags were still buckled close, thonged behind the saddle. He gave the Texan's horse a switch with his own coiled rope and watched it lope on into the brush.

II

Clabe was sitting on the dirt walk, his back against the saloon front. Somebody had brought him a glass of whiskey. He had a swelling on the side of his face and a bovine look in his eyes. Mitch dropped the reins of his horse over the rack, but this time took the precaution to shoulder the saddlebags.

Outwardly there was no change in the attitudes of the Texans, but Atkins knew Federal stock had risen a point. This, he perceived, was one of those towns where you established yourself only by getting proddy.

Atkins and Fisher walked down the street, moving past a Mexican *cantina*, boot and harness shop, and a gunsmith's. Beyond an open space was a larger building, square and solid and with a shed roof. Smoke from its chimney went straight up into the milky blue sky. There was no name on the store, but Fisher remarked: "That's the Widder Satterly's. Reckon we'll find Doc there."

"You work for him?" Mitch asked.

Bat shook his head. "All them boys in the saloon do. That's part of the Cross Anchor crowd. I work for Dewey Cain. Grapevine brand, over across Río Chico. I kind of drift up and down the creek seein' that the cattle don't leave any campfires burning."

A big, black-haired cowpuncher was sitting on the store porch, picking out a one-string tune on a guitar that wanted tuning. He wore a week's stubble on his jaw and his hair was down almost to his shoulders. He nodded gravely at Bat and kept on with the tune. His glance didn't miss so much as the Durham tag hanging from Mitch's shirt pocket when he got around to him. He spat across the guitar.

The Widow Satterly's store was gloomy and warm. The first thing Mitch Atkins noticed about it was the smell. It smelled like civilization. He got the full savor of it into his head; he closed his eyes, a sharp nostalgia choking him. Then his nose began hanging tags on the smells: coffee and ham and twists of tobacco, onions, dried red chiles, ironware. All at once he sensed a miracle. In and around all the other odors, twining like a gourd vine, wound the delicate fragrance of an Irish stew. Mitch felt like crying. He had eaten salt pork and hardtack for weeks.

Bat was making his way familiarly through the gloom. Mitch kept up with him. "Howdy, Widder," the brush-popper said. "Howdy, Doc."

Mitch's eyes found them. The widow sat on a crate by a square iron stove. Doc Barrows leaned back in a chair with his spurred heels resting on the fender.

The Widow Satterly said: "Hello, Bat. Did they finally neck you up and drag you out of the brush?"

There was some laconic banter, and then Barrows's voice, like a file scrape, inquired: "Who's your friend?"

Bat introduced Mitch. A second miracle was revealed to Mitch. The widow was not over twenty-two years old. Jenny Satterly had long, dark hair. She was a pert little trick with lively eyes and rich lips. She had a trim, bare-legged figure, full-breasted, and she carried herself well.

Barrows's grip was dry and cold as the clasp of a vise. Mitch saw in his face the sharp look of a horse trader. He was bald, with dark eye sockets and a black mustache sweeping up to bushy sideburns.

Bat said dryly: "Mitch wants to dicker for some land, Doc."

Mitch inhaled deeply. "First," he said, "I'd like to dicker for a bait of that stew, Missus Satterly. You put the price on it."

Jenny Satterly laughed. "Early in the day for supper, isn't it?"

"It's never too early when you're starvin'."

She brought a tin plate and spooned up a man's helping from the kettle bubbling on the stove. As he reached for it, a strange look came across her face. She was looking at his sleeve. "You were a sergeant?"

"Corporal."

"Your shirt's so faded it's hard to tell what color it was."

Mitch's jaw tightened. "Blue. I was in the Fifth U.S. Cavalry."

The woman straightened. She dumped the stew back in the pot. "They killed my husband at Gaines's Mill, Virginia," she said slowly.

Mitch, feeling the coldness of chagrin and shock, met her stare. "I'm sorry, ma'am. All we lost was a few dozen men, and the battle. I'm sorry anybody had to get killed, and that I lost a finger there myself, but I'm trying to forget about it."

Jenny sat down. "Did you come to talk to Doc about something?"

Mitch looked at the cowman. "I'm looking for land to buy. Bat thought you might be willing to let a little get away from you."

Barrows rocked back in the chair, tugging at a sideburn. "Well," he said, "I'm not trying to get rid of any. What do you want to do, raise sheep?"

The fury was rising in Mitch. He was used to a country where a straight question got you a straight answer, where you were friend until proved foe. He had taken more off these *Tejanos* in an hour than he had taken in all his life, at home. Keeping his temper was mainly a financial consideration. The idea was growing on him that, if there was any money to be made here, he would make it and get out.

He repeated to Barrows the yarn the cattle buyer in K.C. had told him. "It's my notion," he said, "to buy a parcel of land with cattle already on it. I'll hold it a year or two and take the cattle and the increase north."

"In blue uniforms?" Jenny inquired.

Mitch's big angular hands fastened on his knees. "Missus Satterly, the bugles stopped blowin' a year ago. Let's not try to wake them up. We all lost. I lost a finger and my old man. And you don't need to fret yourself about occupation troops taking over. They aren't bothering with any place as small as this."

296

The little nose went up. "Mister Atkins, if you don't like our town . . ."

Mitch turned his glance to Doc Barrows. "We're getting no place," he said. "If you've got anything to sell, let's talk about it. Otherwise, I'll get along."

Barrows sat back, rattled his spurs on the fender, placed the tips of his fingers together. His face acquired the pinched fox look of a money-lender's.

"I might be persuaded to part with my Río Chico pasture," he remarked.

It was Mitch's impression that Jenny snickered. He glanced at her, at Bat, and learned nothing.

"For a price, that is," Barrows said.

"Cattle on it?"

"Twenty-five hundred, range count. That means there ought to be three thousand, with the increase. You've been riding over the land for the last two hours. It's a triangle with the Chico for the western boundary, the Big Sam Road for the northern, and the Frijole Road, one you came in on, for the southern. All the land you'll want for a start."

"How much?"

Barrows chewed his tongue. "How much do you want to pay?"

"I'll be honest," Mitch said. "I've got four thousand. I can pay that much for the works."

Barrows closed his eyes and let pain twist his mouth down. "My God! I could sell the brush on it for firewood at a better price than that." He spat in the sandbox in which the stove sat. "Five."

Mitch shook his head slowly. He was thinking that if there were actually 2,500 cows on the land, Barrows was making the price too cheap. He supposed the joker was in what Bat Fisher had said: . . . *ketching them is the hard part.* If they were there, he decided, he could catch them. He hadn't started punching cows yesterday.

"Forty-two hundred," he said, "is the best I can do. With a guarantee that the cattle are there."

"Oh, they're there, all right! Isn't that right, Bat?"

"That's right."

"If I let it go for less than forty-five," Barrows summed up, "I'd be plumb crazy."

Mitch said: "Done! If Missus Satterly's got pen and paper . . ."

The deed was drawn up. A map went with it. A guarantee was appended that 2,500 cattle had been tallied at the last count. But Mitch's stomach was jumping when the money left his hands. He might never see that much again.

"You'll need help getting yourself squared off," Barrows speculated. "I'll give you the loan of one of my boys, if you want. You seen him when you came in. Moss Coker."

Mitch could hear Coker outside, picking at the untuned guitar and singing deep in his throat. "I'd appreciate it. Bat, I couldn't hire you away from Dewey Cain, could I?"

Bat's scarred, lumpy countenance grinned, but

he shook his head. "You'll find all the men you want. Doc'll probably unload some culls on you, and there's always plenty of Mexicans."

They started out, Barrows lingering to speak to Jenny. Mitch heard her laugh. "Doc, you behave!" His brows pulled in. *Damned old fool.* He was old enough to have played poker with her father. Pretty little thing, he thought; too bad she was so damned ornery.

III

With the crew of eleven men, Atkins set out for his ranch, a clearing in the jungle with corrals and a lean-to. He was paying the four Americans $8 a month, the Mexicans seven *pesos*. Everything about the cattle trade, as these brush-poppers understood it, was primitive. They carried nothing in the way of food but coffee, cornmeal, and salt. Coker explained they would kill a fat steer, render out the tallow, and dry the flesh into jerky. Tallow, salt, and cornmeal made fine cornbread. And there were *chiltipiquínes*—tiny wild chiles—if a man felt the need of spice.

For half a day they followed the road through thickets of black chaparral growing twenty feet, driving a little bunch of neck oxen before them. There was no grass to be seen; without sunlight, it was starved out. The brush made a thorny ceiling that filtered the cool February sunlight. Along the ground ran tough, tangled roots and mats of spined *guajilla*. Stout arms of larger bushes reached higher, twisted, gray, forbidding. Far as Mitch could tell, there was no way in God's world of riding a horse through those terrible thickets.

At dusk, they came to the headquarters. In a cleared, silent acre, brush corrals occupied half the ground. There was a lean-to cabin of weathered gray lumber. There was a well. And there was loneliness. Mitch stood there while the cow-punchers unsaddled; he heard the loneliness rustling in the thickets that locked them in, and in the marbled evening sky. When he wrapped himself in his blankets, he knew he would not stay long in Texas. You could learn to love an ugly woman, but never an ugly country. . . .

In the morning, Moss Coker explained how they worked. He was an indolent man with a face that reminded Mitch of the backside of a flitch of bacon—dark, greasy, and stubbled. But there was confidence in his movements, cockiness, almost, in the man's slow manner of speech.

"We gen'ally go out alone with six or eight *peales* . . . them short ropes the boys are splittin' up," Coker said. "You ketch your ox and leave him tied to a tree if he won't lead. Likely he won't. After you've used up all your *peales*, you come back for a neckin' ox. You bring 'em in one at a time."

There was extra harness in the lean-to. Mitch donned the enormous bull-hide chaps the rest used, and then pulled on a stiff ducking jacket.

He watched the men ride out, squeezing into the mouths of tiny trails he could hardly see.

He picked his own and put the pony into it. In fifteen minutes he had no idea where he was. He was lost in an ocean of twigs. His horse picked its way unenthusiastically through matted catclaw tangles that climbed to its shoulder. The taller trees had fallen behind, so that Mitch was able to see for a little distance ahead. Silence lay upon the jungle.

At noon he found a mossy water hole and stopped. He chewed some of the cornbread. It was poor eating. He tried one of the tiny wild chiles and decided he could do as well by putting lighted matches in his mouth.

About the middle of the afternoon he suddenly discerned the flash of horns in a thicket. Mitch shook out his catch rope. He was within fifty feet of the longhorn when the great horned head went up. Mitch spurred and got the jump. He busted through the screen of handsome green leaves on which the cow had been feeding, yelling as he made the throw. The rope caught on a branch and fell short. Mitch swore and reeled it in. The cow was running now, a dappled red monstrosity with hip bones you could have hung your hat on. It went lunging through the brush with Mitch right behind it.

A thorn ripped his forearm. The pain of it was a fire that went clear to his shoulder. But he kept going, the loop ready. They burst into a clearing about the size of a parlor. Mitch, this time, roped up, catching the hind hoofs cleanly. The longhorn went down. It was up again instantly and turning to fight. Mitch swung the horse, yanking the steer's legs from under it and spilling it once more. He lit down and made his tie. He found a stout chaparral and dragged the brute over to it. He tied it with about six inches of slack.

He saw no more cattle that day.

Toward night his thorned arm grew inflamed. He washed it. The edges of the cut were puffy. For an hour he could not sleep because of the throbbing. In the morning he could barely use his arm. He knew there would be no more roping for him until his arm grew better, so he started back to camp for a neck ox.

Moss Coker was there. One steer stood in the corral and the remains of a second, butchered and cut into strips, were stretched over a slow fire the *caporal* was tending, squatted on his heels. Mitch stared at the single animal in the enclosure. "Is that all we've picked up in thirty-six hours?"

"Kinda slow work," Coker said. "What's the matter with your arm?"

"Thorn cut."

Coker gathered chunks of prickly pear and sliced them up for a poultice. "Be all right," he said.

But no poultice could ease Mitch's discouragement. He rode back for his steer and did not return with it until the following noon. Two and one half days. There were now six cows in the corral. Two a day. 1,250 days to finish—four years. He said to Coker, half angrily: "Sure you've trapped cattle before?"

Coker's smile was bland. "Some days you may catch ten or twenty. It averages out."

For two weeks they worked out of the main camp. They now had thirty-six cattle. One day Mitch worked as far west as the Río Chico, a sandy little stream with a few inches of water in it. He watered his horse and filled his own canteen. As he remounted, he heard movement across the stream. He rode behind a thicket. The creek was his boundary, but, if the cow wanted to cross and wore no other brand, it was about due for a session with a branding iron.

The brush parted. It was a horse. Atop the horse sat Bat Fisher.

Mitch rode out, delighted to see the little limb splitter. If he had a friend in the whole of Texas, it was Bat. They squatted on their heels and talked, smoking. Bat squinted at the Dakotan's scratched and sunburned face.

"Lookin' good," he remarked. "Time you get an eye gouged out, they'll accept you as a Texan."

Mitch jammed the cigarette butt into the sand.

"It's slow death in there, Bat. We had thirty-six critters when I was in yesterday. You can't make money that way."

Bat squinted. "You're the fourth man that's bought the Río Chico pasture from Doc."

Shock was Mitch's first reaction. "You mean there's no cattle here but a few strays? Why didn't you tell me?"

Bat pulled a handful of parched corn from his pocket and began to chew on it. "You didn't ask me. Anyhow, the cattle are there, all right. Only you've got to be around when they are."

"But if Coker's telling me straight about catching them . . ."

"He's telling you straight, as far as he goes. He's Barrows's man, ain't he?" He got up, dipped water from the stream with his hat, drank, and turned to his horse.

"How am I going to get them, then?" Mitch demanded. "Bear traps?"

Bat mounted. He popped corn with his teeth. "If I was working that pasture, I'd look for the best grassed spots. You won't find the cattle there, but, if you hang around, maybe a few hundred will come out of their hiding places over on my side of the river at night and go to browsin'. Cattle aren't dumb, Mitch. That pasture of yours has been worked over so many times the cows have put the Indian sign on it."

Mitch stuck around until dark. About eight

304

o'clock in the evening the longhorns began to come. By pairs, in bunches, cows, steers, and bulls. Atkins got a little excited. Cattle! He'd have a herd to take out when he got finished. Doc Barrows had worked the army game on him. He'd sold the land and cattle for half their value, figuring to buy them back for a train ticket and a pat on the back. This time his buyer was going to stick.

Moss Coker didn't think much of the idea. "Them cattle are Dewey Cain's," he argued. "You're going to run into trouble down there."

"If we find any Grapevine animals or calves nursin' on Grapevine mammies," Mitch said, "we'll turn 'em back. But this is a maverickin' crew and we're going to maverick."

He spent two days rigging up a stout brush corral at the narrow end of a grassy pasture. He had counted seventy-five animals on it the other night. Mitch laid his trap with care, making the men use gloves so that they would leave man smell on nothing. He placed the cowpunchers where he wanted them and gave orders not to move until he gave the signal.

Night invaded the brasada, chilling the air, robbing them of vision and throwing them onto their hearing alone. A frosty rind of moon ascended. From Mitch's point, the pasture was a dark vista of rough ground walled in by brush. What was ahead might be tough. These critters went to fighting when they felt a rope.

He did not hear them, but suddenly he knew they were coming. Against the dark sky before him was silhouetted a darker shape. The bull's head was raised, the vast sweep of the whetted horns glinting faintly. He ducked his head two or three times, struck the earth with one hoof. Then he walked out and began to graze.

The others followed him. They came with no more warning than a creeping armadillo. They simply appeared. Gaunt, cumbered with five- and six-foot horns, they moved as silently as ghosts.

Mitch let fifteen minutes pass. The cattle were all over the clearing. He gave a short, sharp whistle through his teeth. Simultaneously he plunged from the brush to lope up behind the herd. He heard the others coming in, forcing the cattle into the bottleneck at the end of the pasture. Mitch's heart bounded. It was going right. They were leading fairly into the trap.

A horseman spurred hard from the brush near the gate, swinging a rope. Then he faltered, seeing his blunder, and pulled back. But the herd had exploded.

Longhorns split the brush this way and that, vanishing like smoke. The *vaqueros* tried to head them back, but a longhorn on the prod is not a thing to bulldoze. It was over. Someone's blunder had cost them a night's work.

Mitch sat there with a ball of lead in his stomach. He saw the rider who had wrecked the play coming at a jog up the pasture. He recognized the big, blocky shape of Moss Coker. Something Bat Fisher had said about Coker's working for Barrows hit Atkins suddenly.

Coker stopped and fumbled with a sack of tobacco. "Damn' pony jumped out from under me," he grumbled. "We'll try it again another time."

The other men were coming in. They heard Mitch Atkins snap: "It looked to me like he'd been spurred."

Coker's eyes, dark patches of shadow, might have been laughing. Something in his voice was. "Now, why would I do that?"

"Because you've been working against me ever since we came out here. You're Barrows's insurance policy, to see that I botch it up and sell the land back to him. Get off your horse."

Mitch dismounted, but Coker still sat there, sounding pained. "You're tired, Mitch. You know that ain't true."

"Tired of you, yes. Get off that horse, you tick-infested Texan slob."

Coker made a noise in his throat. He got down, in his deliberate way. Mitch walked straight into him. Coker came to life, ducking the first punch the Dakotan threw and trying to close with him. The blunt edge of Mitch's hand came against his neck. It brought a grunt from Coker. He went back. Mitch slammed him on the side of the head. He jabbed him in the belly.

307

Moss Coker was on his knees. He was hurt, but active enough to have an idea left. His right hand moved; the moon struck a silver spark from something at his side. Mitch's boot swung in. The gun popped out of Coker's hand, and Mitch stepped in to slug the downed man repeatedly in the face, letting his fists swing from his shoulders.

Coker made grunting sounds and tried to cover his face. Fury had taken control of Mitch. He wasn't hitting Coker. He was striking out at the whole damned business, at Southern stubbornness, at profiteering, at failure.

With his whole attention focused on Moss Coker, he didn't see the men coming in on him. The Mexican cowpunchers stood around, watching stolidly; the Americans, Coker's *compadres*, had their own ideas about how the fight should finish. The gun barrel took Mitch alongside the ear. For Mitch, it was like a lamp snuffed out. Blackness was sudden and complete. He was not even conscious of falling.

IV

Consciousness was so involved with pain that he had no great desire to awake. Iron thumbs prodded his skull. A pressure seemed trying to escape through his eye sockets. Mitch groaned and stirred. A man said softly: "*¿Ya'sta 'ueno?*"

One of his Mexicans offered a bottle. Mitch nearly finished the mescal. It closed the door a little on the pain. "What happened?"

The Mexican, Ysidoro, made a chopping motion with his fist. "*Como eso*. From behind you, *patrón*."

Mitch lay on his back, staring at the black night sky. The stars up there blinked back at him. "Well, what next?" he asked. "Think we'll ever get a cow across the river again?"

Ysidoro poked at the ground with a stick. "Maybe not at these pasture. Other one, *sí*. Tomorrow night."

"Was it all a stall, the way we were working?"

"Is like that we clean out a pasture . . . *uno por uno*. Is like these we make the big rodeo. Or with decoys." He said confidently: "We get them all, *poco tiempo*. Brand them, ron them away from the river. Is all right." He dragged saddle and blanket off his pony and stretched out.

Mitch caught a little of his confidence. He began to see a plan. The pawns were out of the way now and a few of the bigger pieces were coming into play. One of the controlling pieces was Doc Barrows's intention to move him out. The piece that was going to block it was Mitch's intention to stay. Before he left Texas, he'd have a herd of 2,500 cows under his brand, and all the mavericks he could pick up.

They were in the brush a month. Mitch slapped his Currycomb brand on 1,800 animals and knew where the rest were. Coker had kept them out of his way during the cow hunt. Mitch still hated the brush, but he feared it less. He was learning the tricks that made life endurable in the brasada.

On a windy March day he rode into Frijole.

Outside of town a dozen *vaqueros* ranged slowly about a herd of several hundred Grapevine cattle. Mitch saw a number of horses before the Jeb Stuart Bar. It was prudence, rather than cowardice, that for the moment caused him to avoid it. He was hoping to run into Moss Coker or any of his other recent "helpers", but not with twelve or fifteen men against him.

He walked into the big fragrant gloominess of the Widow Satterly's. Again he tasted the tang of civilization, and all the nostalgia he had locked out of his heart returned in a rush. And he would be damned if the widow wasn't cooking Irish stew again!

He found Jenny in back. She was occupied with a bucket of water and a broom; with these, she was settling the dust on the dirt floor. She paused, leaning with both hands on the broom. Her hair was caught up in a bandanna, Creole fashion, and Mitch irrationally thought of Doc Barrows trying to win a girl like this. A tough old rooster like him, courting a young and pretty . . . he caught himself up short. Put any kind of a face on it you liked, it was still a Texan.

"Hello, Dakota," she said. "I hear you're making out fine."

Mitch snapped out the blade of his pocket knife and leaned over the stew, sniffing it. "Doing all right. Eighteen hundred ears lopped off to date."

Her eyes opened. "But Moss said . . ."

"Moss didn't stay around long enough." Mitch speared a chunk of beef and blew on it. The fragrance was overpowering.

Jenny marched up. "Don't be picking around in that stew, cowboy."

Mitch held it behind him. "Knife's clean," he said.

She hesitated. For the first time he had a good look at her eyes. They were gray, with a mist of violet. He let his glance go on down and the smoothness of her throat and breast was something to make his collar tight. Color tinged her cheeks. She turned quickly away. "You might at least use a plate." She took a tin plate from a cupboard and banged it down. She put out light bread.

Mitch sat down and began to eat. He drew a long sigh. "Missus Satterly, with grub like this in me I could even get sentimental about you."

"That's nice." The smile crept up on her; she snuffed it out.

Mitch sopped bread in the luscious chile-spiced

gravy. "How long were you married before your husband left, ma'am?"

"A week. I don't see that . . ."

"You were fourteen then, I reckon."

"Sixteen. Why?"

"You ought to be about done grieving then. I don't know why you don't quit grieving over the late lamented Confederate States, too."

Her lips pinched. "I don't care to discuss it," she said directly. Then: "You haven't seen a good-for-nothing wagoner out there in the brush, have you? I've got a load of doin's coming in, a month overdue. Sometimes the 'skinners run into trouble. He ought to be coming along the Río Chico Road any day."

"Haven't seen him. I'll look out, though." Four men entered the store. Mitch recognized Bat Fisher and Clabe Lubbock, the man who'd boogered his horse that first day. With a wry twist of satisfaction he also knew the lean, high-shouldered shape of Doc Barrows. The fourth man he did not know.

They came to stand by the fire, Barrows wringing his hard brown hands above the stove. With his small, leathery head and deep-set eyes, he reminded Mitch of an ill-favored bird of prey. "Well," he asked Mitch, "how's the cattle game?" He dug Clabe in the ribs.

Mitch looked soberly at Bat and found the sparkle in the faded blue eyes. "Why, I can't kick. We stand eighteen hundred tallied in."

He saw Barrows's Adam's apple jump. "Eighteen . . . but Moss said you were havin' trouble branding any at all. Fact," he said, "I was thinking I might take that land off your hands. I reckon it wasn't fair to let a green hand loose in that brush."

If there was such a thing as controlled panic, that was what Mitch saw in the black eyes.

"This is going to be my home," Atkins said. "I figure it was dirt cheap."

Clabe cleared his throat. "Hope you ain't branding any of those river jumpers Moss told us about."

"For your sake," the stranger said, "I hope so, too. They happen to be mine."

This man, Mitch realized now, was Dewey Cain, Bat's boss, owner of the Grapevine brand. Cain was a large man with frowning brows and a cutaway beard that exposed his mouth and chin. He had a strong nose, eyes the color of old lead.

"I'm branding everything that doesn't wear a brand or earmark," Mitch told him.

Cain had a big platform voice. "You're ambushing animals that cross the river at night!" he declared.

An idea came to Mitch. "If I am," he said, "you'll have to blame Bat. He tipped me off that a lot of my stuff was hiding out on your side of the river."

Bat's face was completely blank. Cain gave him a steady, punishing look. He said: "What about that, Fisher?"

Blood congested Bat's face. The glance he put on Mitch was dark with fury. "I . . . I just happened to mention that sometimes cows will do a stunt like that. I guess he took the idea from there."

Dewey Cain said: "Draw your time."

Fisher went over and stood in the door, looking into the windy winter sunlight.

Doc Barrows broke the stiff hush. "Mitch, Mitch! I wonder if you know what you're doing? This is a man's game. Cattle stealing is pretty serious business, you know. Now, let's be frank with each other. You know you'll never make out as a brush rancher. On the other hand, I was wrong in letting you try. I'll give back all your money but five hundred dollars."

Mitch was staggered. He had an impulse to grab the offer and get out. On the other hand, he was curious to know why Barrows was so anxious to get rid of him. Maybe there were 5,000 or 6,000 cattle out there, which he had thought were perfectly safe. Maybe . . . but guesses were cheap.

Dewey Cain put an iron glance on him and there was sweat on Barrows's bald forehead. Clabe Lubbock's mouth hung open. Mitch had the impression that he was in the midst of a very important moment.

"I guess not," he said. "Missus Satterly, I'm beholdin' to you for the stew. As the Book says . . . 'I have not eaten better mulligan, no, not in all Texas.'"

Jenny gave him another smile.

Mitch would have left. Dewey Cain's hand arrested him. "Don't be a damned Yankee fool!" he shouted. "Take it while you can get it. I'll put up the other five. It's worth it just to rid the country of Yankees."

Mitch smiled. "*Adiós*, Mister Cain. *Adiós*, Mister Barrows. See you around."

He went out, with Bat right behind him. Bat had his fist cocked, ready for war. Mitch, grinning, caught him by the wrists. "Easy does it. How much salary did I talk you out of?"

"Ten a month . . . best pay in Bastrop County. And I'll have a year's pay out of your hide."

"I'll give you fifteen. I still need a good *caporal*."

Bat hesitated. "Fifteen! Dollars or pesos?"

"Dollars. You don't want to work for an outfit like that, anyway."

Bat wiped his nose. He began to grin. "At fifteen, maybe I don't. If you'll throw in coffee on the chuck list, I might be your man."

"Arbuckle," Mitch agreed. "But we'll seal it with something stronger than coffee."

V

That was how Bat Fisher came to the Currycomb. It was the start of real cow work in the wilderness. Bat's way was to keep about a jump ahead of a longhorn. If a critter wanted fight, he gave it fight. He would fairground it or tail it over, Mexican style. They went down like bulls; they came up like oxen. He knew how to smoke them out of their hiding places. He could figure a month ahead about where any given bunch would be.

It wasn't the end of trouble, though.

Mitch had been throwing the oldest and poorest of the cattle into a day herd at the headquarters place. They would pull a couple of dollars apiece at Laredo, over on the Big River. One night he spoke to Bat about them as they had a last cup of coffee, sitting cross-legged beside a rosy puddle of coals in the darkness.

"How about sending Ysidoro over with the day herd tomorrow?"

"Might as well. We're about cleaned up here."

"Hits Doc right between the eyes that I'm sticking, doesn't it?" Mitch chuckled.

Bat threw his coffee grounds in the fire. The liquid sputtered and steam ascended. "Dewey Cain, too." He frowned. "They never used to pull together before. I'm wondering how come. And how come them to be in such a tizzy to get you out? You'd think they were working against a deadline."

Mitch raised his cup. One instant he was almost tasting the coffee, and the next he was feeling an ache in his finger and realizing the cup was gone. The flat *slap* of the bullet was a profane sound. The cup lay between Mitch Atkins and Bat Fisher with a bullet hole drilled dead center.

Bat went over backward, yelling. Mitch didn't know how he got out of the firelight, but an instant later he found himself lying flat on the ground with his Navy gun in his hand. There were querulous shouts from the Mexicans.

A new sound rolled toward them from the corrals—the rumble of stampeding hoofs. The gate had been opened. Across the clearing, rifle fire punctured the darkness. The broken rhythm of the shots swelled briefly and died. Mitch was on his feet again, stumbling to the horse corral. Ysidoro and another man were already there, gliding into the press of ponies. Mitch snatched a bridle from the corral bar and went after a horse. No time to fool with a saddle. He caught a pony and loped out of the corral.

The first thing he saw was that the attack, paradoxically, had not been entirely successful because it had been such a complete surprise. The cattle weren't streaming out the gate as they should have been; they were milling. Only a couple of dozen were loose, and these, Mitch knew, were as hopeless of capture as moths. The Mexicans took over the gap. One of them jumped down and secured a chaparral bar; he stood there awaiting a chance to get it in place without being horned.

Firing had ceased from the thicket behind the corrals. Mitch, carbine squeezed against his side, quartered around the brush enclosures. Distantly he made out the crashing of brush. Whoever the men had been, there would be no tracking them. He was about to ride back when a horse snorted so close that his own pony jumped sideways. The jump was what saved him.

The sound was a solid impact against his ears and eyes. The flash was an orange explosion that blinded him. It didn't blind him too much to fire back. He fired the carbine once and pulled his Colt. He snapped off two shots in the echoes of the first. He threw himself out of the saddle.

It was quiet then. Quiet until a man let his breath out windily and slumped through the brush to the ground. He lay there in the darkness with the groping sounds of a man bedding down for a long sleep.

It was Clabe Lubbock who they dragged out later.

"If this was Dakota," Bat said, next morning, "I reckon you could freight Clabe into town and claim you were being persecuted." Ysidoro was tamping the earth with a shovel. They had buried the Cross Anchor cowboy where they'd found him.

"What do you do about it in Texas?" Mitch asked him.

"Put out pickets next time you've got a day herd. Yes, sir," Bat speculated, "Doc shore is in a hurry to move you out."

Later, Mitch rode over to Río Chico Road. They hadn't yet laid a loop on the herd Moss Coker had blown up; Mitch had an idea they might be drifting back by now. As he was jogging along the road, he heard a horse racking up behind him. He took the precaution of pulling into a stand of *quebradora*. But it was Jenny Satterly who rode past him. Mitch flagged her.

She turned quickly. He noticed that there was a light saddle gun under her arm. When she saw Mitch, she smiled, and she didn't try to swallow it this time. "I didn't hope to see you, Mitch," the woman said.

"Still looking for that 'skinner?" Mitch asked.

She nodded, frowning. In daylight, her hair was deep sorrel, full of life. "He's six weeks overdue now. He was bringing a thousand dollars' worth of supplies to me . . . paid for in advance. I suppose it's foolish even to look. But a loss like that will hurt."

"I'll ride up with you," he said.

They jogged along for several miles. The road was hardly wide enough for two horses. On its dry surface they found no wheel tracks. They got to talking, and the barrier between them was a low wall a man could almost step across. Their conversation became so brisk that Mitch discovered with a start that the trail now showed two faint wagon tracks.

"But we didn't pass it," Jenny said.

"Not on the road. He may have pulled off. The tracks are old, too."

They rode back. Mitch discovered where the wagon had pulled into the brush on the west side of the road, heading for the river. He rode ahead of Jenny; his nose found the muleskinner before his eyes did. Jenny saw him stop, his glance turning down. "What is it, Mitch?"

"Better go back," Atkins said. He had not seen a completely ripe corpse since the wilderness. This was one. The man's body was bursting its clothes. His legs stuck out stiffly. Buzzards and coyotes had dined richly on him, but the caved-in skull told plainly that he hadn't died of a heart attack.

Beyond the body, Mitch saw a heap of goods covered with a tarpaulin. The wagon was gone. He wheeled his pony. "This is where it happened. The stuff's there, but the wagon's gone." His mind was working fast, trying to figure the thing out.

Jenny saw the body and her face blanched. She let him turn her horse. They rode along a while. Finally she said weakly: "Mexicans. Mexicans did it."

"Why Mexicans?"

"They're whipping up another revolution down in Tamaulipas. They raid a long way from home when they're looking for arms or provisions."

"But they didn't take anything but the wagon."

Jenny did not understand that, but she adhered to the conviction that *revolucionarios* had murdered the muleskinner. "I'm going to get my own wagon and load that stuff in before they come back after it."

"And what if they catch you at it?"

"They won't."

Mitch could not dissuade her.

Next morning he returned with Bat Fisher to the spot where the dead muleskinner lay. They performed the unsavory rite of burying him. Feeling a need for solemnization of the ceremony, Bat threw a handful of dirt on the mound. "Ashes to ashes, dust to dust . . . see you in hell, pardner."

Mitch stood regarding the wagon tracks that trailed on down to the creek. "I'm going to find out where that wagon went, Bat," he said slowly. "It's heading for your old stamping ground. Funny you didn't see it."

"You could hide forty elephants in that brush for a year," Fisher told him. "Your curiosity is going to lose you a pair of ears someday, Dakota."

"I'm going to have a look, anyway."

When he rode across the sandy creek, Bat was

with him. The wagon trail made tracking easy. For an hour they followed it, into a thicket even Bat had never visited. Here the chaparral grew twenty feet high; the grass below was starved out. The air itself was stifling. The encroaching wall of brush gave up a sound—the measured *crack* of someone breaking wood for a fire. They looked at each other. Together they dismounted. Bat reached down to jam his big Amozoc spurs with twigs. They went ahead, slowly and steadily.

Through a broken lattice of tortured branches they had a patchwork view of a camp. For this country, it was a big camp. Brush had been cut back to make room for a dozen wagons and a rope corral of oxen. The wagons were all loaded and another pile of goods was stacked nearby. Four or five men were in sight. Mitch edged closer. He heard one speak.

"What is it, the Twenty-Fifth?"

"Fifth or Sixth," the man breaking the kindling said.

"We ought to be getting word pretty soon." The man sat up; he had been lounging on the back of one of the tarp-covered wagons. It was Moss Coker. "Maybe I'm getting old, Baldy. But I don't cotton to living next door to a dozen wagon loads of black powder."

"If you'd taken care of that pilgrim right, we'd have got out by now."

"Yeah," Coker said. "It looks like we'll have to

fit him out for an ascension one of these days. Damned pig-headed Yank."

Bat was tugging at his arm. Mitch let himself be drawn back. Bat's knobby brown face was perspiring. They returned to the horses.

"Powder, shot, and rifles," Bat said. "I been working for a gun-runner for two years and never knew it."

Mitch repeated Jenny's words. "There's revolution brewing in Tamaulipas. Cain's selling them guns."

"Let's cut a notch in Doc Barrows's ears, too," Bat declared. "Wasn't that his ramrod setting on the wagon? They're in it together. Know why they're burning up to ease you out? Because the wagons have to cross your land to get to the border. When it was Doc's land, that was all right. He figured he'd have it back by now. But you're poison."

Mitch's mind was reaching ahead. He recalled that, although all the wagons were loaded, there still remained much in the stockpile. Wagons, in this section, were at a premium. That was why Jenny's man had been killed. The significance of it came home with a jolt.

"Bat," he said, "she's coming out here to load that stuff of hers in. If they spot her, she may get the same the 'skinner got. They're starving for wagons. And they'll be afraid she'd find their camp and turn them in."

Fisher looked concerned. "Reckon we ought to stop her?"

"What do you think?" Mitch snapped. "She was going to start yesterday afternoon. She might have been out here last night. She might . . ."

"Take it easy," Bat said. "Bet she ain't even started yet." He looked too sunk to mean it.

VI

They cut for Frijole by a lost trail that stripped most of the hide from them but brought them to town two hours earlier than the Río Chico Road. The Widow Satterly's store was in charge of a Mexican youth. Jenny had left that morning.

"*Señor* Barrows loan her a man for 'skeener, *sí*," the kid said.

Mitch received the news with a twist at his heart. He had an impulse to start running after her. So he put himself calmly to the job of rolling a cigarette; he spilled the tobacco and lost half his papers. He tried to think, but his thoughts were falling all over themselves.

Bat said: "You going to stand there making cigarettes all day, or are we going after them?"

"Maybe we missed them on the road," Mitch said. "We took that short-cut."

"Suppose we find out."

• • •

The sun was three hours above the horizon and shone in their faces as they rode. Mitch found himself relying on the Texan for all decisions. All he could do was tag along and worry, building up reasons why nothing could have happened to Jenny, and seeing logic push them over.

Bat reined in, pointing. "Here's where they left the road. Heading straight for their camp."

He swung into the aisle through the brush, but not soon enough to keep Mitch from seeing the footprints in the road. There had been trouble here. Boots had scuffed and a pair of smaller boots had started off at a straight line from the wagons and been overtaken. At the edge of the road lay a scrap of cloth, a red hair ribbon.

They shoved on into the thicket. They had lost the sun now, but its progress was apparent in a ruddy light that stained the sky above them. Before long Fisher was spurring his horse faster than was necessary, racing the night. It went like this, it seemed, for an eternity. Mitch ducked branches, tried to peer ahead, tried to think and tried not to think. His horse bumped into the Texan's.

Mitch knew what that meant. He dismounted, pulling his saddle gun, and found the cowboy already moving ahead. The gray smoke of evening drifted through the brasada, but in the distance a small fire winked, and on the motionless air were faint sounds.

They came to the spot where they had stopped before.

The wagons had been shifted; now they stretched in a long line into the brush. Oxen were being yoked in the rope corral. The last wagon in the caravan was Jenny's, for it was being hastily loaded with crates from the stockpiles in the clearing. They could not see Jenny.

Moss Coker was bossing the loading. "Step it up, step it up! We're leaving tonight, not next week."

Muleskinners were checking their loads. Coker walked along, tugging at ropes. "Take up this slack. Don't jam them kegs in thataway . . . with powder, you never know." He was standing beside a wagon half way up the line.

Dewey Cain and Doc Barrows strolled into view. They had been standing near a small campfire, drinking final cups of coffee. They stopped near Mitch and Bat, and, as usual, they were haggling.

"We could have done without the extra wagon easier than toting her along," Cain's politician's voice maintained.

"Yes, and have her discover the camp before you got under way," Barrows argued. "I did what I had to. You can let her out when it's safe. She can't prove anything, after we get rid of the stuff."

They moved on down the line. Cain dropped his voice, but his last remark was audible. "I'll let her out . . . after we get to Mexico," he said. "She knows enough that we can't afford to have her come back. I'll see to that, too."

Mitch rose. Bat's hand gripped his forearm. They crouched there another five minutes. The rear wagon was being covered with a tarpaulin and ropes were slung across the load. A few drivers had already taken their places. The man Moss Coker had instructed to repack his powder kegs was still working with them. As he watched him, Mitch knew he was their one chance. He whispered: "Cover me. I'm going out."

He moved cautiously until he was near the wagons. Then he walked straight to the powder wagons and made himself busy with ropes. He stood back and rolled a cigarette. He lighted it, and again went to inspecting the loading of the wagon. His hand tugged a corner of the canvas loose and he reached inside. His fingers found the rough oaken top of a keg; they explored it nervously. The bung was jammed home stoutly. He pulled out his knife.

The muleskinner came around the wagon. Mitch palmed the cigarette. He confronted the man irritably. "That's not the way! My God, it's just like Moss says . . . you've only got one chance with powder. Look here!"

He went to the back, with the scowling driver following silently. Mitch threw up the fly and groped among the barrels. "Still too close, see? You've got them jammed forward at the front so they're almost touching. Ever they get to rubbing, you've got a chance of sparks. Haul these rear ones back to the tailgate. I'll help you."

He waited until the man had gone forward to shove the second line of barrels back. The blade of the knife snapped out. He jammed it into a bung and began to work it back and forth. After a moment it came out.

Now he turned and stared at the campfire. He could see Jenny, hunched beside it, hands and feet tied. Doc Barrows stood gloomily behind her. Cain was kicking dirt on the fire. A swamper went by the fire with a yoke of oxen.

Mitch reached under the canvas and dropped the cigarette.

He walked fast, moving up the line to the second wagon ahead. Then he heard the powder—it was like a faint moan, rising, gathering force, becoming a scream as the pent gases searched for a seam. A section of the canvas burst into flames and a spout of crimson *hissed* through the hole. There was a muffled explosion as the keg burst.

Men were shouting. Screaming was a better word. They were yelling at one another to yank the burning kegs out, but at the same time they were all heading away from the wagon. All but Barrows and Cain. They were running toward the powder wagon with some mad idea, perhaps, of hauling it away from the others.

Mitch ducked through the line and walked toward them. It was Barrows who recognized him. Doc made a choked sound. He snapped up his carbine. Mitch was conscious of Cain's throwing himself to the ground, his gun flashing in the firelight. He put a shot into the Cross Anchor boss. Barrows shuffled backward uncertainly and sagged to his knees. He hunched forward with his face in the dirt.

The bore of Cain's gun was on Mitch, but he didn't fire. Atkins swerved his Colt. Then he saw Cain relaxing soddenly on the ground. At the same instant he heard a rifle crack in the brush. Bat had covered him.

Mitch ran to Jenny. Behind him, the explosions began.

One after another the kegs, their staves sprung by the first jolt, took fire. A series of explosions shook the ground. Flame mushroomed above the first wagon. It was inevitable that the other wagons would catch fire. The arms wagons smoked and crackled. The powder wagons went up magnificently, throwing their débris hundreds of feet.

In the ruddy wash of the fires, Mitch saw Jenny crying. He had her in his arms, then. He ran down the border of the clearing, cut across, and found the screened corridor that led to the horses. The face of terror hovered over the freight camp. Men were dying in the explosions; oxen were stampeding over the teamsters, sprinting for the brush. Here in the brasada wilderness, Doc Barrows and Dewey Cain had found the end of the contraband trail.

They reached Frijole an hour before midnight. Jenny had been too shocked to say much on the way in. Bat took the horses around to the stable and she and Mitch went into the store. The only light in it was the warm, flickering redness of the stove. Jenny took his arm.

"We've been terrible to you, Mitch. You're worth ten of any of us, and we've snubbed you and tried to run you out. Now I suppose you'll take your cattle and leave."

For a change, Mitch liked holding the reins. "Matter of fact," he said, "I'll probably be around a couple of years yet. Then I'm going to trail north with every cow I can get my brand on. I'll make enough to buy a ranch in a country where you don't have to wear cactus poultices three days out of the week. Say along the Red."

"I . . . I think I'd like a country like that, too," Jenny said. "It gets lonesome down here, sometimes."

"Maybe I can fit you in somewhere," Mitch said easily.

Jenny turned and let her arms go around his neck. "Take me with you, Mitch. Frijole will just be a cow camp after you leave."

"If you're done grieving, Missus Satterly," Mitch told her, "I'd be proud to have you come along."

Jenny reached up and took him by the ears. She pulled his head down, and from the warm sweetness of her lips Mitch judged that the Widow Satterly had finally put grieving behind her.

About the Author

Frank Bonham in a career that spanned five decades achieved excellence as a noted author of young adult fiction and detective and mystery fiction, as well as making significant contributions to Western fiction. By 1941 his fiction was already headlining Street and Smith's *Western Story* and by the end of the decade his Western novels were being serialized in *The Saturday Evening Post*. His first Western, *Lost Stage Valley* (1948), was purchased as the basis for the motion picture, *Stage to Tucson* (Columbia, 1951) with Rod Cameron as Grif Holbrook and Sally Eilers as Annie Benson. "I have tried to avoid," Bonham once confessed, "the conventional cowboy story, but I think it was probably a mistake. That is like trying to avoid crime in writing a mystery book. I just happened to be more interested in stagecoaching, mining, railroading. . . ." Yet, notwithstanding, it is precisely the interesting—and by comparison with the majority of Western novels—exotic backgrounds of Bonham's novels that give them an added dimension. He was highly knowledgeable in the technical aspects of transportation and communication in the 19th-Century American West. In introducing these backgrounds into his narratives, especially when combined with his firm grasp of idiomatic Spanish spoken by many of his Mexican characters, his stories and novels are elevated to a higher plane in which the historical sense of the period is always very much in the forefront. This historical aspect of his Western fiction early drew accolades from reviewers so that on one occasion the *Long Beach Press Telegram* predicted that "when the time comes to find an author who can best fill the gap in Western fiction left by Ernest Haycox, it may be that Frank Bonham will serve well." Among his best Western novels are *Snaketrack* (1952), *Night Raid* (1954), *The Feud at Spanish Ford* (1954), and *Last Stage West* (1959).

About the Editor

Bill Pronzini was born in Petaluma, California. His earliest Western fiction was published under his own name and a variety of pseudonyms in *Zane Grey Western Magazine.* Among his most notable Western novels are *Starvation Camp* (1984) and *Firewind* (1989). He is also the editor of numerous Western story collections, including *Under the Burning Sun: Western Stories* by H.A. DeRosso, *Renegade River: Western Stories* by Giff Cheshire, and *Tracks in the Sand* by H.A. DeRosso. His own Western story collection, *All the Long Years*, was followed by *Burgade's Crossing, Quincannon's Game* , and *Coyote and Quarter-Moon.*

Additional Copyright Information

"The Texan Buys a Gun-Bride" first appeared in *Action Stories* (Summer, 49). Copyright © 1949 by Fiction House, Inc. Copyright © renewed 1977 by Frank Bonham. Copyright © 2007 by Gloria Bonham for restored material.

"Whiskey Creek Stampeders" first appeared in *Dime Western* (1/49). Copyright © 1949 by Popular Publications, Inc. Copyright © renewed 1977 by Frank Bonham. Copyright © 2007 by Gloria Bonham for restored material.

"Bonanza Railroad" first appeared in *Blue Book* (12/45). Copyright © 1945 by McCall Corporation. Copyright © renewed 1973 by Frank Bonham. Copyright © 2007 by Gloria Bonham for restored material.

"Cowman-on-the-Spot" first appeared in *Dime Western* (5/47). Copyright © 1947 by Popular Publications, Inc. Copyright © renewed 1975 by Frank Bonham. Copyright © 2007 by Gloria Bonham for restored material.

"Dakota Man" first appeared under the title "Head Back North, Dakota Man!" in *Dime Western* (2/47). Copyright © 1947 by Popular Publications, Inc. Copyright © renewed 1975 by Frank Bonham. Copyright © 2007 by Gloria Bonham for restored material.

Center Point Large Print
600 Brooks Road / PO Box 1
Thorndike ME 04986-0001 USA

(207) 568-3717

US & Canada:
1 800 929-9108
www.centerpointlargeprint.com